MW01171342

CARNIVAL

a collection of stories by members of the
Northwest Independent Writers Association

Published by the Northwest Independent Writers Association
www.niwawriters.com

ISBN: 978-1-719877-13-8

The stories and poems contained within this volume are fiction. Names, characters, places, and incidents are either fictitious or used fictitiously. Any resemblance to actual events is coincidental and unintentional. No endorsement by any persons, institutions, organizations, or localities should be implied or inferred from inclusion within.

Cover © 2018 by Lee French

The Parade © 2018 by L. Wade Powers
The Ferris Wheel © 2018 by D. L. Gardner
Duck In a Dog Show © 2018 by Stephen Hagelin
Mardi Gras Creek © 2018 by DK Ritchey
The Mask-Maker of Fogg © 2018 by Jonathan Eaton
The Trapeze © 2018 by Nia Jean
Carnival Humanus © 2018 by Kamila Z. Miller
The Girl on the Boardwalk © 2018 by William J. Cook
Something Old and Forgotten © 2018 by Emma Lee
Bambi's Revenge © 2018 by Connie J. Jasperson
The Fiji Mermaid © 2018 by Roslyn McFarland
The Monkey Bug Circus © 2018 by Steven C. Schneider
The Unmasking © 2018 by KateMarie Collins
Cat Carnival © 2018 by Sheila Deeth
Stark Naked © 2018 by jl courtney
The Last Beer © 2018 by Suzanne Hagelin
The Night the Carnival Came to Town © 2018 by Eric Little
Captivating Luna © 2018 by S.L. Brown
Round and Round She Goes © 2018 by Liam RW Doyle
The Essence of Her © 2018 by April La Delfa

All Rights Reserved

NIWA and the NIWA logo are trademarks of the Northwest Independent Writers Association and may not be reproduced without permission.

The scanning, uploading, and distribution of any portion of this book via the internet or any other means without the permission of the affected copyright holder(s) is illegal. Please purchase only authorized electronic and print editions, and do not participate in or encourage electronic or other piracy of copyrighted materials. Your support of the authors' rights is appreciated.

CARNIVAL

a collection of stories by members of the
Northwest Independent Writers Association

NORTHWEST INDEPENDENT
WRITERS ASSOCIATION

Editor's Note

The members of the Northwest Independent Writers Association chose this year's theme because we wanted to party. Specifically, we wanted to play with words that had nothing to do with politics or the political landscape. We wanted to tell stories of hope, madness, and even horror without the pall of current events in these tumultuous times hanging over our work.

Inside, you'll find parties both festive and somber, fantastical and mundane. Our authors cover a variety of genres and cross the boundaries between them.

Put on a mask and join the fete within.

—Lee French

Table of Contents

L. Wade Powers is the pen name for Lawrence W. Powers, a retired academic biologist. He lives in Eastern Oregon with his exceptional wife and a very strange cat. He has published a number of technical papers in medicine, biology, and history, as well as a critical essay on John Steinbeck. His first novel, *The Home*, was released in 2017 and he has two short stories in print. He is currently the nonfiction editor for Timberline Review. This is his first published poem.

The Parade

L. Wade Powers

A long life, if one is lucky,
from the dark side alley through the side streets
onto the main boulevard, and finally to the park
riding, gliding to the end.

Off the float, off your feet on a bench
to rest, recalling the trip and marking the miles,
the moments passed, the people passed
waving, calling to the end.

Waiting crowds line the sidewalk,
children's faces turned upward seeking
trinkets and candy raining down, producing
laughter, the scramble, and on you go.

To the next block, the next throw,
next stage of your big ride in the big show
from dark shadows to bright street lights
your first deep breath and your last gasp.

Life is a carnival you were always told,
believe it or don't, the parade will start with
or without you, your choice to play your part,
an appearance, a role, a place to go.

THE PARADE

Wear a mask to a masque—
strut and stroll in the grand parade of
glittered faces, littered traces on streets
of busy places, always a place to know.

Ponder this upon your bench:
was the ride what you expected and
were your companions who you wanted,
how did they come and go?

On the ride of life, the festive float,
are memories gay, future shining bright?
Is the trip completed, reaching journey's end
with business still unfinished?

Can you grab some beads and find a Krewe,
hitch a ride down Mississippi Avenue, grab a brew?
Is it Mardi Gras or life's last chance to celebrate
Oregon spring before winter's chilly grasp?

Events in life pass like city blocks,
a carnival parading in beads and feathers,
life's many moments tick like clocks, passing
time, passing by, passing away.

D. L. Gardner loves telling stories for young people, and for people young at heart. She writes all genre of fantasy, with a special love for historical fantasy. She appreciates the classics, both visual and literary, and believes a story should be good enough to hand down from one generation to the next. Her books have been on the Amazon Best Seller's list and the Hottest New Release; winner of Best Urban fantasy at Imaginarium Convention; and *Cassandra's Castle* was a finalist in the Book Excellence Award, along with a host of screenings and trophies for the screenplay adapted from that book.

The Ferris Wheel

D.L. Gardner

Richie Barber always rode his bike up and down the sidewalk in front of our house just to tease me 'cause he knew I didn't have a bike to ride. He knew I'd stare out my window, peering through the old lace curtain in my bedroom on the third-floor, wishing I was Richie Barber. Ma didn't have money to buy a bike. Not with the Depression and all but Richie Barber's folks, they were land owners, had a big daffodil farm, and Richie had everything he wanted.

"Hey Tommie!" he yelled up to me. "The carnival's in town!"

He wasn't telling me nothing new. I saw the painted wagons yesterday rumbling down Meeker Street from the train tracks. I saw all the kids chasing after like a bunch of chickens called out for seed. Richie just wanted to make me feel bad cause I can't afford the carnival rides. I plopped on the bed and pulled my socks up to my breeches and laced my boots.

"Hey Tommie!" he called again trying to wake the whole neighborhood.

I pushed the curtains aside and yanked the window open. "I hear ya. Ain't nothing I can do about it. Go on and pick on someone your own size."

"I'm not picking on ya this time. I'm asking ya to go with me."

"Get out of here!" When has Richie ever asked me anywhere?

"Uncle Dan's helping set the rides up," he said. "Got a bunch of us kids some free tickets. Better hurry though 'cause I'm not waiting on ya."

He pushed his bike off and started peddling. I flew down the stairs like a colt being chased by a bumblebee, grabbing my hat off the stair railing as I headed out the door.

"Where you scrambling to, Tommie Benson?" My sister called after me.

"Out!" I answered. Bridget didn't need to know where I was going. What did she care? She had her book and her apple.

"Be back for dinner. Don't be late."

What was she, my ma? Ma was gone working in the factory today and she wouldn't be home for dinner.

I high-tailed down the street. Richie just about disappeared he was so far ahead, but I ran as fast as I could. I knew he'd be meeting the boys at Kupfer's Corner, so if I lost sight of him it didn't matter that much. The gang always met there. I slowed enough to catch my breath and then started running again.

Sure enough, there they were. Richie, George and Al standing around looking like small-scale hoodlums, smoking cigarettes. George leaned against a willow tree, his cap pulled down halfway over his eyes. Not my favorite person, George always told everyone what to do. Usually he told me to go home. They all had bikes.

"Look what's coming," Al laughed at me. The other two just snickered.

"Richie invited me," I said when I got close.

"Yeah. I heard."

"Let's go." George didn't say nothing to me. He doesn't talk much except to boss us.

The three walked side by side pushing their bikes, and I trailed behind. They were older than me so trailing was my place. Least that's what George once told me. Told me if I didn't mind my place he was going to take me to the railroad tracks and toss me on an old freight car. Told me I'd never see my ma again. I didn't know if he was serious, but I played it safe.

We went up to the baseball field and turned right where the parkway changed to dirt. Richie waved to some kids playing catch and they came running. Pretty soon there was a whole bunch of us flocking to the fairgrounds—me still bringing up the caboose.

My heart started jumping out of my rib cage when I saw the Ferris wheel. It towered way over the barn roofs and the roller coasters. I've seen Ferris wheels before. Every year, but this one looked bigger, especially since I was going to get to ride on it.

"We gots to meet Uncle Dan around back," Richie told us, and we all started running, kicking up dirt and dust. I coughed a couple of times

6

and stumbled once 'cause there were rocks all over the road.

Richie's uncle was there, guess he'd been expecting us, and I heard him mumble something about too many kids. He started shaking his head as Richie and them filed by. He held his hand up when me and another kid got to the gate.

"There aren't enough tickets for every one of you," he said. Richie and the others were laughing as they dropped their bikes in a pile and ran on into the carnival. I could smell food frying. My stomach gurgled and, boy, I could almost taste the hot dogs. I heard the Carnies barking at George to toss a bean bag into a basket, but he kept on running toward the Ferris wheel. I would try my luck if I had a penny. Richie's uncle kept us back.

"Please Mr. Barber. We just want to watch the show," the kid next to me begged. He chewed on a piece of grass and looked all nonchalant. I was too awed at all the sights to talk. I've never been to a carnival before, just seen them from on top of the hill every year coming back from church.

"Well if that's all you want to do I guess there's no harm in letting you in. Just I don't have any more tickets for the rides."

He lowered his arm and let us through, slapping me on my back a little rough as I walked by.

"What's your name?" I asked the kid.

"Frankie. You're Tommie, aren't you?"

"How'd you know?" Didn't recollect how Frankie would know me.

"The boys talk about you all the time," he said. He pulled a can of snuff from his pocket, opened it, and pinched off a wad. When he offered me some, I was going to say no because I'd never chewed tobacco before, but what the heck. I took a nip, stuffed the shreds into my mouth and started chewing. He laughed.

"Don't eat the stuff," he said. "No wonder everyone laughs at you. Put it under your tongue. Like this." He opened his mouth to show me. I about gagged it looked so gross.

By that time the tobacco burned my mouth, so I spat everything on the ground. Couldn't get rid of the taste. He took my arm and pulled me to a refreshment stand. The greasy smell of frying food hit my nostrils and I perked up some. He laid a nickel on the counter.

"Get my friend here a coke." Then he laid another one down. "Me too."

"You got money?" I asked.

"Sure, I got money," he said. "You ain't nobody without money in this world."

"How old are you?" I asked 'cause he acted older than Richie and maybe even George who was fourteen. I wondered why he wasn't at the front of the line with them to get those tickets.

"I'm twelve," he said.

"Same as me," I said. "So, where'd you get your money?"

"Grandpa hires me at the stables. I can get you a job too."

"That sounds good. I could use money. Maybe then the gang wouldn't pick on me."

He laughed. "The gang's always gonna pick on you. You're Tommie."

I didn't like the sound of that, but I wasn't going to argue with Frankie. Not after him being nice to me by buying a coke.

I swished the cold, fizzy liquid around in my mouth to cool the burning, and then swallowed. After that I drank almost the whole bottle's worth in one gulp. Frankie already drank his. He set the bottle on the ground and I put mine next to his. They looked like buddies, the two coke bottles propped up together. Made me think maybe I had a pal now.

Frankie headed for a big red and white tent and I jogged alongside him.

"We really just going to watch the show?" I asked, my eyes fixed on the Ferris wheel. I had to lean back to see the top cause we were almost directly under it. Richie and George and Al were getting into one of the seats.

"Yeah. Why?" Frankie asked.

"Just wondering." I didn't want to seem greedy, asking if he'd buy me a ride so I didn't say nothing.

"You want to ride that thing?" he asked as if he read my mind.

"Nah," I lied.

"Ever been on one?"

"Nope," I said.

"I don't have enough money for two," he told me. So, there was the answer.

We dodged into the tent and immediately I felt a hundred degrees hotter. And damp. Frankie pulled up a chair in the front row and I took a seat next to him. There was a crazy man standing on the stage. He wore a top hat like the kind grandpa had, and a black cape wrapped around his shoulders. There were black marks around his eyes and his brows were thick. I thought maybe they were fake they were so hairy. He looked like Dracula. He stared out at the audience which was just me and Frankie and a couple of adults in the back row with their little kid, a girl with a big balloon. I think he was waiting for more people, but no one else came in. We could hear screams from the rides outside.

He grumbled something fierce and then opened his cape just as an organ started playing a creepy song.

"Ladies and Gentlemen," he said. I looked at Frankie wondering if we were supposed to be the gentlemen he was talking to. "You are about to embark on an adventure to the mystical marvel of Monsieur de Moovalle's Magical Extravaganza!"

He shut his cape closed as he talked and then quick swung it open again and a flock of winged critters flew out of him. I near jumped off my seat and my mouth dropped open. I never saw a man give birth to a bunch of pigeons like that before. He had my attention. I didn't even hear the Ferris wheel riders after that.

I watched him perform magic for near half an hour, pulling scarves from his sleeves. He tossed rings in the air and they started burning up, and he even put a lady in a box and cut her in half. Only she smiled the whole time. When he was done she jumped up. Not a scar on her.

The organ stopped playing and Mr. Moovalle walked across the stage glaring out over the seats. I looked over my shoulder and glory be the whole tent was filled up with people chewing gum and eating cotton candy and staring back at him.

"I need someone—a daring soul, from the audience to come be my assistant," he said, pointing at all of us. My heart pounded in my chest because I thought it'd be fun to be his assistant, but I was scared to death he might cut me in half or something. I held my breath, but Frankie jabbed me in the ribs with his elbow.

"Get up there."

"Me?" I said it too loud and the next thing I know, Mr. Moovalle pointed at me. "Yes, just the young man I need. Come up here son!"

I never heard anyone call me son that I can remember. My mom just called me sugar plum and mushy names like that. The blood drained out of me, and I grew cold. Frankie jabbed me in the ribs again and when I stood up he pushed me toward the stage while Mr. Moovalle took my arm and helped me up the steps.

"What's your name?" he asked.

I almost forgot. Everyone stared at me eating their popcorn and all. "Tommie," I whispered.

"Tommie! I want you to do something for me, Tommie."

Just when I gathered my senses, I saw Richie and them take seats in the back row. They whispered and laughed and I knew they were making fun of me again. I think I looked at them too long, because Mr. Moovalle glanced that way too and then he looked long and hard at me as if I were a squished stinkbug.

"Yes, sir." I said.

"I want you to hold this hat of mine."

He took that big old top hat off and I held it with two hands. It smelled greasy like the pomade my granddad used to wear. Dapper Dan is what it smelled like. I held back a sneeze so as not to embarrass myself, but it wasn't easy.

"Now, hold it steady. Don't drop it no matter what happens, do you understand?"

"Yes, sir." I got scared cause I knew if I wasn't supposed to drop it I probably would.

Mr. Moovalle pulled a long black scarf from out of his pocket, held it up for the audience to see, and then stuffed it into the hat.

"Got it?" he asked.

"You go Tommie!" someone called out from the back row where the gang was. I looked and the whole row made faces, waved, and carried on. I think they were trying to make me drop the hat.

"You know those boys?" he asked me quietly.

I wasn't sure what to say. I didn't want to know them at the moment. I just shrugged. Mr. Moovalle grunted.

Frankie still sat quietly in the front with his hands crossed over his chest pretending nothing of interest was going on.

Mr. Moovalle then took a white kerchief from his other pocket and laid it neatly over the black scarf. "Hold it tight," he whispered to me, wiggling those black hairy eyebrows. He put his back to the audience, looked up at the top of the tent and shouted some magic words that scared the bejeebers out of me. The hat suddenly got heavy and started wiggling. I swallowed. My throat got dry and everything in my gut wanted to drop Mr. Moovalle's top hat and then run.

"Hang on!" he whispered to me again, his dark eyes scowled, and I could see he was a real man under all that make up.

I swallowed and nodded. He spun back around, did a fancy dance with his cape and stepped aside, pulling the white scarf out of the hat all in a split second. A big white rabbit appeared in my arms. The thing must have weighed a ton and it was thumping its back legs something crazy. I was glad Mr. Moovalle had it by its neck or it would have been hopping off the stage.

Everyone clapped. Mr. Moovalle bowed low. He handed the rabbit to the lady he cut in half who was still walking around, and the organ started up. Everyone in the audience got out of their seats and made for the aisles, heading back to the carnival. Richie and George and the other guys left too, and I saw Frankie follow them. I stood there like a doodoo bird not knowing if I was coming or going.

When the tent was empty, Mr. Moovalle took me by the arm again and led me to a chair.

"Tommie, thank you for being brave and coming up on stage with me," he said. He still looked scary, but his voice had changed. He pulled those hairy eyebrows off and smiled at me.

"Wasn't nothing," I said even though I'd been scared out of my gourd.

"You were brave standing up in front of those boys."

I didn't think it was brave, because I wouldn't have done it if I had a choice. But I didn't tell Mr. Moovalle that.

"I always pay my help." He took his white gloves off and reached in his pocket. "It's not much. I don't make a lot of money doing these tricks, but maybe you'd like a hotdog, and a ride or two in the carnival?"

"Wow!" was all I could say when I saw the tickets. "Wow!"

"You earned this. Thank you."

"Yes sir, and if you ever need me to hold the hat for you again, I'll be here every day just to do that. Just give me a holler."

"I'll do that!" He laughed and patted me on the back when he stood. He had a kindly grin. "Have fun," he told me.

I shot out of that tent like a bullet from a .45 and headed straight for the Ferris wheel.

You can bet your bottom dollar I rode it twice!

Stephen Hagelin wrote his first novel at the age of nine, and by the time he reached adulthood, had written several more. Writing was always his first love, though he got a BA in Japanese at the University of Washington and studied engineering for several years. He is currently working on The Commission Series, of which the first two novels have been released, *The Venomsword* and *The Viper's Chase*. *The Lich's Blade* is expected to release late 2018, and *The Mountain Fang* in 2019.

Duck In a Dog Show

Stephen Hagelin

Monroe, WA
Evergreen State Fair

"Today's the day," Harriet thought as she sauntered through the gate, showing off her armband to the distracted youth who barred the way. Her mallard waddled dutifully behind her, giving a quack at the teenager, nearly causing him to choke on his vape. Feathers, her duck, wagged his head as they moved down the lane, and nearly tripped over an extension cord when he did a goose-necked double-take toward one of the carnival games. Harriet stifled a laugh at his expense when a particularly meaty little boy tossed a ring around a plastic duck's neck. She snapped her fingers and continued toward the back where the dog show would be held, confident that she'd be walking home with the prize.

Avoiding an oil-slicked puddle by the Gravitron ride, which whirled with its screaming occupants a little too quickly, like a dented-quarter—she flicked her wrist and slowed it with a harmless charm just so. Now passing it wouldn't mess up her hair. It had taken a long time to style it so that it looked worn and natural yet appealing. Harriet felt her hair with pride and pushed up one of its dark unwound curls as she passed a girl who was a bit too done-up. "Less is more," she explained, glancing down at Feathers, who was puffing along; she half imagined that he was sweating trying to keep up with her pace. She slowed; the organizers wouldn't mind if she missed the introductions of some of the regular pets.

There'd be setters and Basset hounds, and Labs and retrievers galore...but the look on their faces when she went in—well, it would almost be worth the price of her charm's ingredients. The garnet dust alone was worth, what, 12 dollars? Small price to pay for a bottle of Westland.

Only three days since she turned 21, and this was her chance to come of age in style!

Most girls would have their girlfriends take them out...but the only other girl her age was Mary, and there was no way in Hell she'd do something nice for her. No, the Monroe Magical Academy was too small. The only other student in their class was four!

As if he'd sensed her coming bad mood, Feathers quacked purposefully, and she looked up. Apparently, doing her hair had taken a lot longer than she'd thought, because the event organizer, a red-faced, fat man, who wore a poorly-attached and slightly off-colored toupee, was already standing in the center of the show floor giving a vegan dog treat to a rather disappointed chihuahua. The people in the stands applauded for whatever the little rat-dog had done, and it trotted off to its master intolerably pleased with itself.

A veritable child stopped her at the door, his messy hair straightened and combed over his face. "The stands are full miss," he said, giving Feathers a confused look. Feathers chuffed and looked away.

"I'm a participant. Harriet," she said self-importantly, scanning the crowd through the door.

"Oh, alright then. Can I see your entry-form?" he asked helpfully.

She stared at him. That worthless piece of paper was important? She'd thrown it in the trash! Eyes bulging, she replied, "I must have lost it," and she made a show of looking in her purse before she looked back at him with shoulders slumping. "I've got my duck right here!"

"I'm not supposed to just let people in," he explained, almost looking smug.

Swallowing her pride, she tried to flutter her eyes at him, using just the slightest bit of a charm to actually make it work.

He covered a laugh but relented anyway and waved her through. She went in, Feathers forgotten, beet red in the face for several reasons. Skirting the aisle, she spared a look at the arena, where a glossy black lab sat before the fat man, watching his mouth, not the biscuit in his stubby-fingered hand. Harriet stopped in her tracks and scanned the room. Three chairs away from her sat a beautiful young woman with flowing blond hair, in a form-fitting trench coat, wearing a smug grin.

"Eat, drink, and be Mary..." Harriet breathed angrily. Her duck

14

was still at the door, so she snapped her fingers and it padded over carelessly. She sat in her chair and pointedly avoided meeting Mary's taunting look.

"I think you should duck your tail between your legs and go home, Harriet," Mary commented coolly, watching her black lab as it leaped through one hoop, then another, and ran around a pattern of cones in an intricate dance; and the audience gave such appreciating responses, and the incessant notes of praise wafted into her ears like mosquitoes on a…she added a charm to keep mosquitoes away, and watched cheerfully as one landed on Mary's exposed neck.

The mosquito sizzled with an electric-blue pinprick of light, and the ash blew off in the breeze. Mary, it seemed, had warded herself just in case.

The lab climbed up a few stacked boxes and did something clever, so Harriet scoffed for good measure—but only earned a few odd looks from the other contestants. He cantered back down the boxes and sat obediently before the organizer, panting, but patient, until he was given the promised treat, and an unwarranted bout of applause as he ran back to his master and sat nobly on the chair beside her. It was just as well that she and Mary were separated by the animals, since they were content to ignore each other, though Bozo (as she referred to him) looked at Feathers in an awfully condescending way. It was all water off Feather's back, and he didn't care; he was a duck.

After Bozo's circus act, the people were disappointed when an untrained and wildly affectionate border collie pranced around the confused organizer, who tried to instruct it to sit down and to enlist the help of its owner to no avail. The collie's owner was a distracted 8-year-old who chased after it laughing. The crowd's disappointment dissipated and there was a chorus of "aww's" and Harriet's heart sank as the organizer heaved his bulk up the blocks and around the cones, leading a jumping dog through the course, to open cheers and laughter.

The other dogs faired far better, and received far less praise, but none were as obedient as Bozo, or as loved as the collie; and she nearly fell out of her chair when she realized it was her turn next. The organizer stood in the center with a dog biscuit in hand, as he read "Feathers" from the list, and looked up in shock as the duck flew over and landed at his feet with a smug "quack".

"O-ooh! Well, um, let's see, I think, ah…" the organizer stammered, running a hand over his head, knocking off his toupee, "I don't think I've ever, really, seen..." He ran out of breath and labored to suck in another gulp of air before he decided to meet the reality of his situation with a cold, hard, gritty set to his teeth. He bent down and held the treat before the duck's beak and pointed to the set of cones. There'd be no leading this duck through them; Feathers snorted and waddled off, going around one, then another, and another, as he looped through the cones like a belt in a car engine.

This earned him some impressed mumbling in the crowd, and Harriet sat a little straighter in her seat just in case anyone looked in her direction. A duck in a dog show, well who'd ever heard of a thing like that!? She'd get this prize, tear off the foil, open it up, and take a quick swig right out of the bottle—just to rub it in Mary's snooty, stupid little face.

Feathers returned to the Awestruck Wonder, who'd recovered enough of his self-awareness to find his dirt and hay-covered toupee and slap it clumsily on his head. "Right!" He declared, rising triumphantly, as if he'd told the duck to do all that. It had taken weeks of preparation to get her duck in a row!

Her heart raced as he held a hoop just off the ground, and Feathers hopped through, and then, the organizer pointed to a series of hoops. They were arranged on different boxes at assorted height levels to really give some dynamics to the show. Feathers would not be bothered waddling up and down and hopping through all that. He simply ran toward the first hoop, flapped furiously, and flew in a tight circle, navigating all the hoops, before settling down to an open-mouthed audience. Silence reigned; a silky gray feather drifted to the ground.

Dumbfounded, the organizer held out the dog treat, as if he expected the duck to eat it, and Harriet laughed when Feathers' head snaked forward and it bit the man on his thumb! A good number of the audience clapped when he jumped back and rubbed his sore hand with embarrassment, and they clapped until Feathers had flown back over and settled comfortably on the chair beside her, nestling his head in his fluffed feathers.

The wait, oh, the unbearable wait! They watched three more stupid animals stumble around the cones, and the last one, well, he just stole the treat and was dropped from the contest. At last, the organizer, more of a performer than any of the animals (indeed, he'd done the circuit himself more than once) brought out the three prizes: a bottle of Westland Whiskey, for the first place winner, a basket with crackers and a wheel of Brie for the second place, and for third a large tin of kettle corn.

The Collie was ushered out with the little boy, and above the baying of the hysterical animal, the organizer's words were unintelligible; but to both Mary's and her relief, the boy was given the Brie and crackers.

"...not nearly old enough for his deserved prize..." he was saying, to the applause and joy of everyone else. He pinned a large frilly blue ribbon on the boy's chest, and his idyllic story-book parents stood beside him glowing with pride.

Well, even if Feathers didn't take first, the Westland was still available.

"And now, for the Westland, for the most remarkable performance I have seen in a long time, and for his good manners and obedience, Mary Johnson, and her black lab Berlin!"

Mary didn't say anything. She didn't have to. She merely sauntered down the stairs, out onto the floor with her Black Stallion of a dog, to overwhelming approval.

Anything would have been better than seeing Mary delicately removing the foil at the cork and unstopping it with her sultry smile as she placed her nose over it. She was too proper to taste it there, but she met Harriet's eyes as she laughed and praised her dog with a few repeated 'who's my good boy's.

Nothing could be worse than hearing her name next. Feather's head peaked out of his wing and he waddled abjectly beside her as if he were waddling to his grave. She stood beside Mary, blushing not with pride, but rage, as the Kirkland Signature tin of kettle corn was unceremoniously deposited in her hands.

"Such a spectacular show, truly!" The organizer declared, "I have to say that is the first time I have seen a duck participate, but it was well trained. Well done, Miss Harriet, well done." He looped the overlarge ribbon around Feather's neck, and leaned back with a smug, self-satisfied smile.

As the people cheered, and they all walked toward the exit, her familiar, Feathers, shrugged off the ribbon, leaving it where it fell, and commented in a perfectly pitched monotone: "this is degrading." No one else could hear him of course, but his, no her, humiliation was too much to bear.

Mary strutted out the door before them, sparing a haughty glance over her shoulder as she scratched Bozo's ear. Harriet, stomach churning at this new outrage, stared daggers at Mary and her stupid black dog, and her stupid bottle of whiskey, and her stupid coat and stupid good grades, and everything stupid she represented.

"This *is* degrading!" she whispered to her duck.

He gave a disheartened quack and fluttered up to perch on her shoulder. He at least could stomach the kettle corn, and she gave him a sideways, suspicious glance…he might not be sufficiently upset after all.

He stuffed his head in among her assuredly warm curls, and whispered so no one else could hear him, "At least she got second to that border Collie."

"Hmph," she replied and decided not to say or think anything more of it until she was safely back in the confines of her home.

In her day job, DK Ritchey is an operating room nurse at a Level 2 trauma center near Portland, OR. In a former life, she wrote user technical manuals for Oracle and IBM and was a technical publications manager at PeerLogic in San Francisco. In an alternate universe, she would have been a lady gambler in the Wild West, a barn-storming aviatrix, or a lady bootlegger in the 1920s. Check out her website www.dkritchey.com, follow her on Facebook at DK Ritchey author, or send her a tweet at @DKRitchey.

Mardi Gras Creek

DK Ritchey

Mardi Gras Creek, Oregon 1870

Marny O'Neill peeled the second to last card out of the silver dealing box, her slim white fingers in stark contrast to the green baize of the faro table. The Queen of Hearts floated down beside the glossy silver box amongst the chips, silver coins, and small bags of gold dust on the field of green. Ten rumpled bearded men sitting around the table peered down with reddened eyes at the final two cards in the smoky lantern light. Shot glasses littered the edge of the table, and one slumping miner dropped his whiskey glass to the floor. Several onlookers, including the saloon's owner, Sheriff Gillette, sat at the bar behind the table engrossed in the game. The Sheriff leaned forward, a black shadow, only his silver revolver handle winking in the flickering light.

"And Hock, gentlemen," Marny said, as the Ace of Spades remained in the box. She brushed red curls over one creamy white shoulder. Her plum-colored dress clung in all the right places, revealing a respectable amount of décolletage. A single jeweled dagger, a gift from her father, a riverboat gambler, rested at the point of her cleavage. She leaned back and took a delicate pull from a small black cigarillo, carefully assessing all of the hands on the table through half-closed eyes. Ever her father's daughter, she watched the curl of smoke that hovered above the table as she felt for her derringer in a pocket in the folds of her dress. Several drops of sweat dewed her forehead and trickled down her back. Would the punters notice the card she palmed? She squashed the frisson of fear with the delicious thought of the piles of silver coins and gold dust that could be hers.

A chorus of groans went up around the table as one by one the dusty miners pushed back from the rickety wooden table. Jack, the coffin keeper, sat directly across from Marny clutching the abacus-like card counter in his undamaged left hand. He winked at her.

"Thank you all," Marny said, smiling as she scooped the silver coins and bags of gold dust into her plum-colored reticule tied to her waist. Her father taught her everything she knew and would certainly approve of her haul, especially since it would allow her to travel back to the Idaho Territory to find him. "A last drink for the road? On me." Marny imagined her father's scowl at her gesture of atonement. "Never give anything away for free," he always said. "The punters will think you owe them."

Sid, the dark-haired bartender, nodded to Marny as she shot him a knowing glance. Girlishly handsome, Sid clinked the glasses as he set up a round of whiskey with small, deft hands. Speculation had run rife about Sid's manhood when the beardless young man arrived in town with Marny.

"It's a pleasure to be beaten by such a woman, Miss Marny," Shorty said, his red face wreathed in smiles. He tipped his brown felt hat to the back of his head. "Lady Luck is certainly smiling on you."

"So kind," Marny said, rewarding him with a winning smile. She reached down to pat Lucky, her deer-sized black dog of uncertain parentage resting in the sawdust at her feet. The dog's tail thumped the floor as he put his black head in her lap. "Lucky found me wet and smoky on the riverbank, and we've been together ever since," Marny said as she patted Lucky's head. "We've seen a lot together, haven't we boy?" Marny laughed and ruffled Lucky's ears as he licked her face.

"Last call, gentlemen," Sid said to rest of the patrons in the saloon, his high voice pierced the rumble of conversation and laughter.

Shorty and the other miners stumbled to their feet and lurched to the bar. Lucky got up and lumbered to the swinging door at the back of the room behind the bar.

"You are off to the Idaho Territory tomorrow, Miss Marny?" Jack asked as he handed Marny the faro counter. He scratched at gray whiskers on his chin as he palmed the silver coins Marny surreptitiously gave him in return.

"Alas, yes. I've heard that my father is dealing at one of the mining camps at the new strike near Boise. I haven't seen him since the riverboat fire when we got split up a couple of years ago. But I've always held out hope." Marny smiled wistfully. "Besides, the gold's played out here, I fear."

"Ah, well. We'll miss you."

"It's been a good run, and I've made a good stake here, but you know how it is. I've been chasing my father in saloons throughout the west. Maybe this time I'll find him."

Jack nodded, his weatherbeaten face creased in a frown.

"There'll be one less woman in town," Jack said, shaking his head sadly as he stood up.

"There's still the House of Joy next door," Marny said, winking at him as he strolled toward the bartender.

"They're not as beautiful as you," Sheriff Gillette said, leaning down from his barstool at her elbow, an inky shadow. Fastidiously clad in black, he looked out across the gambling tables in his saloon. "Or as talented."

"You're too kind, Sheriff," Marny said, frowning down at the whiskey stains on the green table top and fanning herself with her black lace fan. Had he seen her signals to Jack during the game?

"You've been such a draw here in my saloon," the Sheriff said. "They never came in such numbers when I was dealing." His dark eyes bored into her.

"Perhaps you weren't offering the proper inducement." Marny smiled and waved her fan slowly back and forth in front of her face.

"Is there nothing I can say to get you to stay on longer?" Gillette gazed at Marny, his eyes wide and dilated, lips pulled back showing sharp teeth.

Marny stopped her fan mid-flight at his ice blue stare. She stifled a trickle of fear and pulled her shoulders back.

"You know how it is, Sheriff." Marny looked down at her fan, then back up at his hungry face. Marny's smile didn't quite reach her eyes. "My father must be in one of those mining camps near Boise. I might miss him if I don't go now. Besides, once a woman gets a notion in her head to go, it's time to go."

"It's a woman's prerogative to change her mind." He smiled, wolf-like teeth bared in the lantern light. He reached out and grasped her hand. "I was thinking of a more personal attachment."

Marny resisted the urge to snatch her hand back from his grip. She had seen the black eye Gillette had given to one of the French soiled doves from next door.

A crash of pans and string of invective came from the swinging door to the kitchen and brought the bar's babble of voices to a halt.

"You no good thief! That's my steak!"

All eyes turned to the kitchen. The black dog streaked out the door chewing a red hunk of meat as Wing Lee the Chinese cook charged after him, cleaver in hand.

"I'll skin him for a new hat!" Wing Lee shouted at Marny, shaking the cleaver in the dog's direction. The dog ran straight to Marny, then sat at her feet to gulp down the meat, tail wagging.

"Oh, Wing Lee!" With a swirl of plum skirts, Marny was on her feet in front of the large dog, her hands out in front of her, placating the small man in his white apron, black skullcap, and long black pigtail. "It's my fault! I've been playing cards so long he didn't get any dinner."

"He should not eat my dinner!"

"I know it, and I'm sorry." Her face flushed. "I'll make it up to you."

"How about you buy me the tea and rice wine you didn't want before?"

"Whatever you want," she said, white arms up, her palms out. "You win."

He nodded once, lowered the lethal-looking cleaver, and stalked back to the kitchen.

"And you're taking my cook!" the Sheriff said, squinting at her.

"I'm doing you a favor," Marny said, frowning. "We've been 'negotiating' about rations like tea and rice wine since I hired him back in Denver. And he keeps saying he wants to move on to Portland. What kind of a backwater town is that? I ask you!"

The Sheriff smiled and looked down at his turnip-sized gold pocket watch, hung with several jeweled fobs.

"All right gentlemen, just a few hours before sunup. I've got to get some work done. Closing time!"

The gamblers stumbled out the front door. As the last tipsy patron left, the Sheriff leaned down behind the bar to put the bar's share of coins and gold dust in the combination safe in the floor and locked it with a twist of his wrist. He straightened up and walked to the front door, keys in his hand.

"See you in the morning, Marny. Think about my offer." The sheriff nodded to Sid. "Clean up and put out the lights."

"Yessir." Sid stood at attention, nearly saluting.

Marny sauntered up to Sid at the bar, taking Sid's hand.

"About packed?" she asked. Sid glanced over at the figure of the Sheriff made wavy by the glass of the front door. They heard the click of the key in the lock as Sheriff locked it from the outside. Sheriff Gillette stared at them through the glass for a moment before striding down the boardwalk toward the House of Joy.

"I don't like this," Sid said, watching the dark figure move across the windows. "He's not going to let you go without a fight."

"But we're leaving in the morning!" Marny said, eyes wide.

"We should go right now." Sid locked eyes on Marny. "While he's occupied."

Marny stood still, face white, biting her lower lip. "All right. Let's go. I'll go change clothes." Her face cleared. "Tell Wing Lee? He's been raring to go for days."

Sid smiled, his dark eyes softening as he gazed at Marny. He reached out with a gentle hand to push a stray red curl from her face.

"Sure." Sid squeezed Marny's hand softly. "The mules are out back."

They could hear tinny piano music and raucous laughter through the wall from next door. The House of Joy wouldn't close until sunup, and with luck, they would be a long way from town by then.

After changing into her comfortable calico traveling clothes, Marny stood with a lantern held high as Sid strapped Marny's foldable faro tabletop to one of the loaded mules. Dark shadows draped the back of the rough board buildings as two saddled horses picked up their feet nervously. Wagging his black tail, Lucky stood at the feet of the second mule with a riding saddle. The full moon illuminated the ribbon of road out of town.

"What is taking Wing Lee so long?" Marny said, glancing down the dusty street. The House of Joy's windows spilled yellow light and raised voices into the alley. Marny jumped as a scream of laughter and French curses burst through the air.

A row of square shacks loomed in the shadows across from them on the other side of the narrow track. Red lanterns in the crib windows provided an eerie flickering light. Scantily clad women with dark skin and black hair gyrated in the windows, whistling and calling out in pidgin English to the men who passed by.

The pack mule's ears swiveled backward as a small figure detached itself from the shadows between the shacks and collapsed to the ground.

"What the...?" Marny said as she stood still watching the collapsing shadow across the street. Then she sprinted to the fallen figure's side. Marny's lantern revealed a black-haired girl, eyes purple with bruises, the girl's cheek gashed. The girl shivered in her short black dress, the sleeves and hem torn. Bruises on her wrists and ankles mushroomed in lurid color. The girl opened her almond-shaped eyes to gaze at Marny as tears spilled down her bruised cheeks.

Marny kneeled next to the girl. "Who are you?" Marny narrowed her eyes and clenched her jaw. "Who did this to you?" Marny asked through tight lips. An image of herself as a teenager beating against the locked cabin door of the burning riverboat came unbidden to her mind. Marny pushed the thought down but started to feel that suffocating fear again. She shivered, closing her eyes for a moment.

"Let's go now!" Wing Lee said, breathing heavily, as he appeared in the dark between the cribs. He glanced down the alley apprehensively, then spoke to the girl in Cantonese.

Her frightened face softened as Wing Lee spoke gently to her. "Mui tsai," she said, nodding at his question, long black hair cascading down her back. She stood up gingerly as he took her hand.

"The girl can't go like this!" Marny said, noting the ragged clothing and bare feet. Marny felt her face getting hot, and the trickles of sweat under her arms. Should she throw caution to the wind by taking the girl away from here?

"I'll hold her up on my mule," Wing Lee said, his face set in a rigid mask of anger. He glanced down the alley between the cribs again. "They'll be looking for her."

Marny nodded decisively.

"Let's give her your coat to cover her," Marny said, helping Wing Lee to slip his blue coat over the girl's bare arms. "You've got an extra pair of trousers?" Wing Lee nodded. "Let's get them on her. What's her name?"

"In English, it is Lily." Wing Lee relaxed a little as he looked from

Marny to Lily.

"Nice to meet you, Lily," Marny said. "We've got to get you out of here."

Wing Lee smiled.

Marny and Wing Lee put their arms around Lily's shoulders, supporting Lily over to the waiting mules.

Sid appeared in the shadows next to the mules.

"Another passenger, Sid," Marny said. Reading his searing look, she agreed. "I know it's crazy. But I can't leave her here like this."

Sid said nothing as he helped Lily up on Wing Lee's mule, but quietly observed Lily's bruised face and disheveled clothing. The corners of Sid's mouth turned down as he worked out the implications. Once Sid settled Lily carefully in front of Wing Lee, he patted her hand, then he swung up on his horse behind them to lead the pack mules.

Marny led the parade on her buckskin mare into the dark. Lucky fell into line at her horse's feet. "I didn't think I'd be slipping out of town in the middle of the night," she said to the dog. Marny knew her father would not approve of this gamble. Sheriff Gillette was smart. The odds were against her.

As the moonlight faded and the first rays of sunshine dappled the road in front of them, Lily swayed and nearly fell off Wing Lee's mule. Marny turned her horse at Wing Lee's shout.

"I had hoped to get further from town before stopping to rest," Marny said. "But we have to play the hand we're dealt. We'll rest here." Marny reined in her horse at a grove of pine trees. "Let's make a fire and cup of coffee."

The sun had risen higher in the sky when a plume of dust indicated approaching visitors. Lucky whined, ears pricked up, as he looked up the road in the dust's direction. Marny pulled one of Wing Lee's wide-brimmed straw hats off a pack mule and gave it to Lily. "Here, put this on." The hat hid Lily's face. "Let's tie back your hair into a pigtail." In Wing Lee's garments, Lily looked like any other Chinese miner.

Hoofbeats sounded, and five men led by Sheriff Gillette rode up on horseback in a whirlwind of dust. Marny noted that all had played cards with her recently, including Jack and Shorty. She nodded to the group.

"Gentlemen. What brings you out so far and so early, Sheriff?"

Marny said, sitting down on one of a pair of blankets near the fire. She stifled a yawn. "Coffee?"

"Missed saying goodbye to you this morning," Gillette said. "Thought you'd have something to say to me."

"No. I said I was going, so I'm going."

Gillette scanned Marny's group around the fire. "I've lost my property. I want it back."

"What property?" Marny asked, yawning.

"One of my Chink whores is missing. Ran off," he said.

"Why would you think I've got her?" Marny asked, rubbing her eyes.

"You were missing this morning. You've got a Chink cook." He shrugged. "It's always worth looking for a stray. She cost me more than my horse."

Gillette slid off his dark horse, the revolver on his right hip glinting in the sunlight.

Lucky flattened his black ears and growled at Gillette's sudden movement.

"Tie him up if you don't want me to shoot him," Gillette said, his hand on the butt of his gun.

Sid grabbed Lucky's collar and tied him to a tree next to the pack mules.

"Sit," Sid said. Lucky sat down, hackles still raised, his eyes never leaving Gillette. Sid patted Lucky's head. "Good dog."

Gillette continued his scan around the little group, noticing two Chinese figures sitting on the ground next to one another.

"So who is this?" Gillette asked, walking up to the pair.

"Just my cousin from Canton," Wing Lee said, looking up at Gillette.

Sheriff Gillette knocked the wide-brimmed straw hat off Lily's head with one hand. Her bruised face stared up at him, her eyes wide in fear.

"This one is mine. Bought and paid for." Gillette smiled. Wing Lee's arm went around Lily's thin shoulders. Marny's eyes narrowed.

"Kept running away, so the mistress taught her a lesson." Gillette grabbed Lily's chin and turned her face from side to side. "Pity about the spoiled face though, can't work for awhile like that. Customers don't like it."

He turned to Marny as she appeared to sit unruffled on her

28

blanket. "You've stolen my property."

"I didn't know she was yours," Marny said calmly. "But obviously you haven't taken good care of her. An injured horse carries no rider."

Gillette's eyes blazed. He looked to the group of men at his back, as they shifted uncomfortably on their horses but said nothing.

"Even a beaten dog runs away from his master," Marny said.

"I want what is mine," Gillette snarled, hands curling into fists.

"How about we wager for her?" Marny said. "Being that she's like one of your horses." Her lip curled slightly. The men on horseback broke into laughter. Gillette hesitated, scanning his men's faces. He saw no support for just taking what he wanted.

Gillette's granite face split into a smile. "All right, I'll do the gentlemanly thing and play for her. But what stake are you putting up?" Gillette asked Marny, eyes like razors.

Studiously avoiding Sid's gaze, Marny smiled up into Gillette's face, eyes sparkling, and poked the tip of her pink tongue to the side of her mouth. "What did you have in mind?"

Gillette's eyes dilated. "You deal for me for a month without pay. I keep the winnings."

"I can make more in a month than she's worth," Marny sneered, cocking her head in Lily's direction. "She's damaged goods. Look at her! You've seen me acquire the amount for a fine horse in a single hour of play." Marny leaned forward. "One day."

"One week."

"One weekend." Marny hitched her skirts up to reveal shapely ankles in trim black boots. "I'll make it worth your while."

Gillette hesitated and licked his lips. He could see a few inches of her pink petticoat. He looked over at Sid who glowered and twitched the lead rope tied to the pack mules. "Done."

The men of Gillette's posse relaxed and broke into conversation amongst themselves. Now, this was something! Two of the town's best dealers pitted against each other, and one a woman! What a tale this would be!

"A hundred dollars says Miss Marny beats the Sheriff!" Jack said.

"I'll take that bet," Shorty said. "He's the best I've ever seen! Better than any woman. Begging your pardon, Miss Marny."

Marny looked at Gillette. "So if you win, you keep your Chinese woman and get my services for a weekend. And if I win, she's free, and comes with me," Marny drawled.

Gillette nodded woodenly.

"Let's sit down by the fire. Might as well get comfortable." Marny gestured to the Sheriff's men. "Gentlemen, have a cup of coffee. Sid, if you would serve these gentlemen, please." The men scrambled down from their mounts to get a good view of the game.

"All right," Marny dusted off her hands and stood up. "My table and cards are packed up on the mule. I'll get them."

"Not faro," Gillette said, shaking his head. "My wager, my game."

Marny looked at him narrowly.

"Poker," Gillette said, smiling evenly. "My cards." He pulled out a greasy, dog-eared pack of cards from the pocket of his black coat.

Marny schooled her features. With faro her favorite game, she was not as used to playing poker. Poker narrowed many of her advantages.

Shooting a triumphant look at Sid as he sat down on Sid's blanket, Gillette pulled out a pair of blue spectacles from his vest pocket. "The sun gets in my eyes," he mumbled.

"I agree," Marny said, sitting back down on her blanket. She pulled a blue velvet spectacle case out of her reticule. "Positively painful." Dark glasses meant a marked deck. Marny hoped she could read the signs on the back of Gillette's cards. She took off her dusty brown traveling hat and untied the matching ribbon holding back her hair. A cascade of red curls flowed around her face and shoulders. Marny reveled in the rumble of appreciation from the onlookers.

"Much better," Marny said. She fingered the pocket of her brown calico traveling dress, reassuring herself that her little gun was handy.

"Your game, your cards, but my deal," Marny said snatching up the cards. As she shuffled, the pasteboard cards felt stiff and unwieldy in her hands. The spectators drew close to the fire and the game. Marny made the mistake of looking over at Lily seated next to Wing Lee and noted the glimmer of hope in her eyes. She pushed down a feeling of nausea and continued to shuffle the cards.

"Five card draw," Gillette said. "High card wins."

"Surely." Marny dealt five cards face down in front of Gillette. She was pleased to see that the painted diamonds in the corner of the cards varied slightly on each card. Gillette's eyes softened as he gazed at the cards in his hand. Marny gave herself five cards, carefully covered the backs of the pasteboard with her fingers. A pair of queens jumped out at her.

"How many cards?" Marny asked. Marny's practiced face

remained placid as her mind whirred. An image of herself as a frightened, bedraggled teenager sitting on the bank of the river with a burning riverboat came unwanted before her eyes. This game could decide the freedom for two women, she thought. Marny gritted her teeth and forced herself to look into Gillette's eyes. Stomach twisting, Marny prayed that Lady Luck would be kind to her.

"Three," Gillette said. He placed three cards face down on the blanket. If she was right, he had discarded a deuce, three, and eight. Marny dealt him three new cards. She was sure he kept two aces. The three new cards looked like a pair of nines and a ten. Gillette showed a glimmer of a smile. Marny took a breath.

"Dealer takes three," Marny said, giving herself three new cards, a queen, and five and six of clubs. Would her hand be enough to win?

"Call," Gillette said, with a piercing glance at her cards covered by her hand.

"Three of a kind. Queens," Marny said as she flipped over her cards. A collective roar from the spectators made her flinch.

Gillette snarled as he threw down his two pairs. "Take the whore then." The spectators slapped each other on the back as money changed hands.

"Thank you," Marny said, scrambling to her feet to walk over to her horse.

"But don't think you're going to get very far!" Gillette whipped his pistol out and pointed it at Marny. Marny opened her eyes wide, her hands held out to her sides

"No!" Sid said, one hand on the rifle in the saddle holster, too late to fire. With a frenzy of barking, Lucky lunged free from the rope around the tree. At the sound, Gillette pointed past Marny and shot at Sid, then fired a second shot at Lucky. The booms nearly deafened Marny. Tree bark scattered near Sid's head, and Lucky fell to the ground with a yelp at Marny's feet.

Instinctively Marny whirled to fire her derringer. Gillette fell to his side holding his arm, blood blossoming from his gun hand. Marny took two strides to Gillette, and struck him across the temple, knocking him cold.

"Sore loser," Marny spit, her eyes flinty. She whirled to reach the bloodied body of her black dog. She cradled the dog's head gently in her lap, petting his back.

"He oughtn't've shot at your partner or your dog," Jack said shaking his head as he looked down at Gillette. "You won fair and square."

Marny bent over the form of her dog as he labored to breathe. Bloody foam came from Lucky's nose and mouth. With a last tail thump, Lucky stopped moving altogether. Marny looked up at Sid with tears wetting her cheeks. Sid stood mute, a tear trickling down his face.

"You'd better do something about that arm," Marny said after a minute. Her lip curled as she shot a cursory glance at Gillette's still form on the ground. "And get him out of here before I shoot him again."

Jack bent down to wrap a bandana around Gillette's wound. "We'll get him fixed up back in town. You better git while you can." Jack winked and nodded.

"Thanks," Marny said. "We'll move on to Idaho after we bury Lucky." Jack turned to Shorty and the other men standing by their horses.

"You need any help?" Shorty asked Marny somberly.

"I can do it," Marny said, suddenly very tired.

"No, I will," Sid said, reaching for the shovel tied to the pack mule. Wing Lee followed Sid for the second shovel.

"Lucky was a good dog," Wing Lee said.

Marny nodded.

Jack and Shorty loaded Gillette on his horse, then mounted their horses, saluting as they left. Tongues loosened, the garrulous group of men took off back toward town in a cloud of dust. "Did you ever see such a game?" Shorty asked.

Several minutes passed. Dirt and blood staining her brown traveling dress, Marny knelt on the fire ring-sized mound to give the earth a few final pats. She scattered pine needles over the rounded top as if they were flower petals. Sid and Wing Lee stood watching a few steps away holding their shovels. As she stood, Marny looked down at the ruin of her dress as if seeing it for the first time. Marny looked at Sid.

"I've got to change clothes. And so do you," Marny said to Sid. "Please, put on one of my dresses."

"I haven't worn one of those since I was a kid," Sid said dubiously, feet planted. "I've lost the knack."

"I know. You haven't worn a dress since you were 'Sidonie'. Way before I met you as a drover in Oro City," Marny nodded. Sid squinted past her at the mules.

"But please. I know it's a lot to ask, but we need to move in disguise," Marny pleaded. "We'll just be two sisters with their two Chinese manservants on their way to Idaho. I've got to save you, even if I couldn't save Lucky."

After a moment, Sid looked directly at Marny's tear-streaked face and nodded slowly.

"We shouldn't go to Idaho," Wing Lee said. Marny looked over at him, her shoulders slumping.

"You're right. The sheriff knows that's where we're headed." Marny chewed her lip, standing forlornly with her arms hanging limply. "Then where?"

"Lily needs the herbs and medicine from my people." Wing Lee pulled Lily close, and Lily leaned her dark head on his chest, closing her eyes. Marny looked at them with a curious feeling of pride. Despite the girl's bruises, Lily stood taller and straighter.

"There's a large population of Chinese in Portland, north of here," Wing Lee said. "It'll be safer for us there." He looked down at the ground, shuffling his feet. "Besides I want to marry her."

"I see," Marny nodded slowly. "That's why you broke her out of the crib." Wing Lee looked down at Lily's sleek head and nodded. "Portland, huh?" Marny looked over at Sid with raised eyebrows. Sid shrugged.

"Papa wouldn't approve, but he's not here," Marny said, hands in fists at her side. "I'll guess I'll have to wait a little longer to find him." Marny smiled faintly, unclenching her hands. "I've got to take care of the family I have left. We'll just have to strike gold in Portland!"

Jonathan Eaton grew up in Texas in the 20th century and moved to Oregon in the 21st century, where he writes about Texas and the southwest in the 19th and 25th centuries. He is the author of the western novel *A Good Man for an Outlaw* and the sci-fi novel *The Prairie Martian*. As "The Space Wrangler" (https://www.facebook.com/SpaceWestern), he amuses friends with flash fiction and, idiosyncratic art work. He is married to percussionist Cyndi Lewis and has a cat named Sherman.

The Mask-Maker of Fogg

Jonathan Eaton

Sam Clarity, founder of the Clarity Logging Company, was one of the first in that industry to embrace the use of steam power, and his foresight paid off. He became a wealthy and powerful man—powerful especially within his realm: a hundred-thousand acres of pine forest in northwest Oregon. In the town of Fogg on the Nehalem River, the hub of his prosperous and growing logging operation, his word was law.

Though Sam Clarity was not a grave man, neither was he given to foolishness, and his word-laws were correspondingly serious and reasonable, with one exception: It was his command that on Fat Tuesday, no citizen or visitor to Fogg would show their face in public. This is not to say that everyone stayed home—very much the opposite. Fat Tuesday was a day unlike any other in Fogg, given over strictly to merriment with friends and neighbors. There was even a parade, led by the Carnival King, and featuring a procession of 50 strapping lumberjacks, who carried on their shoulders the de-limbed, de-barked, skin-smooth trunk of a sugar pine, upon which rode (side-saddle, for the sake of modesty) the Carnival Queen. And yet none of the revelers broke the law and showed their faces in public, as every one of them wore a mask.

Anyone caught in public in Fogg on Fat Tuesday not wearing a mask was subjected to a flogging and a forfeit. The flogging was done with a whip especially made for the purpose—the so-called "Carnival Cat." The Carnival Cat was composed of nine long and colorful strips of silk, braided at one end to form a handle, and was incapable of inflicting any harm beyond chafing the recipient's dignity. The forfeit was to sing a low and vulgar ballad unmasked, so that friends and neighbors might judge the character of the transgressor by the color of their cheeks. In truth, the color didn't really matter: maidens and youths were sure to be gleefully reproached for blushing too little, and married folk too much, during the performance.

As to how the idea for this strange, truncated version of Carnival got into Clarity's head in the first place, there is little consensus. That he came to Oregon from somewhere else is all that was known for certain concerning the origins of the man. Some believed he was Cajun, others Irish, and still others that he was the child of German missionaries stationed in South America, and that he grew up in Columbia (some said Venezuela). But all of that is mere speculation, and as far as our story is concerned, where he got the idea is neither here, nor there, nor even somewhere south of the Panama Canal.

It should be noted that despite the harmless nature of the chastisements, the law was taken seriously by the citizens of Fogg, and was rarely violated except by the newly arrived, who were, for amusement's sake, often kept unaware of the town's unusual Fat Tuesday customs.

Having described and explained the tradition as well as we are able, we may commence with the story proper. It concerns a young woman with the appropriately charming name of Miranda Birdsong, who was also known as "The Mask-Maker of Fogg."

Miranda grew up in Fogg, and had exhibited, at a tender age, a remarkable talent for making masks. As a child Miranda made masks for herself and her family, and these were so much admired by all who saw them that by the age of seventeen, the making of masks for Fogg's one-day Carnival celebration had become, without any particular effort on Miranda's part, a lucrative profession. She worked at her masks all year long, and on carnival day, one could fairly say that there was hardly a "face" in Fogg that did not carry the touch of Miranda Birdsong's artistry in its countenance.

A few hours before dawn on the last Fat Tuesday of the 19th century, Miranda was still working on one mask—the last she had to make for the year. It was a mask for a young woman recently betrothed to Sam Clarity's personal secretary, Isidor Steadfast. The couple was well-matched and deeply in love, and Miranda meant for the mask to show the joyful contentment the bride-to-be felt as she looked forward to a June wedding. When Miranda was done, though she had been a bit rushed, she was quite pleased with her work—until she put the mask on and looked at herself in the mirror. Her own face grew hot as the mask grinned back at her. It wasn't joyful contentment that she saw on that simulacrum of a face, but a sort of mad ecstasy—the look of a starving man about to stab his fork into a heap of gravy-smothered broiled beef. It was too much, even for Carnival.

Miranda took the mask off and cursed softly to herself when she realized that although the lamp on her worktable had gone out, the room was growing lighter. Desperate for some quick way to fix the mask, she alighted on the idea of painting a tear on its cheek, and immediately did so, in the hopes of restoring some semblance of dignity to its aspect. The tear, though brilliantly executed (it looked as though it might roll off the mask and fall to the ground with a plop at any moment) was too large. *Mama would scold me if I used that much water to moisten flour for a piecrust*, Miranda thought to herself, *that's no tear, it's a lake a soul could drown in.*

Though Miranda felt the artistic merits of the mask had been ruined, she had run out of time. And anyway, the enormous tear did have the desired effect of diluting the overtly sensual appearance of the mask, and Miranda felt she could wear it in public without fear of ridicule. It was, of course, a mask she had made for herself.

She put on the mask and walked in the light of dawn to a certain grassy hill overlooking the Nehalem River. She had become quite familiar with this hill over the past several days. She came here hoping to see a boat coming up river. Perhaps it goes without saying that she was hoping to see a particular boat carrying a particular passenger. Isidor had been sent to Tillamook to transact some business on Sam Clarity's behalf. He was supposed to return to Fogg by boat in two weeks, and almost three had passed.

Miranda only meant to sit by the river for an hour or so in the morning before returning to town to join in the festivities, but the hours of morning drifted by, followed by the hours of afternoon, and soon the sun would be settling into the pine-quilled hills across the Nehalem, and Miranda could not bring herself to abandon her vigil and return to Fogg.

She became suddenly aware that she was not alone—a man was sitting next to her.

"Who are you?" she demanded, startled.

"Isidor," the man said.

The voice was Isidor's, but the mask wasn't, or at least, it wasn't the mask Miranda made for him, and gave to him, and received high praise for from him, before he left for Tillamook.

"Isidor!" she exclaimed, taking in a deep breath of relief, and releasing a great puff of annoyance. "How you do sneak up on a body!"

"I'm sorry," he said, "I didn't mean to frighten you."

But he did frighten her—or rather, the mask frightened her. It had some resemblance to his face, but was rounder and smoother, as though swollen. In color, it was a gray that was almost white. The eyes were thrown open as if in alarm. The mouth was open too, and in the darkness between the teeth, two little eyes peered out, as if some small creature had taken up residence therein. Miranda turned away—the mask gave her a most unpleasant feeling in the pit of her stomach.

"I hate that mask," she said. "Why aren't you wearing the one I made for you?"

"I left it at home," Isidor said.

It was a perfectly reasonable answer. He thought he'd be returning to Fogg days ago, so he left the mask at home. Had he walked through town on his return to get the mask, he would have undoubtedly been caught and made to suffer the consequences, and the consequences would have delayed their reunion for another miserable hour at least, and so Miranda forgave him—mostly.

"It's horrible," Miranda said. "Where did you get it?"

Isidor touched the mask with his fingertips, tentatively feeling the pale, rounded cheeks, the open eyes and mouth. "It *is* horrible," he said, "I wish I could have worn a more pleasant one for you."

"I've been watching for your boat," Miranda said. "I didn't see it."

"I disembarked downriver a few miles."

"So you could sneak up on me in that horrible mask and scare the daylights out of me?"

"It wasn't by choice," Isidor said. "The boat turned over."

"Oh!" Miranda gasped, "how awful. Thank goodness you're okay!" She grasped his hand. "You're chilled to the bone! Let's go back to town. I'll make you some soup."

"Miranda," Isidor said, "there's something I have to tell you."

"What is it?"

"The wedding is off."

"Don't say things like that," Miranda said, alarmed. "Not even to tease me."

"I'm not teasing. The wedding is off."

"Why? What have I done? Is there someone else?"

"There's no one else, Miranda, and I would marry you if I could—but I can't. There was a certain gentleman on the boat—I didn't recognize him, but he knew me. It seems some arrangement was made when I was born—perhaps before I was born—and this gentleman—has come to collect."

"Collect? Collect what?"

"Me."

"You are promised to *me*, remember? I won't let him have you."

"I'm afraid he will insist," Isidor said. "Miranda, you have to listen to me. It was with the utmost difficulty that I was able to persuade the gentleman to allow me to come here and speak to you at all. I don't have much time. I want you to know that I love you, and I want you to be happy. Forget about me and find someone else."

"I'll never—"

"Here he is now," Isidor said.

Miranda saw the gentleman Isidor referred to approaching them. He was a tall man wearing a long black coat, and though Miranda doubted he was ever before in Fogg, Isidor had apparently informed him of the tradition of the day. The gentleman wore a mask, though like none Miranda had ever seen before—entirely black and featureless.

"It's time to go, Isidor," the gentleman said. His voice was gentle.

Miranda grasped Isidor's hand as tightly as she could, but when he stood up, his hand slipped through her fingers like mist through the pine trees.

Sam Clarity had been searching for Miranda for some time, and while he searched, he had put together what he believed was an appropriate speech—short and to the point. Having found her, sitting on this hill overlooking the river, his carefully chosen words seemed to stick in his throat. He was wearing the mask Miranda had made for him: the face of a man who has made a place for himself in the world above his natural station, through exertion, cunning, and good fortune. Disregarding his own decree, he removed the mask. The face behind it was older, less certain, and tired. Clarity wiped a few beads of sweat off of his brow with his sleeve.

"I have received…news…that I…though I wish…" he said, and then stopped. This wasn't going at all the way he had planned. He took a breath, collected himself, and was about to start over, but hesitated.

Miranda was still looking across the river, and Clarity wasn't sure she even knew he was there.

"I have received news that concerns you," Clarity said firmly. "Do you hear me, Miranda?"

She did turn toward him then, and what a face he saw: a grimace of horror, and a tear on the cheek big enough for a soul to drown in. How strangely that face was reflected in the mask that lay next to her in the grass, staring up through empty eye sockets into a sky all but drained of light.

"I know what you have come to tell me," Miranda said. "The boat carrying Isidor Steadfast back to Fogg has turned over in the Nehalem River, and Isidor is drowned."

Nia Jean has always loved books and stories. As soon as she could hold a crayon, she began drawing pictures that told a tale and was soon writing novels instead of doing schoolwork. As a teenager, she published a multitude of stories online via fiction and fan fiction websites under a couple different pseudonyms. A gifted artist, she set aside writing to pursue art and other areas of interest. Recently, she decided to return to her love of writing and invest her imagination in a novel started a few years ago. Her YA fantasy novel, *Influence* is expected to be released early in 2019.

Trapeze

Nia Jean

Luna was lost. Darkness stretched around her, amaranthine shadows and fog, from which she could just make out the shape of trees. A shiver crawled down her spine, as she turned in place in search of a direction to go. Just as she was about to give in to fear, she saw it; a light up ahead. Relief breathed through her body as she took one hesitant step after another, making her way through the dark.

It didn't take long, though she felt damp and cold after pushing through the evergreen branches of the forest around her. It wasn't raining now, but it must have been not too long ago—the boughs were soaked with the evidence. Several times her hair, frizzed up by the moisture, caught on the branches as she pushed her way through them. Drawing nearer to the source of the light, her steps slowed, and bewilderment washed over her. This…was not what she had expected.

Carnival tents, large and colorful, were pitched in a great clearing surrounded by trees. Yellow lights hung in strings, connecting each tent and stage in a tangle of strands, drew her sight inward toward the center. Had there always been a carnival in the Olympic peninsula? In all the times that she had been to visit her dad out here, she had never seen it. Perhaps she simply couldn't remember passing it on her way. Curious, she stepped up to the ticket counter and peered inside the stand. A single sign hung on the wall at the back. "Welcome," it read, in bright yellow letters.

Music began to play to her left, and she turned to face an open tent decorated in white and red stripes. Almost without realizing it, she found herself moving toward it, and her steps carried her through the flap into the warm shadows of the tent. Several rows of chairs had been set up, most of them already filled with people. She chose one near the back and seated herself.

There was a wide circle in the center of the tent with performers doing their acts—clowns, trained dogs, a seal on a ball. A lean and lanky man, garbed in a checkered purple suit, grabbed her attention. He stood in one place, spinning large hoops in circles and circles, directing them around a young child in the center, no more than ten years of age. Holding a flute to her mouth and closing her eyes, she played a simple melody. "Faster!" cried the man spinning hoops. The flutist picked up her speed.

It was a tune Luna had once known so well that she could have played it backward. When she was ten, she used to stand in her room and practice with her flute, over and over, wanting so badly to be able to shine when she performed at school. She used to think that if she could only be better, *they* wouldn't fight so much.

The familiarity of the performance left her with a strange feeling at the back of her neck, like an itch that lay under the skin. "I don't need to hear this," Luna whispered. The audience applauded, and she took the opportunity to get up and slip out the back.

She had only taken a few steps when she caught sight of a small crowd of people gathered around a stage. Their gasps of shock and delight piqued her interest, and she found herself making her way over to join them. It took a few tries to elbow her way through the throng, but at last she made her way to the front.

Atop the brightly colored platform stood a magician. He wore a white mask with a glittery, painted mouth, and a triangular-shaped eyebrow on one side. Depending on which way he turned, he would go from looking amused and playful to severe and cold. Sweeping his coattails behind him with a flourish, he presented an empty suitcase laying open upon a table.

It was just like the one she used to have in junior high, that she had covered with baggage claim tickets from her flights to and from her dad's place. The first time she made the trip, she had painted her name with cheap, acrylic purple across its plastic side. L-U-N-A, only the "A" had rubbed off some and looked more like a crooked "I." Her dad nicknamed her Luni-bin because of it. She always liked that. Seeing him only twice a year was hard, but it made every visit special.

A gasp from the crowd startled her from her reverie. With a twist of his hands and a puff of smoke, the magician gestured toward the bag, closed it tight, and began drawing the broken zipper closed. It stuck in the same place hers always had, right beside the handle in the middle. Jiggling it back and forth, he flailed and wrestled with it, the audience laughing at his attempts, before it finally became unstuck. Once the bag was successfully zipped closed, he stepped back with fists raised in victory, bowing as the crowd cheered. He picked up his cane and gave it a twirl in one hand, then brought it down to rap the top of the suitcase. *Tap, tap-tap, tap-tap.*

The sound was so familiar, it reverberated through her as though she had been struck. *Tap, tap-tap, tap-tap.* She had always knocked on her dad's door that way, she would knock first, and he would answer before she set foot inside.

It was their secret knock.

How could they know? Luna thought, her throat feeling tight as she scanned the crowd of people around her. But no matter where she turned, there were no answers for her. Each face seemed blank, featureless, less distinct the more she tried to analyze them. Who were these people? Why couldn't she see them clearly?

"Behold!" the magician cried. The sound of his voice jolted her like an electric shock, and her head snapped back toward the stage. Her eyes were fixed on the suitcase, on the baggage claim stickers and sloppy purple letters covering its surface, as the zipper by itself began to unzip.

At first it was just a hand, stretching out from inside the bag. It searched for the table with artful, exaggerated movements, and pressed flat against it. But soon, more followed. The arm came next, and then the head, revealing a girl with a painted face, dressed in a skin-tight, glittery suit. The contortionist was young, no more than thirteen, her eyes bright as she slithered and crawled, unfolding herself in impossible ways until she was standing upright beside the bag, her face turned skyward.

Tap, tap-tap, tap-tap, the contortionist stretched out her hand, and knocked against the air.

It was only then, after the faceless audience burst into applause, that Luna was able to move again. Hurrying away from the stage, she stared about her with a growing sense of alarm. Something was not right. These were more than just performances, they were glimpses into her past, an unexpected and uncanny breach of her memories. Her mouth opened, her voice too quiet for her words to be heard over the crowd of shadows she no longer believed were people. "I want to leave."

The music changed, shifting from lively carnival music into something more like a radio tune, a popular song she was well familiar with, but didn't much care for. It was just noise, something in the background so that she didn't feel so alone in the car on the way to her dad's place. The long drive through the peninsula was always boring and eerie without music.

Luna shuddered, her chest painfully constricted. "No," she whispered. "I need to go. He's *waiting* for me."

Legs feeling weak, she pushed her way through the onlookers and staggered away from the stage. She scanned for the exit but saw only tents and more tents around her. It couldn't be far, she had only just entered. Hadn't she?

Luna began to run. She didn't care anymore which direction, it was just a carnival out in the middle of the rainforest. As long as she made it to the edge, she could just walk out.

She scurried around a large tent, glancing over her shoulder, unable to shake the feeling of being watched. Not by the crowd—they were only shadows observing the show, oblivious to her and her fear—but by the performers who followed her wherever she went. They were everywhere. The magician with his mask, the amused side turned as though fixed upon her, following always at the edge of her vision. The flutist sat on top of a nearby tent, her face painted so that it appeared almost porcelain, obscuring her expression. Three clowns juggled school books back and forth between themselves, one of them laughing, another crying. The third stared right at her, its mask painted to look like her face.

Luna turned down a narrow gap between two tents, her lungs aching in her chest. There was a tear in one side of the larger one to her left, and she dropped down on all fours to crawl inside. It was dark, and music was playing, but no one noticed her as she crawled into a corner and huddled up against the far side of the tent. For a few moments, all she could do was breathe anxiously, trying to calm her racing heart. Her eyes closed, a cacophony of questions swirling in her head.

What was this place? *How did they know?*

A quick-tempoed melody began to play from the direction of the stage, once again familiar. It was a piano concerto, her least favorite one. Her ballet teacher always used it for tendu and dégagé, and she could never seem to do them to her teacher's satisfaction. But then, having her mother as her ballet teacher, she could never do anything well enough.

Luna opened her eyes, peering through the stands to watch. Seven heavily costumed performers danced across the stage in leaps and bounds. Despite their sparkling tutus and animated steps, each movement was robotic and sterile. It reminded her of how lifeless she felt each day in her mother's house, flitting from one activity to the next, attempting perfection, and never finding it.

All I wanted was for you to be proud of me, she thought. Tears welled up in her eyes.

Pushing against the ground with both hands, Luna sprang to her feet and raced toward the entrance of the tent. She was desperate to escape before she had to see anymore, and her steps were careless. A stone in the dirt caught her foot, and she fell and landed with a clumsy roll, knocking the wind out of her. For a moment, she thought she could hear the sound of tires, screaming as they gripped and slipped across a wet road, before she picked herself up and kept running. She ignored the ringing in her ears, not wanting to think about what it meant, fighting to force air into her winded lungs. Yet no matter how fast she ran toward the exit, it remained a fixed distance away, pulling ever further back the closer she got to it.

This was a dream. It had to be a dream. It couldn't be real.

Behind her she could hear the sound of the radio, and her mouth tasted like the blueberry energy drink she'd been sipping during the drive. Her steps slowed, a heavy resignation settling over her.

She couldn't outrun this.

Luna turned. Once more she was in a circus tent, a massive one, stretching high above her head and far out in all directions. But this time, she alone was watching.

A spotlight circled around the stage, finally settling on a lone announcer, standing upon a pedestal. His body was crooked, head craned sideways at a shocking angle, and one arm bent the wrong way. He lifted a megaphone to his red and white masked face. "And now," he declared, "The Final Act!"

She could only lift her eyes, following the spotlight as it turned upward to the top of the tent. A trapeze artist, young and vibrant, no more than seventeen years old, raised both her arms in a proud "Y". She smiled, her teeth glinting in the light, cheeks dimpled and head turned just the right way. She always smiled that way, because it looked best in photographs.

But Luna didn't have to see the face to know who it was. She already knew.

The trapezist leapt from her perch, her body arching through the air with spectacular grace. With both hands she caught the swing and followed its path to the middle of the tent, only to leap once more to the swing flung toward her from the other side. Back and forth, she cut through the air like she was flying, and the props and stage changed with each trick. Through evergreen trees, looping around mountains, up and down rolling hills. A particularly dazzling flip brought her soaring over the cool dark gray of the Sound.

She stood once more on the precipice before the trapeze, body relaxed as she bent her knees and made the final leap. Her arch across the tent was graceful, but it was wrong. Her eyes were fixed not on the swing, but upon a simple phone she held in one hand.

Too fast, too low, her body began its descent far too soon to reach the rope. By the time her eyes lifted, it was too late. A frantic cry seized her chest, she made one final grasp at the rope.

Her hand missed its mark, and she fell into darkness.

Kamila Miller also writes as EM Prazeman and Tammy Owen. She mainly writes secondary world historical fantasy with romantic elements. In other words, you get the beautiful clothes, the intrigues, and deadly duels with wit, rapier and pistol without the baggage that comes with the history of our real world 18th century. She's a world traveler who prefers direct research like firing a flintlock firearm, paragliding, and sailing on a square-rigged ship, because it's fun and because her readers deserve the best she can give. For more information check out these links: http://wyrdgoat.com/ http://emprazeman.com/

Carnival Humanus

Kamila Z Miller

They're gathered in a cathedral of massive Douglas fir trees whose branches make shadows that block the stars. Dozens of lanterns hang from iron garden hooks, set in no particular pattern. At the edges of the darkness beyond, a hint of metal and cloth—tents. Because this, whatever this is, will go all night. The only rule is that you can't come as yourself. You can only be someone else.

A trio of eighteenth century ladies in wedding dresses smile from behind Venetian masks. A lone Viking sits at the foot of a Douglas fir. His clothing is detailed with embroidery, and the leather boots look hand-made; he's a picture of re-enactor perfection. He's drinking from a polished horn edged and tipped in silver. The rest, though relatively modern, span from the eighties to the present from a dozen cultures: working ranch hand with dirty shit kickers and a cowboy hat with tiny bits of hay stuck to it, a biker and a head-banger side by side forming a wall of leather and metal, an office worker in a corporate monkey suit, and so on. I wonder how many of them cheated. Did those ladies borrow those wedding gowns from former brides, or did they wear them to their own weddings? Is the guy in the greasy mechanic's outfit with the company logo on an oil-stained pocket a mechanic by day? Maybe that isn't really cheating. Maybe we aren't ourselves at work, or on our wedding day. But then, who's working? And who got married? Someone other than ourselves, and then we just collect the paycheck and end up having a long-term affair with someone else's husband?

That sounds about right.

There aren't many women here, not nearly as many women as men anyway. That's normal. The invitation said, *come to this unique mixer to fall in love.* I suspect the men are here to find long-term access to sex, and the women are here to meet someone special, maybe make a friend, though there might be one or two in it for casual sex.

I'm not in the mood for anything casual. I take the phone out of my pocket. No signal. I take a few pictures and put it away. There are a couple of others making love to their phones. One of them is playing a game. The other is sweeping and tapping in a way that makes me think she's creating words.

Despite the lanterns, it's pretty dark, and the campground parking lot seems a horror-movie distance away. If werewolves attack, we'll never make it in time.

The redneck, or rather possible fake redneck, approaches me with beer-in-hand. "Need help bringing your things from the car?" He doesn't have an eastern Oregon accent, that not-quite-drawl that's softer and less enthusiastic than Texan. I miss hearing it. I didn't know that about me, or rather this me, until now. His beer breath isn't right, either. It's not Hamm's. I'm not even sure if they sell Hamm's anymore. Everyone buys microbrews because they're everywhere around here.

"I, uh, didn't bring a tent," I tell him. "I'm going to sleep in my car."

He grimaces. I try to figure out who he might be. Clean-shaven, round-faced, round-cheeked which makes him look like he's packing extra weight but I think he's just muscular and strong. Not in a cut way, though. Not like a bodybuilder. Maybe a warehouse worker. I'm surprised that it matters to me, that I can't judge him by his job or his clothes. It's just him, as not-himself, and me, as not-myself, and I should be fine and good with this. I don't like the idea that I might be prejudiced.

"It's going to be pretty uncomfortable," he goes on. "You know, they set extra tents up, just in case. Check it out." He gestures and I follow him. They're watching us, looking at us like they want to figure out if I've already claimed him, or if he's already claimed me, or both. They're chatting, laughing, and it has that nervy energy of a mixer with an added tension because the darkness is pushing everyone closer together. It's like we're underwater and subject to a wall of pressure all around us. If the lights go out, we'll drown.

We pass a line of six-foot tables draped in black tablecloths with food on top and coolers underneath. Everything is marked: beer, wine, champagne, brandy, vodka, whiskey. The cookies, sandwiches, and baked goods have lists of ingredients on folded cards near their silver platters.

Some are gluten free. The cheese platter looks great. I snag some cheddar with a toothpick, make plans to get into the brie and crackers later, and follow him to the tents. They're spaced far apart, like a hundred feet apart, and each has a lantern and a rug in front of it. There are signs on some of the garden hooks that say Vacant. "There's a trail over there that leads to heated restrooms," he says. "It's a pretty nice setup."

And then he leaves me there, heading back to the group with a little duck of his head as if to say 'pardon me, ma'am'. I don't know why I feel abandoned. I'd become attached to him for no reason.

I pick one of the tents and stake my claim by tossing the sign inside, then make my way back to the group. There's nowhere to sit except the ground. That seems like an oversight. The lack of music seems odd too, though it shouldn't.

It's August, but I can't tell from the chill in the air.

There's no one here who's my 'kind.' I struggle to figure out what that means as I try to see past the masks both literal and figurative. I look for a fellow bookworm, a fellow foodie, a fellow gardening nerd. I have to laugh at myself because so often at these singles things I dress up 'nice' instead of wearing my favorite LotR t-shirt that says *You Shall Not Pass.* I think about that line every time I'm on the freeway in a construction zone where they paint the solid white lines. And people pass each other anyway, because they're special and rules don't apply to them, only to suckers like me.

I don't wear that shirt to dates because it seems off-putting and confrontational. Maybe I was over-thinking it.

Maybe I over-thought my 'costume' too. I was going to cosplay but I realized that cosplay is more me than I am myself, so I asked a friend if I could borrow her clothes. Amy is always adorable, with her all-natural fiber clothes, mostly in hemp and bamboo, both of which feel silkier and heavier than I'm used to while still breathing really well. Something about the colors of the natural fibers lend themselves well to crazy combinations that I wouldn't dare on my own: earthy green, dusty purple, soft but rich red, a kind of slate blue. I'm glad she made me take the scarf. It has all those colors and more: gold, tan, and charcoal in ripples that remind me of my grandmother's knitting, but without being frumpy. It's bespoke, assuming I'm using the word right, and it's keeping me warm. Her boots didn't fit but she told me to wear my hiking boots that I've worn all of five times. Her socks are wool, also multicolored and not scratchy at all but soooo soft. I wish they showed above the hiking boots against the tights I wore underneath the boho skirt because the socks are multi-colored glory. I'm not crazy about the fair-trade necklaces and bracelets but they're all part of the look, right? Anyway, my feet are the warmest part of me right now, backward from my normal self.

And this is so not me. I think I should win a prize, but instead I'm standing alone and waiting for some guy or girl to come over and say hi. In my defense, Amy, who I sort of am tonight, would wait too. But I'm tired of waiting.

Someone else has arrived, and he looks like a vampire LARPer. Except, he might not be into live-action role-playing at all. Cheater, or not a cheater in his long black canvas coat, frilly shirt, sparkling cufflinks, red ascot, top hat, and sword cane? I decide to investigate, to be the first. He glances at the eighteenth century ladies who clearly planned to come together this way. None of them have ventured from their clique, nor has anyone been brave enough since I was here to approach the carnival wedding.

The way he looks away from them to me seems dismissive, cold, and I'm not sure I like that. "Greetings," I say, and immediately feel like an idiot. Who says greetings anymore except super-nerds and SCAdians at events? I wonder if the dim lighting hides the heat of my blush.

"Hi." He avoids my gaze. "Are you the hostess?"

"I don't think there is one. I can show you around, though."

"Okay." He bows his head and follows me dutifully as I show him the food, the tents, and the way to the restrooms. I can see an emotional reflection of myself, as if this vampire was in a weird way a mirror of me. In his mirror I was silent, shy, and uncommunicative while the ranch hand showed me the ropes.

I don't want to abandon him like I'd been abandoned. "Do you need help moving your stuff in?"

"I don't know if I'll stay. I don't think this is my kind of thing."

"What is your thing?" Come on, vamp. Say reading. Say roses. Don't say video games because while I love them too I've been second place to video games before. No, call it tenth place, behind just about everything someone can do at home besides housework.

"I should probably stay in character and say blood." No smile.

Something was up with him. "I should say upcycling." I curtsey, trying to get some sort of reaction out of him. Was that a tiny smile? "Pleased to meet you, Mr. Darcy."

"Mr. Darcy?"

I chuckle, though it feels a little mean. "Okay, now you have the quizzical brow thing going too. Tall, dark, quiet, shy," a little rude…"From —"

"Oh, right. Pride and Prejudice. I haven't read it."

"Or watched the movies, I take it. Which is cool because if anyone found out they might take your man card."

"I'm a firefighter, so I'd just get another one."

"Are you supposed to admit that?" I ask, surprised. I try not to think of a cop friend of mine chuckling and teasing me about talking to a hose monkey.

He shrugs. "I'm glad I'm not the only one who dressed up like a nerd."

Hackles officially rise in anticipation that he might dis my people. "Oh?"

"Although I guess it doesn't really mean anything, unless they cheated." He points his chin briefly toward the Viking, who's still sitting alone, drinking. "What's that dude's thing?"

"I don't know. I haven't talked to him. So, did you borrow an outfit?"

"I do paintball and one of the guys is a LARPer. He knows a guy who's tall like me."

"Ah, two orders of removal. Nice."

"How about you?"

"Friend of mine is the same size as me. I took the easy route."

I thought we were done then, but there's nowhere to go except to excuse myself with a nod. I open my mouth to suggest that we go back to the party, if that's what it is, when he looks up. I follow his gaze. There's a tiny patch of sky, and a few stars twinkling there. "I tell people I'm a firefighter, and that's all they see," he says. "I probably shouldn't have told you. Don't tell anyone, okay?"

"No worries. I get it. A friend of mine is a cop. There are all these preconceived notions people have about him because of that. Even me, I have to admit. I see him as a cop."

"Is that the lesson we're supposed to learn?"

"Is this a class?" I counter, though I wonder too.

"I don't know if I want to stay. I don't like this sort of thing." He looks down at me and I look anywhere but at him.

Something's going terribly wrong with me. Now that I know his job, I should be on familiar ground. But the woods and the lights and the lies that we wore have somehow become more genuine than the reality of who we were. And I'd become a part of this 'we' while he, who's revealed too much, has become an outsider. I want either to go or to reel him back, but to what?

I walk away, thoughts spinning out of my mind and into the surroundings. I'm in the dark, among the lanterns, the trees, and the cold air creates mist from my breath on an August night.

He's following me. "Did I say something wrong?"

"No." But he was wrong, and I'm wrong. I stop on the verge of where most of the people are gathered, and make eye-contact with the ranch hand. And then I know. "I was wrong. This isn't about playing a part. I'm not my friend Amy tonight. But I'm not me. I'm not the person who is second to fucking video games and Netflix and answering emails. I'm not the cosplayer who never gets stopped for a picture in the halls or that obsesses about what fucking t-shirt to wear on a date. And why am I stuck being me anyway? Why are any of us stuck being who we are on the job, at home, in our families? Why do we have to be those people, trapped in our boxes, predictable and so easily taken for granted because we'll suck it up, or walk away, or start drinking, or whatever it is that we *always* do. And," I have to laugh because I've done this, "I've spent so much time trying to find myself, when really what I wanted was to lose myself. To not be me anymore. But I don't want to be anyone else, either. I've seen their lives from the outside and the last thing I'd want is to be inside their lives. I want to be right here, in these clothes, talking to him." I point to the ranch hand. "And next week I'll want to be in different clothes, talking to whoever I want, doing and being whatever I want and for once, please, not have a damned thing assumed about me because of what I wear, what I look like, or whether I have balls, or long hair, or wear sneakers in the rain."

The group had electrified. I sense a kinship in some of them. I don't know how deeply my feelings have touched them, though. I want to explain more, about how identity could be fluid, how we could become beings of water and life instead of earth and subjugation, a subjugation where we choke ourselves to death with expectations that we think others have, expectations we assume but don't actually know.

When I garden I'm happy. I'm not some cosmic Gardener with a capital letter, defined by the mud on my knees, nor was I single and unhappy when I was gardening. I don't have to be anyone, not even myself, because my self is ever changing, ever learning. I'm not a damned tree stuck in one place destined to grow one kind of leaf, spreading roots ever-wider over the same ground until gravity, disease, insects and my own unwieldy, decaying size drag me down.

I don't say these things, but I think they understand. I look into the vampire's eyes, and I sense that he gets it. Maybe he was lying about being a firefighter. I would never take him for one. He's aloof, confident, quiet, an outsider not because he's not one of us, but because he's not really alive unless he's hunting.

We talk all night, about all those things and more, anything and nothing and it's glorious. We commit to meet here again next month.

Then the next month we meet the following week, and we grow and morph, as we must. There are the Maskers. There are Costumers. There are Players. There are the Chameleons. Members drift from group to group. We have no names. We don't live in cages. We're opening our first clubhouse soon. I'm researching churches and how to build and organize one. My ex thinks I've joined a cult. He's so blind, blinded by who and what I was to him, blind to his own restrictions.

I no longer wake up and have a routine personality. I rush to the clubhouse every day because there's so much work to be done. Every day is so different, so new, I feel privileged to work at it.

We need a big storeroom, and there's talk of a physical storefront to fund the someday-plan of changing the clubhouse décor daily. Our patrons will never know what space they'll be walking into on a given night. But in one corner there will be the round, bark-covered section of a tree, and a lantern hanging from a garden hook.

Outside, the Douglas firs cast deep shadows over the formerly defunct face of a decaying restaurant that closed for lack of business. It's not that out-of-the-way, not for us. We'd all been willing to travel a long distance that formative night to camp with strangers. A little drive out past Hillsboro is no big deal. Come join us, and shed your corpse-encapsulated life. Come be with us, and be free, at the Carnival Humanus.

William Cook's most recent book is *Catch of the Day*, a "salad of short fiction." His previous works include *Seal of Secrets: A Novel of Mystery and Suspense*, *The Pietà in Ordinary Time and Other Stories*, and the novel *Songs for the Journey Home*. Four of his stories have appeared in NIWA anthologies. He is a transplant from the East Coast to the Pacific Northwest, where he divides his time between babysitting for his fifteen grandchildren and writing. Visit him at https://authorwilliamcook.com

The Girl on the Boardwalk

William J. Cook

I step out of my car and inhale the pungent smells of salt and seaweed. The surf pounds in my ears like the beating of my heart. My breath catches in my throat. "Lara," I say to the wind.

I had vowed never to come back, never to poke the scar. But here I am on the Spit, that small bar of sand along the bay, where we hung out as teenagers. There were no malls back then, but we had something better— a boardwalk. Built in the 40's by some forward-thinking city planners, the Driftwood Boardwalk rivaled its more famous cousins in southern California. It ran east to west, parallel to the shore of the bay, stopping just before it reached the heavy surf of the Pacific. On the north side were quaint little shops, filled with trinkets and treasures and the forerunners of fast foods. It was a go-to place on the Oregon coast until Friday, July 21, 1967—fifty years ago to the day.

I'm here in Driftwood on business. I have a staff of paralegals working for me, but I like to do some of my own research. Besides, anything that gets me out of the Portland office on a summer day is a good thing. The hour and a half drive to the coast was pleasant, and the Friday morning traffic was light.

I slip off my suit coat and tie and lay them on the back seat. Then I reach in for our token—the secret gift Lara and I had shared every summer. The sun is warm on the Spit. My shiny black shoes aren't meant for beach-combing, but I don't care. I walk by a few sunbathers lying on blankets and hear the cries of children splashing in the bay.

All that's left of the boardwalk are a dozen support pillars, rising above the incoming tide like the rib cage of a dinosaur picked clean by scavengers. The expense of rebuilding it after the fire had been far more than the small town of Driftwood could afford, so it had been abandoned to the waves.

As I approach the mouth of the bay, where it empties into the ocean, the sounds of the crashing surf become louder. In that white noise, I hear the calliope music of the carousel and the Ferris wheel, children squealing on the tilt-a-whirl, barkers shouting to draw crowds to their attractions. The carnival that camped along the boardwalk the third week of every July has come to town.

And I remember everything...

FRIDAY, JULY 21, 1967

I couldn't wait to show Lara my new car. I had just driven off the lot in a 1960 Ford Falcon—my *Green Machine*—paid for by working almost every night at Rosco's Burger Heaven. I was king of the world.

I pulled up in front of Stan's house at about noon. He was waiting at the front door.

"Jeez, Jimmy, you did it! Holy shit! A car! Our summer just got a whole lot better."

Greg came running from across the street. "No way, man! You never told us you were getting a car. Damn! No chick is safe!" He ran his hand along the hood. "I'm in love! C'mon, let's take it for a test run to Newport. Practice our cruisin'."

Forty-five minutes later, crooning along with Scott McKenzie's "San Francisco" blasting from the radio, the new cocks-on-the-block made it back to the Spit. Our usual routine was to walk the beach and check out the babes, then head up to the boardwalk for fries and pop and continue our *perambulatin'*, as Greg liked to call it. Of course, during the third week of July we walked the midway, maybe even took a ride on the Ferris wheel or the carousel, if they put the rings out. Greg snatched the gold ring yesterday and turned it in for a teddy bear, which he hoped to give to one of the girls who prowled the carnival in groups as we did.

"Nothing smells quite like the carnival, does it?" I said. The odors of sweat mingled with the aromas of french fries and fried clams, the sweet perfume of burnt sugar from the cotton candy and candy apples, the smells of grease and exhaust from the engines operating the rides.

"Picked up the new *Sgt. Pepper's* last night," Stan said. "You guys gotta come over and listen to it with me." He frowned. "Oh, I forgot. Jimmy's never free at night anymore."

"Sorry, guys. It's only for a week. It's the only chance I get to see Lara. She has to wait till her old man falls asleep. But I can come over till about 9:30."

"He goes to bed that early?" Stan said.

"Gets drunk and passes out every night."

"Sounds like my kinda guy," Greg quipped.

"She's afraid to introduce me to him. But I've seen him. Works the ring-toss and the shooting-gallery on the midway. Sometimes runs the tilt-a-whirl. Looks angry all the time."

"We'll have to stop by and relieve him of some of his prizes," Stan said.

"Hey, can we hit the boardwalk before I take a bite out of one of you guys? I'm starving." I preferred our local fare to the carnival's offerings.

They didn't need any persuading, and in moments we were scarfing down french fries and slurping sodas.

"Hear the news?" Stan kept us up-to-date on current affairs. "Race riots in Newark? 26 people killed, 1500 injured, 1000 arrested."

"Now why do you wanna go and spoil this beautiful summer day with downer shit like that, nerd?" All Greg cared about was getting laid this summer before he went off to college. With Vietnam getting worse, we all worried about the Draft, and getting into college seemed the best way out.

"Just sayin'. This country's a powder keg. You wait. Lots of other cities are going up in smoke before it's over."

"Well, thank you, Walter Cronkite. Now shut the hell up."

We were quiet for a long time after that. Greg finally broke the silence. "You guys are holdin' me back. I gotta do some cruisin' on my own." With that he went down the stairs and back to the carnival.

Stan shook his head. "I think I'll head home early, Jimmy. I can walk." He looked unhappy.

"But we just got here, man. Stick around. Greg'll be back."

"Yeah, well, my dad wants me to finish painting the house this

61

summer, and I got a long way to go."

I shrugged my shoulders and waved as Stan walked away. With nothing better to do, I sat on a stool under the awning of an ice cream shop and ordered another pop. I decided to count the minutes till I could see Lara.

I had met her four years earlier, the summer of my freshman year. It was the first night of the carnival, when it stayed open till midnight. I had wandered around behind the carousel, where the workers parked their trailers. On the metal stoop of an Airstream sat the most beautiful girl I had ever seen. Her blonde hair glowed silver in the moonlight, which reflected off the tracks of tears on her cheeks. The shadows turned her red lipstick black.

"You're not supposed to be here," she said. "This is private—carnie crew only."

"I'm Jimmy."

"Well, Jimmy, you're trespassing."

I wasn't about to be brushed off so easily. "Why are you crying?"

I expected her to tell me it was none of my business. Instead, she sighed. "Wanna go for a walk? I don't wanna wake him up, talking under his window."

"Who?"

"My father. C'mon."

In moments we were on the midway, then up on the boardwalk. The wind had died, and moonlight speckled the swells of the gunmetal sea.

"You must live around here," she said.

"About half a mile down 101 and then up on the hill. How about you?"

"In the Silver Twinkie." I'm sure she saw the confused look on my face. "The Airstream trailer. Looks like a Silver Twinkie, doesn't it?"

"I guess it does. Never thought about it before. But where's your house?"

"No house. Just the trailer. School?"

"Driftwood High. You?"

"Oh, I get some schooling when we winter in Florida. But I'm way behind."

"You guys come here every July, don't you?"

"Ever since my mom died eight years ago. The central coast is good for us. People come down from Pacific City and Netarts and Oceanside. Even Tillamook. Up from Depoe Bay, Newport, and Waldport. Sometimes Florence."

"Where else do you go?"

"Usually bigger cities. Salt Lake City and Phoenix on the way out here. Seattle and Spokane afterward. Then it's mostly Florida. St. Augustine, Tampa, Orlando, Miami. But you can't beat July on the Oregon coast."

"You like living out of a trailer?"

"It sucks."

We walked down the boardwalk and back. I became oblivious to the sounds of people around me, to the smells of popcorn and cotton candy. My world had shrunk to the presence of this beautiful creature at my side.

"How come I haven't seen you before? I spent every day at the carnival last year. I would've remembered you."

"Daddy usually makes me stay inside. Afraid I'll meet some bad boy who'll do me wrong." She stopped and looked me up and down. "You a bad boy, Jimmy?"

I didn't know what to say. My heart began to pound and my hands started to shake. "I-I guess I've dreamed about being one, but I'm not. I think my mom and dad would say I'm a pretty good kid." I returned her gaze. "Hey! You know my name but I don't know yours."

"Lara." Her voice sounded like an angel singing.

And I was head over heels. We met every night after that. By the second day, we were holding hands as we strolled the boardwalk. On the fifth day, while we stood at the end of the pier, looking at the moon and the lights of the fishing boats on the horizon, she kissed me. I staggered home, drunk on the pleasure of it.

On the evening of July 21st, the day before the carnival would pack up and leave for Seattle, Lara greeted me at the trailer with a finger to her lips. "Shh! He's having a hard time falling asleep. I don't want him stumbling out here and seeing you. Go to the boardwalk and wait for me."

I left immediately. The minutes passed with agonizing slowness. I kept looking at my watch, pacing back and forth.

"Heavy date comin'?" It was a gray-haired lady standing behind the counter of Driftwood's Best Fried Clams. Her voice sounded kind. She had my mother's smile. "So who you waitin' on?"

"My girl," I blurted out.

"She must be somethin', havin' you all antsy like that. What ya got for her?"

I shrugged my shoulders.

"Girl like that needs a gift. I'm closing up shop now, so here, take one of these. My husband, bless his heart, brought me some flowers today for our anniversary. Careful of the prickles." She handed me a single red rose.

"I-I don't know what to say."

"You just give her that. Don't hafta say nothin'."

A half hour later, Lara came running, out of breath. She threw her arms around me and buried her face against my chest. I felt her warm tears through my shirt.

"I'm going to miss you so much, Jimmy. Promise you'll come back to see me next July?"

"Of course I will."

She pulled away. "It isn't fair to tell you not to see any other girls while I'm gone. But don't forget me. Please."

"Forget you? I love you, Lara. I don't want to see other girls." I drew her close and kissed her lips. "You're my girlfriend. My only girlfriend." I gave her the rose.

"How sweet!" She took my hand. "Walk me to the end."

I felt my soul warring within me, joy and grief locked in combat. I was desperately in love with a girl I wouldn't see for a whole year. And a year was forever.

Fortune smiled and gave us another glorious evening with the breeze off the sea cool on our faces, the stars whirling overhead. When we reached the end of the boardwalk, she turned to me and held up the rose. "Do you love me?" she said, as she pricked her finger on a thorn.

My eyes grew wide as I watched a small red drop stain her white skin. "Yes, I love you. You know I do."

"Then prick your finger and mix our blood together."

I winced as I did and wrapped my bleeding finger around hers.

"Now we have a sacred pact, sealed in blood. That thorn is all the things that try to tear us apart, the obstacles that block our path. But we'll overcome them all. Now throw it in the water."

I threw the flower as far as I could, and we watched it tumble into the waves. We gave our souls to the night.

I moped until school started again, too sad to enjoy being with my friends, too bored to read a book or go to a movie. Lara had punched a hole in my heart. How could I be so hopelessly in love with her after only a week? Yet why did I feel I had always known her? I couldn't explain it to myself, let alone to my parents or my school guidance counselor. I didn't come out of my cocoon until after Christmas, when at last I gave myself permission to enjoy things again.

At school, Christie Aaronson wanted me to take her to the Valentine's Dance, but I pretended to be sick. I finally relented in May for the last dance of the year, but I actually felt guilty the whole time. That cured her infatuation with me. I just wanted school to be over and the carnival to come back.

My prayers were answered. Like magic, the carnival appeared full-blown on the morning of July 15th. When I went to see Lara that night, I was terrified. What if she had found another boyfriend? What if she didn't care about me anymore? I crept up to the trailer without making a sound. I didn't see her on the stoop, and my heart sank. I waited for several minutes. Then I heard shouting from inside. Her father's voice, drunk.

"You can get some fresh air, but stay close by. And don't you let any boys come sniffing around. You know all they want is to get in your pants."

Lara came running out. Even in the moonlit darkness, I could see her eyes were puffy from crying. She grabbed my hand and pulled me toward the midway.

"He's getting worse. I'm so afraid of him."

"Does he ever hit you?"

She turned away and didn't answer. Several minutes passed. "I need to be on the boardwalk with you."

We never talked about her father again. Instead, we treasured every moment, if only sharing a burger and a soda, nibbling a candy apple, or splitting an ice cream sundae. Each night we strolled the boardwalk hand in hand, watching the water and the moon. "You come in like the fog off the ocean, and you disappear just as mysteriously."

"So you're a poet now?"

"You make me want to write poems and sing songs and dance like a madman." I took a deep breath and plunged ahead. "And be with you for more than just a week every summer."

I'm not sure what I saw in her eyes. She took my face in her hands and kissed my mouth. "Take me back to the Twinkie now."

And almost before it began, the week ended. We repeated the ritual of the rose on our last night and I was bereft again.

But this time we had the experience of weathering a whole year without each other and had proof we could do it. I threw myself into my studies and spent the weekends with Stan and Greg. In the blink of an eye, it was July again, and the carnival returned.

The summer of my junior year, we became more intimate. We would hide in the shadows behind the Ferris wheel and let our fingers and our lips explore our bodies. It was always gentle and loving. Though we both felt the hunger—the desire that grew in us—we never went all the way. Without saying it, we both knew we were saving ourselves for marriage. The bloody rose sealed our love once more.

When the carnival returned during the July after my graduation, something was different. This was the summer of decisions. Would I go off to college? Would Lara? If so, would we see each other next year? Lara had changed, too. Though she had always been beautiful, she was radiant now, her cheeks rosy and full, her curves more obvious even in the baggy clothes she wore. And how I wanted to show her my new car!

The hours dragged by. I made small talk with little children who came to the shop for ice cream and cold drinks. By five o'clock, the marine layer had moved in from the ocean, blotting out the sun and dropping the temperature almost ten degrees.

"Rain before long." It was the shopkeeper, a twenty-something guy with long black hair pulled back into a ponytail. "You've been sitting here all day, man. You'll wear that stool out. What's up?"

"Waiting to see my girl." I looked at my watch. "Another few hours if you don't mind me taking up space."

"I don't mind, man, but she must be some hot chick. Here, have an ice cream cone. On the house. Gotta support the true romantic."

As nine-thirty approached, I got up and stretched and walked to the Silver Twinkie. The hours alone with my thoughts had convinced me. I would buy a ring and ask Lara to marry me.

I found Lara weeping on the metal steps of the trailer. She got up and ran to me, hugging me with an embrace that took my breath away.

"I'm here, honey. Everything is OK."

"No, it's not." She took my hand and walked toward the pier.

"I've got something to show you first. It's in the parking lot." I didn't answer the quizzical look in her eyes, but pulled her in the other direction.

"Ta da!" I said, introducing her to the *Green Machine* with a sweeping motion of my arm.

"You own a car?" Her eyes went round with disbelief.

"Bought it myself today. Here, hop in and check it out." I opened the door for her and she scooted into the passenger seat. "The radio works. And the heater. Supposed to be pretty good on gas, too."

She stroked the dashboard as if assuring herself of its reality. Then she turned to me with a look in her eyes I had never seen before. "Let's run away together." I heard desperation in her voice.

"What?"

"Let's just go. Somewhere far, far away, where nobody knows us, and we can start a new life together. You've graduated high school. You can find a job anywhere." She became thoughtful for a moment. "And if you're worried about the Draft, we could go to Canada."

She had caught me completely off guard. She saw and heard my hesitation.

"I'm sorry. That wasn't fair. Your parents are here. Your friends. I have no right to ask you to do something like that." She leaped out of the car. "Let's go to the boardwalk."

I didn't know what to say. We walked to the wharf. I couldn't hear the sounds of the crowd, the cries of children on the Ferris wheel and tilt-a-whirl. My vision went in and out of focus. At the end of the pier, the wind was strong, whipping her hair across her face. The sky was starless.

Lara took both my hands and pulled me close. Her eyes brimmed with emotions I couldn't decipher. "I'm pregnant."

I rocked back on my feet as if she had slapped me across the face. What she said didn't make sense. How could that be possible? Confusion and shock became anger. "You didn't tell me you had another boyfriend." My pulse pounded in my ears. My breathing came in tortured gasps. I felt dizzy and out of control.

"I don't have another boyfriend."

I let go of her hands and slammed my palms into either side of my head. "Of course you have a boyfriend!" I pointed an accusing finger at her belly. Then came words I would regret for the rest of my life. "You're nothing but a slut!" I shrieked. "How can I compete with boyfriends in Phoenix and Seattle and Miami? I'm such a fucking idiot for believing you loved me!"

I can't remember what else I said, but ugly words spewed from my mouth, vile and unclean, slashing at her like knife blades. I watched her face crumple in despair, her eyes drain of all hope. I turned and ran, stumbling on the rough wood of the pier, regaining my feet without looking back.

When I reached the parking lot, I jumped into my car and started the engine. Before I put it into gear, I pounded my fists on the steering wheel until the pain stopped me. But that hurt couldn't match the agony in my heart. I raced toward home as fast as the little car would go. Without saying a word to my parents, who sat in the glow of the television in the den, I ran upstairs to my bedroom.

I was awakened at midnight by the wail of fire engines speeding down 101. I looked out the front window and saw the whole of the western sky aflame, billowing clouds of black smoke silhouetted in the crimson glow. I threw on my clothes and ran to the door.

I drove as close as I could get to the fire. Police cars had cordoned off four blocks to keep the gathering crowd of spectators safe. I left my car and hurried to the barrier, where a grim-faced policeman cautioned me back.

The whole carnival and boardwalk were ablaze, flames raging

above the Ferris wheel, engulfing the carousel and shops, a storm of hot ash and sparks streaming across 101. Firemen were hosing down the roofs of nearby buildings to prevent the holocaust from spreading. It had not rained during the night, but the wind had risen to gale-force gusts, creating a blast furnace that consumed everything in its reach. The roar was deafening; the heat, scorching even at this distance.

"Lara!" I cried to the inferno.

I stood there for hours, until the wind diminished and the day dawned weakly through an amber haze of smoke. Engines from as far away as Salem and Cannon Beach had come to the aid of the Driftwood firefighters, and with the dying of the wind, they finally gained control and containment. By noon the hoses were quenching the last of the smoldering hotspots. Exhausted, I staggered back to my car and drove home.

The evening news said the fire was "of suspicious origin." Police said it had burned so hot it was difficult to identify the bodies and even to determine how many had died. It could be weeks before they finished their investigations. The carnival and the boardwalk were total losses, every trailer reduced to ash. I wanted to believe that Lara had escaped, perhaps made it to shelter in Seattle, where she could have her baby and live in peace away from her father.

By the next summer, my therapist said I was doing well enough to be weaned off my medication. I was eating and sleeping better, and it had been a month since my last nightmare. I still wept whenever I remembered my last conversation with Lara. I sought absolution from the priest at our church, but my guilt was resilient.

My adolescent brain hadn't believed Lara. She didn't have another boyfriend, just as she had said. So I devoted myself to school—first college, then graduate study. When I got my J.D., I knew exactly what kind of law I wanted to practice. It was the least I could do.

So here I am on the Spit, on the 50th anniversary of the worst day of my life. I have a long history as a district attorney, prosecuting child molesters. And I'm good at it. The judges like me because my cases are so air-tight, and the defense attorneys cringe when they see who they're going up against in the courtroom.

I walk to the end of the bay and face the booming Pacific surf. A wedge of brown pelicans flies low over the water, and two seagulls argue over a dead crab on the beach. With a slow and deliberate motion, I raise the rose I hold in my right hand, prick my finger on a thorn, and hurl it into the waves.

Emma Lee is a native Californian wanderer currently living in the Puget Sound region. She writes contemporary stories about life, love, and family. When not indulging that hobby, she travels to exotic locales like Detroit and Denver, tries not to ruin the flowers growing wild in her garden, and makes serious attempts to understand what her teenage kids are talking about at any given moment.

Something Old and Forgotten

Emma Lee

Rain thumps on the roof of the airy shelter where I sit with my coffee, huddled under a worn, ratty blanket. The structure has three walls and a ceiling held together by two dozen coats of paint. Dandelions grow unchecked through the cracked asphalt. Hundreds of colored light bulbs hang everywhere, but I haven't bothered to turn them on. They use a lot of juice.

My metal crutches lean against the side of a bowl-shaped bench with a circular table in the middle. Once, the bowl held smiling, laughing people who made the whole thing spin by pulling on the center disc. Years ago, my dad dragged it into the dubious safety of this former cafe to use as a dinner table.

Outside, metal squeals as the rain turns the wind- and watermill made from the remnants of a giant swing ride. Dad was handy and clever, unlike his son. If any of his contraptions break, I don't have the first clue how to fix them. Maybe I'll just sit in the dark and let myself starve to death.

Whenever the rain stops and the ground dries, I'll get out and oil the mill. A tall order for early spring in Tenino, Washington, where water falls out of the sky more days than it doesn't.

I hate the place. I hate everything about it.

The coffee isn't warming my hands anymore. I sip it, still expecting heat for some reason. Stupidity, maybe, or stubbornness. When I discover bitter, tepid water, I toss it behind me as if that act can banish disappointment. My metal cup sloshes brown liquid and clatters on the ground. I'll pick it up and clean it later.

The rain keeps falling.

I don't want to remember a worse time in a worse place with the same rain, but I can't help it. They say there's never any new water; it goes around and around in a cycle. Maybe some of this water also fell that day all those years ago, plastering dark hair to a lovely face.

Lan and I stood in the middle of a Saigon street in a sudden downpour. Everyone else at that festival did the sensible thing and headed for shelter. Not us. She clung to me, her delicate hands clutching my Army uniform, both of us soaked to the bone in under a minute. I kissed her and forgot about the world.

She tasted like mango ice cream and smelled like cinnamon.

A shadow in the rain throws me out of the memory. I can't tell what it is until a silhouetted figure stumbles into my shelter. They crumple to the ground, shivering so hard I can hear it.

"Who's there?" Though my voice cracks and I have to cough to clear my throat, I try not to sound harsh and uninviting. It's raining, after all. Even if this person is trespassing by a wide margin.

My visitor looks up and shrinks from me but doesn't leave. "I'm sorry. I didn't know anyone was here." He sounds young and scared.

I remember being young and scared in a strange place.

"Don't apologize for seeking shelter, kid. There's a switch on the wall back there." I wave toward a counter that separates the empty space with my bowl from a defunct fast-food kitchen. "It turns on lights that give off about a billion degrees of warm. Should be enough battery to run them for a little while."

The kid doesn't move. He stands there in the dim, gray light, an unreadable shadow in my domain.

"I promise there are no booby traps or landmines on the way."

He huffs what might be a laugh and hurries to the back wall. The lights blaze into multicolored life, hanging in metal panels taken off the broken-down rides in this godforsaken hellhole. Within seconds, heat presses down from the banks of incandescent bulbs.

"You weren't kidding," my visitor says, his voice full of wonder. He's maybe sixteen, wearing soaked jeans and sneakers. As he approaches my bowl, he shrugs out of a waterproof jacket covering a bulging backpack with an extra bag strapped to the bottom. Under that, he's got a quilted blue flannel. His short hair is soaked—I think it's sandy blond.

"I don't joke about landmines. That's serious stuff."

74

As he gets closer, I see light-colored, uneven stubble on his chin and cheeks. Dark circles frame his eyes. Water drips from his hair. His mouth quirks up on one side, just enough to tell me he thinks I'm amusing.

"You live here?" He sets his backpack on the floor and checks it, maybe for water damage to its contents.

"Yeah. I'm Jake. What's your name?"

"Andy. I didn't know anybody lived in this place. Thought it was an abandoned junkyard."

"It's definitely a junkyard. My dad built the carnival here because the land was cheap. Always said it was cheaper to just drop it on this spot than pack it into trucks and haul it from place to place. Can't say whether that was true, or just what he said to try to convince himself he'd made the right choice."

I have no idea why I blurt all of that to a random teenage boy caught in the rain who just wants to warm up. Maybe I haven't talked to anyone in too long.

"Kinda seems like maybe it wasn't true."

"Eh, it worked for a few decades. He shut it down in the nineties."

The way Andy looks at me makes me feel older than usual. He wasn't even born yet in the nineties. By the time that decade rolled around, I'd lived through a lot more than I ever wanted.

He pulls a towel out of his backpack, which surprises me, and uses it to dry his hair. My high school years happened a long time ago, but I don't remember carrying a towel to or from school for any reason. Then he surprises me more and gets a thin blanket out of the bag strapped to the bottom.

Curiosity piqued, I watch him step out of his soggy shoes, then wrap the blanket loosely around his waist. He wiggles and squirms until he's draping his jeans and socks over the side of my bowl.

I can't decide whether to ask the obvious question or not. Kid seems like he's not afraid of me, and I don't want to abuse that fragile trust. Strangers had done me the kindness of simple decency a fair few times, and I remember how it felt. One of those strangers even became my wife.

Lightning flashes outside and I see a different carnival, this one on the other side of the country.

Tess and I stood in the paltry shelter of a narrow overhang covered with garish lights. Rain fell in a thick sheet less than an inch from my shoulder. Our newborn son hung between us, strapped to her chest by a peach-colored sling and suckling from her breast.

We should've stayed home. The forecast had called for rain in the afternoon. But Tess wanted to get out of the house, and I worked mornings. No matter how hard I tried, I couldn't say no to her.

I touched the silky fluff on Brian's head with my thumb, careful not to distract him. My gaze slipped from him to her. She smiled at me. Leaning close, I brushed my lips against hers. The world narrowed to these two people, both depending on me for everything.

Thunder cracked, startling all three of us. The boy squalled. I clutched Tess while she fumbled to shift him to the other breast.

Instinct, I realized, led me to protect them. I suddenly felt like a father instead of a man who'd gotten his girlfriend pregnant. The shift threatened to knock me on my ass. My father must've had the same revelation with my big sister. That meant he could relate. When I got home, I decided, I'd write him a letter. The old bastard had never gotten a phone installed at that damned carnival.

Thunder rumbles in the distance. Andy sits opposite me in the bowl, the dingy blanket wrapped around the lower half of his body. "Are you okay?"

I figure I zoned out for a minute, thinking too much. "Yeah, just old."

He chuckles. "My grampa used to tell me not to get old if I can help it."

"Smart man."

"Yeah." His smile fades. I know what comes next. "He died about five years ago. Cancer."

"Sorry to hear that."

Andy nods like condolences don't mean anything to him anymore. I can relate. "What about your dad?"

"Ten years ago. Heart attack."

Dad and I sat together in the bowl, finishing dinner. Rain tapped on the roof and asphalt. He told a story about a bunch of teenagers at the carnival in the seventies. I laughed so hard, I snorted rice through my nose. It hurt like hell. Dad started laughing because he'd never seen anything like that.

I rub my eyes with a finger and thumb to banish the memory, wishing I had another cup of coffee. Why am I talking to Andy? He's dredging up all the worst things in my head.

Andy goes quiet. When I open my eyes again, I see him looking at his hands in his lap. A kind of quiet desperation clings to him, pulling down his shoulders.

"You live out here by yourself?" he asks, soft and meek.

"Yeah."

He squirms in his seat. Whatever he means to say or ask next, I brace for the worst.

"Do you think there might be space for me out here?"

The kid surprises me again. Then I think about the towel, the blanket, and the likelihood of someone stumbling here for no reason in a downpour. Maybe I'm not so surprised after all.

"Why the hell would you want to stay in this dump?"

Andy squirms again. "I left home, but I still want to finish high school."

This statement makes no sense to me. As two separate things, I get it. I'm not stupid. Put them together, though, and I have no idea how that works. "You don't think they might find you if you keep showing up at your school?"

Anger twists his mouth, giving me another surprise. He has venom inside him. "They'd have to want me in their house," he snarls.

I can't imagine a parent not wanting their kid. The idea makes me sick. "Did you kill somebody or get a girl knocked up?"

His eyes snap wide open. "No!"

The force of his honest outrage makes me flinch. "Okay. Then what's going on? If you want to stay here with me, you have to tell me what I'm getting into. All of it."

Andy deflates until his head droops enough for his chin to touch his chest. He tells me about alcohol, oxy, screaming, and beatings. Everything started in a slow creep downhill when his grampa died and left them with nothing but medical bills.

To prove it, he pulls off his sweater and the T-shirt underneath. Bruises from yellow to dark purple decorate his torso. I notice the shape of a boot heel. A cluster of tiny, round burn scars decorate his left shoulder.

"My mom is the smoker," he says as he puts on his shirt.

I don't know what to say. Each new statement in his story makes the last one sound tame. My gut churns at the thought of a teenager trying to bear this burden by himself.

Though I prefer solitude, I can't justify it to his face. This kid needs someone. I'm far from the best choice, but at least I won't beat the crap out of him. "You can stay here as long as you want, Andy."

One side of his mouth twitches like he wants to smile but can't after saying all those things. "Thanks."

My hips hurt because I've been sitting on my ass for too long. I grip the edge of the bowl and haul myself to my feet, letting the blanket fall to the ground. The left leg is paralyzed from the knee down. Everything else still works, at least, so I can avoid dragging the foot when I'm not tired.

Sometimes, I wish they'd lopped it off so I could use a fake leg. Then I hear another story about phantom pain and decide to appreciate my numb lump of withered, useless meat.

Andy hops to his feet, arms outstretched to offer help. "I didn't even realize you had a problem with your leg."

"Crazy how sitting works." I'm surly and I don't care.

He grins at me. Maybe I remind him of his grampa. "Do you need help?"

"If I needed help, I'd be long dead by now." I take my crutches and slip the cuffs over my arms.

"Oh. Do you want help?"

I pause, because no one asks me that. In the forty years since the accident, no one has ever bothered to ask me what I want, just what I need.

"I suppose I wouldn't mind if you picked up that cup and took it to the sink back there to save me the hassle."

Andy smiles and hops to the job, holding the blanket around his waist. I watch him hurry to the kitchen and find the latch to swing open the counter.

Determined to get some exercise, I stump my way around the cafe. All the memories creep back into their dark corners.

Water runs. Metal clanks. The kid is doing my dishes. I'm not sure how I feel about that, because I don't want him to think he has to work for me in order to stay. Besides, I'm not helpless. I can do things. On the other hand, standing and leaning at the sink takes a lot out of me. He's young and spry. The effort probably costs him nothing.

After a few minutes of walking, I can feel sweat on my forehead and lower back. I debate braving the rain to go to bed and decide not to abandon Andy. If I'm too tired later, it won't be the first time I've slept in the bowl.

Another lap leaves me panting. I push myself to do one more. Halfway through, I have to stop and catch my breath. Andy slips under my arm without a word and helps me shamble to the bowl. We sit. I pant. He watches me like he thinks I might keel over any minute.

"There's a pair of ferris wheel cupolas around back." I want to make sure he knows this before I conk out for the night. "They're made up as beds. Take the one with the blue stripe."

"Okay."

"Bathroom is that way. Marked and all. Don't let the octopus arm mess with you. It's a shower. There's a handle you pull to make the water go. No water heater, so it's cold."

"Good to know."

I try to think of anything else important. "Food in the kitchen is mostly canned. I go into town once a week to get more."

He nods, then he looks at me and his body cringes just a hair. Like he thinks I might swat him if he asks the wrong question. Something to work on, since I don't plan to swat him for anything.

"Is it okay if I cook sometimes?"

"Is it okay?" I laugh. "Boy, if you want to cook, you go right ahead and do it. I'm not the worst, but standing isn't my favorite place to be."

With all the energy of a jackrabbit, he bounces out of the bowl and rummages through his backpack. He comes back with two old, worn books and sets them on the table so I can see them. One is an encyclopedia of edible plants in the Pacific Northwest. The other has instructions for setting snares and other wildlife traps.

Andy's eyes light up as he babbles about catching and skinning wild hares, foraging for tubers, and drying herbs. I don't understand most of it, but the gleam in his eyes makes something old and forgotten unfurl in my chest.

Hope.

Connie J. Jasperson lives in Olympia, Washington. A vegan, she and her husband share five children, a love of good food and great music. She is active in local writing groups, is an active member of the both the Northwest Independent Writers Association and Pacific Northwest Writers Association and is a founding member of Myrddin Publishing Group. Music and food dominate her waking moments. When not writing or blogging she can be found reading avidly.

Bambi's Revenge

Connie J. Jasperson

Lisa rinsed the remains of her cold tea down the drain. Through the window, movement on the Wonderland side of the fence caught her eye. It was only seven a.m., but already a handyman could be seen piling a few more decrepit statues next to the property line. The pile of junk from the abandoned theme park frustrated her, just one more thing she couldn't deal with.

The kitchen was clean, immaculate, unlike her life. With everything done, she couldn't put off the hour she dreaded any longer. Sitting at the table, she began opening her mail. Nothing but demands for money she didn't have.

Jason had always handled the bills, controlling their money as absolutely as he controlled everything else. She had learned early on not to ask her husband about anything. But that meant she'd had no idea just how close to the edge they were.

A new envelope, one from the county assessor's office, struck fear into her heart. Feeling disassociated from the moment, she read the final demand for property taxes.

She sat staring at the paper, unseeing. Jason hadn't paid their property taxes for more than a year, and now the county was going to foreclose on the house she couldn't sell.

Lisa fought the urge to scream, biting back sobs. Rage bubbled up, threatening to burst forth like the poison it was. With all her willpower, she stuffed it down, fighting the ever-present feeling of powerlessness that giving in to her anger wouldn't help.

Jason was safely hidden away in jail, insulated from the shame he'd brought on her. When he was arrested, she'd had no idea where to get the money to post his bail. Fifty thousand dollars—despite his threats and demands she'd been unable to find it. Now his trial date was approaching, and the newspapers all said he would get at least ten years. Maybe she'd never have to look at him again.

The prosecuting attorney's revelation of her husband's duplicity had been the final straw. Because of him, she had been questioned, treated like a criminal. He was still lying, keeping his secrets, still playing some game only he knew the rules to. But with him safely locked away from her, she'd found the courage to file for divorce. Life should have been wonderful, but she was losing everything.

Despite having sold most of her furniture, she was nearing the limit of what she could put on her credit cards. The day after Jason's arrest hit the news, she'd been "downsized" from her job of fourteen years. She knew it was because her ex-husband was a thief, and everyone thought she was guilty by association. Her unemployment compensation was running out, but while it came nowhere near to covering her bills, it was something.

How could he have done it? How could Jason have kept the magnitude of his theft a secret for so long? Like a rat trapped in a maze, her thoughts always returned to that conundrum.

The worst thing though—Lisa's aunt had called that morning, letting her know her father had suffered a heart attack and died. He'd left her with a forty-year-old mobile home on a sand dune out in Westport to somehow dispose of, but that was something she could deal with. What she couldn't cope with was the horrible feeling of loss. Her dad had been calm and supportive when Jason's disgrace hit the news, swearing it would pass and offering her a place to get away from things if she needed it.

Lisa hadn't taken him up on it, hadn't taken the chance to say goodbye, to tell him she loved him, and now it was too late. The guilt was like a mountain on her chest; she couldn't breathe.

She had to have air, so she went downstairs and out to the patio, hoping to find peace. But even there, she couldn't escape the misery. She had to walk through Jason's disgusting man cave to get outside, and then she was faced with another disaster.

The gaping hole in the ground that was her unfinished swimming pool had to be filled in, but she couldn't afford to hire anyone to do it. Her agent had warned her that before she could sell the house, she was going to have to shovel all that dirt back into the hole. Walking around it, she stood with her back to the shambles of Wonderland, trying to think of what to do.

All through her childhood, Lestrange's Wonderland had been a mainstay of their small town, and Lisa had enjoyed having the old theme park as a neighbor. The lights of the distant midway had been pretty, glimmering through the trees. Even the sounds of the carnival on summer nights had been nice, a distant but comforting buzz of music, laughter, and happiness. With the many hidden gardens in the Fairytale Forest, featuring scenes from every famous tale, it had seemed a magical place to her as a child. Old Mr. Lestrange had truly made it a place of wonder.

As an adult, she had loved the way the sounds from the midway drifted in the evening air when she and her daughters sat out on the patio, playing Candyland. But now, twenty years on, Lisa's daughters had left home. Mr. Lestrange had died, and his son had never returned to take over the theme park. Now she heard many rumors about the place and the Lestrange family.

It was odd that René had only come home to bury his father and then left again, letting everything fall into disrepair. Of course, he was in the military, fighting the war in the Middle East. And at least, unlike her life, someone was cleaning up the old theme park.

The familiar feeling of hopelessness stole over her. What was the point? She would never be able to sell her house. And even if she could resolve that, there was the problem of Bambi. What was she supposed to do about that elk?

Wonderland falling to pieces, the gaping hole that was her swimming pool, and Bambi's perfectly preserved corpse in her basement —everywhere she turned she was faced with the disillusionment and failure that was her life.

A noise sounded behind her, and she turned away from the hole, seeing the handyman from Wonderland in white coveralls, pushing a wheelbarrow loaded with more statues for the pile. This time it was a deer and a large, grotesque gnome.

She wanted to say something, to tell him to stop piling junk next to her yard but didn't have the courage. Then she realized he wasn't just a handyman. "René?" Lisa walked to the fence. Joy coursed through her, followed by fear that she had made a mistake. "René Lestrange, is that you?"

He looked up, weathered and older now, but it was still him, still the boy she had secretly admired, the lucky boy whose father had owned Wonderland. "Lisa Allan? I didn't know you lived here."

"I heard you were in the Middle East."

He nodded and looked away. "I was. I'm retired now." He gestured to the rundown jungle that Wonderland had become. "I've managed to find a buyer for the old midway and carnival rides. They'll be here next week to haul it away, taking it down the coast to Oregon. Once those are gone, and the junkman comes for this stuff, I'll be rid of the property. A developer has purchased it."

René's hair was long, and his smile was no longer that of the carefree eighteen-year-old she had graduated with. He seemed worldlier, slightly disillusioned. Despite the changes, his eyes twinkled as they took in the great hole that was her pool. "Ellen Mahoney at the grocery store told me what Jason did. What have you been doing? Digging his grave?"

She didn't know how to answer that. Finally, she managed a smile, ignoring the reference to Jason as she had become good at doing. "It was supposed to be a pool. I lost my job right after Jason was…and I've run out of money. I'm going to have to fill it in. Who knows? Maybe I'll make it a garden." After a little small talk, nothing important or serious, René went back to work.

Relieved that René was resolving the problem of Wonderland, Lisa went inside and continued dealing with her mail.

She was just finishing when a sound in the driveway out front alerted her to visitors. Praying it wasn't another reporter, she went to the window in time to see her car being hooked up to a tow truck. Tears of frustration ran down her face as she watched her Prius being repossessed.

She now had no transportation…unless…she had never driven Jason's Jeep, but she probably could. She'd never had a problem driving a manual transmission. It was just that she detested it. The Jeep represented the start of his obsession with hunting. He'd ordered it specially painted in shades of green and brown camouflage, and whatever else he had let fall to ruin, he had kept the engine and tires of "his baby" well maintained. However, it was ten years old, paid for long before the embezzlement, and still insured.

Two years before, Jason had insisted on transferring it into her name and now she knew why. She hadn't decided what to do with it, but it was in the garage, which is why her Prius had been out front in the driveway.

That Lisa would now have to drive the disgusting, smelly thing was a given, but she had to erase Jason and his filth from it. Unfortunately, if she wanted to cover that camouflage, she would have to pony up the cash for cheap paint.

She could take the money from her slim food budget.

Gritting her teeth, Lisa started walking down the street to the hardware store. She had barely walked beyond her property line when Betty June Murray stuck her head up from her front flower bed, a snide glint in her eye. She'd been the mean girl at school, and little had changed. Divorced and with no apparent source of income, Betty June lived well.

"I saw them hauling your lovely new car away. How sad for you." The ever-present diamond and sapphire tennis bracelet glinted on her wrist, scattering and reflecting the light, just as Betty June herself seemed to. It had appeared on her wrist at Christmas, and she was never seen without it, always holding herself in such a way Lisa couldn't avoid noticing it.

Betty June's glee was hard to take, but Lisa nodded as politely as she was able. "My car was three years old. But you're right, they took it."

Betty June smirked a little brighter. "How sad for you. It looks like your whole life is falling apart."

Lisa offered a hard, bright smile of her own. "It consoles me to know I have your support and friendship."

As if a switch had been thrown, Betty June became apologetic. "You do have my support, although you don't believe it. The gossips in this town are something else."

Lisa thanked her again and walked briskly down the street, confused as usual by Betty June. She'd been Jason's girlfriend in high school but dumped him for a middle-aged neurosurgeon.

Jason claimed he felt sorry for Betty June and insisted on socializing with her and her shallow friends, a rich crowd that was out of Jason's league. At first, Lisa was flattered, as Jason clearly was. She had wanted a friend, but soon found she had nothing in common with the woman. One minute she was malicious, the next she was forcing her castoff clothes on Lisa as if that meant they were friends. Something about her gave Lisa the chills.

Awash in her gloomy thoughts, Lisa managed to make it to the hardware store and back with no further sympathy from her neighbors. Tenino was a small town, and some folks had small minds.

First, she cleaned every trace of Jason's presence from the Jeep's interior then pulled it out of the garage and onto the front lawn, where she washed off years of caked-on mud.

Before she began painting, she set the video camera up on the tripod, filming the event for Jason. She'd been making a video record of the dismantling of their marriage as each of Jason's possessions were sold or hauled away, making sure he knew what had happened. She knew it was mean, but it was her way of hitting him back, repaying him for many bruises he'd given her.

Lisa stood a ladder beside the Jeep and climbed up with her paint tray and roller at the ready. Starting with the roof, she rolled paint onto the Jeep, satisfaction growing with each pass as the disgusting camo was covered. Paradise Pink wasn't a color she would have chosen, but it was enamel paint and had been on sale. The small can of Purple Passion held just enough to make a perfect racing stripe.

She knew you were supposed to spray the paint on but didn't know how to do that or even if Jason owned a sprayer. From her perch on the ladder, she noticed Betty June staring through her windows, wearing a look of shock and horror. Why it mattered to her, Lisa didn't know. Nothing about Betty June made sense.

It surprised Lisa that she found such satisfaction in her creativity. She had used all her paint, even the leftover white and yellow from painting her kitchen. The painted daisies on the corners of the doors, just above the running boards, made her happy. When she was done, she looked forward to driving what was now *her* Jeep whenever she could afford the fuel. She poured a glass of wine and officially named it Daisy Duke.

The next morning, Lisa began shoveling dirt into the hole. After fifteen minutes, she had to quit. She'd hardly made a dent in it before she became too tired to continue. The sting of her blistered hands raised the fear that the job might not be done before the county evicted her, and then they would fine her for leaving behind an unsafe hazard.

She sat on her patio drinking cheap burgundy, the bottle resting beside her, as she attempted to read but couldn't concentrate.

"Hey." A shadow fell across her and Lisa looked up, seeing René. He grinned, holding up a bottle. "I see you're drinking the same fine vintage I do, and before noon at that. My pension doesn't allow for champagne. I know you're not reading. Want to talk about it?"

Lisa shook her head. "I do, but I don't have the words. It's too big, and I just can't. But I'm glad you came. Sit and help me enjoy the silence. I haven't had a friend for…a long time."

"I imagine it's been tough." René nodded, sitting on the lounger facing her, and leaning back, he closed his eyes. After a long, comfortable silence, he said, "I never intended to come back, you know. I left my dad and never looked back."

"Why?"

"The bloody, never-ending parade of bizarre new statues, my dad's eternal obsession with the Brothers Grimm, Mother Goose, and fairytales in general. They were more real to him than I was. When I was four, my stepmother died, and he retreated into his fantasies. You can't imagine what it was like growing up with Pinocchio as your babysitter. I had to get away from it. The military was my ticket out of town." He opened his eyes, meeting her gaze. "Do you know how many statues I've found so far, tucked all over the twenty acres?"

Lisa shook her head.

"As of today, one hundred and seventy-three." René's chuckle was slightly bitter. "I'm not done yet. But soon, hopefully. Finding a buyer for the rides and the midway was the difficult part. It takes a semi-truck to move them and a driver who has experience with transporting carnival rides. I was lucky to find a buyer willing to make the trip up here from Oregon."

Lisa held up her bottle, and René held out his glass. Setting the bottle back on the table, she said, "I'm embarrassed to say how small my problems are compared to yours. Jason was a liar and a thief, and a bully. Every time I open the mail, I'm faced with some new example of his deceit. I can't understand how I was so blind to what he was doing. But I was afraid to question him about anything."

He shrugged. "Jason was adept at intimidation."

"I've found a home for most of the corpses, but no one wants Bambi. Figuring out what to do with him seems impossible. But the Ferris wheel and such…those are big problems. It's wonderful you found a home for them."

René's eyebrows rose. "Corpses? Bambi?"

"I'd better show you."

She gestured to the patio door behind her. "In here." Sliding the door open, she led him into the walkout basement, to Jason's man cave. They went past a badger, a marmot, a raccoon, a small bear, and a lynx, all on display and posed as if still alive. Around the empty space where the giant flat screen TV had hung, the wall was decorated with the severed heads of four deer and two antelope, several dismembered antlers, and a bighorn sheep's head. But no matter who entered the basement, their eyes immediately went to the corner where, taking up as much space as a car, Bambi stood, his immense rack of antlers nearly touching the ceiling.

"This is Jason's man cave or, as I think of it, the Mortuary for Murdered Mammals. It's where some of the money Jason stole went. I haven't found what he did with the rest. My daughters and I did without vacations, clothes, books, and other luxuries for years and years, while... this." She felt some pride that her voice didn't shake when she added, "All those years he shorted us, made me feel guilty for wanting a nice home and all the while, he was lying. He stole that money from the soccer league, from children. These corpses represent everything that could have been in our life but wasn't."

"Corpses indeed." René just stared, shaking his head. He gestured at Bambi. "This one is definitely a problem. How did he get a Roosevelt elk down here?"

"It took four guys and a forklift. They had to lay him on his side, and even then, he barely fit. It took a lot of maneuvering." Lisa gripped her hands together, fighting the urge to break something.

He looked around. "But you said you found someone who'll take the others?"

Lisa forced herself to speak calmly. "A natural history museum in Tacoma is coming on Wednesday for them."

René shrugged. "Well, since you've shown me the skeletons in your basement, I should show you mine. Did you ever wonder where I grew up?"

Lisa shook her head. "You were popular, a normal person. Not an outsider from the trailer park like me. I just assumed you lived in a real house somewhere."

René shrugged. "I *yearned* for a real home. A home in the trailer park would have been a place I could bring friends, like normal people, as you say." He saw her surprise, sensed her curiosity. "Come and see. I'll make sure you get back home before dark."

Lisa had forgotten what it felt like to be adventurous but walking through the ruins of Wonderland with René made her remember the girl she had once been. He pointed out places where he had made inroads in clearing up. Several large dumpsters were filled with debris, and one was partially full. "The garbage service comes twice a week for this stuff, although I could fill these bins every day. I still have a lot to do. Once the rides are gone, I'll use my dad's old Kubota to finish cleaning things up. The tractor was how he maintained the grounds."

They came to the abandoned food court, a small motorhome parked beside it. A motorcycle stood beside a firepit, and a lawn chair with a book resting on the seat showed that someone lived there. "My place of residence, for now," he said, gesturing. Walking around back, he unlocked a side door of the food court, with a faded sign that read *Employees Only*. Leaving that door open, he led her through the storeroom and stood before a nondescript door labeled *Private*. "Come on in. You're the first guest I've ever brought home." His handsome features bore an expression she'd never known him to wear, one of wariness. "I haven't had the courage to go inside here since my father's funeral." Taking a deep breath, he unlocked it, pushing the door open.

Lisa entered the room, which was illuminated by high windows, covered with dusty lace curtains. She turned and turned, unable to comprehend what she saw. It was a large studio apartment, divided into living areas by the furniture. The layout made sense, but nothing else did. Life-sized statues in various poses were everywhere, as if they were the numerous family members living there. Snow White stood at the stove, apparently cooking a meal. Rumpelstiltskin waited beside the wood stove, his arms full of wood. Opposite a large 1980s television, Prince Charming sat on an ancient sofa, his outstretched hand holding the remote. Cinderella and Alice played cards at the table, while the White Rabbit offered a cup of tea to a dusty Rapunzel.

The room was crowded with statues, so many that Lisa couldn't take it all in. Some were characters from fairytales she had never heard of. Two beds stood in opposite corners of the apartment. Pinocchio stood beside the child's bed, holding a robe and several other small garments. Tinkerbell perched on the headboard of the adult's bed, welcoming the sleeper with a smile.

"My job when I got home from school was to sit quietly and pretend to be a statue, which I became quite good at." René's lips twisted into a smile, but his eyes gave away his discomfort. "My father never got over Vietnam. Wonderland was how he coped with what he saw over there. Wonderland and alcohol."

Lisa laid her hand on his arm. "And you? How do you cope?"

Startled, René laughed. "I see a shrink regularly. The VA does a little more now for us vets than they used to."

"Not enough, I'd wager." Having seen the magnitude of René's secret, Lisa could only laugh, stricken by the similarity of their problems. "What a pair we are, both trying to escape the immortal dead."

He shook his head, chuckling. "In high school, just when I thought nothing would ever surprise me, you always did. And you still do. How did a smart girl like you end up married to an asshole like Jason?"

Lisa laughed. "I was nineteen and naïve. It seemed like an escape from my mom's drinking. My dad was on the road all the time, so I couldn't live with him. Jason's a master at playing the good guy, and everyone trusts him."

"He was one of the more likeable bullies in school, I'll give you that. But underneath it all, he was a thug."

"I didn't realize that until after the girls were born." She corrected herself. "I guess I didn't want to know it."

They walked back to Lisa's house. "What's your plan for tonight?" René asked.

"I'm going to figure out what to do with Bambi. Then I'm going to start photographing the tools in the garage and get them posted on Craigslist. That way I should be able to pay some of my bills."

"I've been doing much the same over at Wonderland, and tools will fetch you a good price, especially certain brands."

Later, as Lisa closed and locked the garage door, she saw Betty June's Mercedes backing out of her drive way, probably heading off to some fancy party. All her bigwig friends were in Olympia, yet she chose to live in a Podunk town like Tenino. It was a mystery. Sighing, Lisa screwed up her courage, deciding to face the beast in the basement.

Bambi towered over Lisa, and she was sure he weighed at least as much as a refrigerator. But his base was on castors, so maybe she could shove him toward the slider, to make it easier to have him hauled away. Each wheel had a little lever that locked it in place. They were stiff, but she finally got them unlocked. Getting him moving was difficult, but she braced herself against the wall. With a huge shove to the base, she had Bambi rolling.

At least, the elk was rolling until suddenly he stopped and began tipping. Lisa panicked, vainly trying to stop his fall. With an almighty crash, he toppled over, almost crushing her and just missing the raccoon.

A greasy hunting magazine had somehow gotten stuffed underneath Bambi's platform, and the wheel had caught on it, jamming.

It figured—Jason was the worst slob. As Lisa picked the magazine up, a handful of papers fell from it. Feeling slightly disassociated, she found herself looking at several statements from a bank in Olympia.

At the top were two names, neither of which were Lisa's, along with an Olympia post office box for the address.

Betty June with no income and all that jewelry. How long had Jason been sleeping with her? Long enough to have acquired a joint bank account. Jason had taken every penny Lisa had ever earned before she even saw her paycheck. How much of her wages had gone into supporting her cheating husband's mistress?

For a moment Lisa was stricken dumb. Then the rage she had kept bottled flared, burning, turning her vision red. She stared down at the prone elk taking up all the floor of her basement, and a wordless scream erupted from her. She grabbed her keys and stalked to the garage, raising the door, and backing the Jeep into the yard.

The halogens lit the yard as well as a solar flare, and she dropped it into four-wheel drive. A wild, vicious glee coursed through her veins as she drove through the backyard, bumping over Jason's precious rose garden, laughing at the sound of snapping bushes. With some effort, she got the Jeep parked so it faced the sliding door, its lights shining across the unfinished pool and into the walkout basement, illuminating the room. Lisa walked around the hole and set the video camera up on the tripod. This was one event that had to be filmed for Jason.

Hooking the winch to the slider, Lisa went back to the Jeep, kneeling beside the front bumper and flipped the switch on the winch. She couldn't stop chuckling, enjoying the noise as it yanked the door out of the wall. Once it was free, she shoved it out of the way. With the slider gone, she took the chain and walked toward Bambi.

René's shadow looming over her woke Lisa. Sitting up, she looked around. "Oh, god. My head hurts." She was in the lounge chair outside on her patio, an empty wine bottle on the concrete beside her. From the sun's position, it looked like she had slept until noon, or nearly so.

He held up a plate. "I made breakfast. Tacos—a surefire hangover remedy."

"Thank you. I can't remember the last time anyone made me breakfast."

"I can't remember the last time a friend of mine buried an elk. It's a good solution, although the finishing touches seem a little macabre."

Lisa looked at the gaping hole in the wall where the slider had been, then at the trail of damage leading to the pool. Standing at odd angles on the dirt pile ringing the hole in the ground were several of the statues from René's junk pile, draped in black and staring down. "I kept thinking how he was a victim too. Jason murdered him. Bambi deserved a funeral."

Rene grinned, handing her a plate. "I heard a lot of noise over here, but figured it was Betty June having one of her parties. Now I wish I been here when you did it."

Fighting the desire to howl, Lisa showed him the receipts. "Betty June and Jason—that bitch is wearing ten thousand dollars' worth of the stolen money on her scrawny wrist. She knows where the rest of it is. The proof was under Bambi's platform." Rage bubbled up she shouted, "He knew I'd never look there. The bastard!"

"But think about it—when he fell over, Bambi had his revenge. Jason always was arrogant and careless." René's gaze turned hard. "So is Betty June. I have an idea as to how to knock a little of the shine off her if you're interested."

Lisa sat at the table, scanning the receipts she had found and saving the images into a file. For once, her ancient, touchy printer seemed to want to help, and the task went smoothly. "I'm going email it to the prosecutor's office now, or I won't be able to relax." She composed the email, made sure the images were attached and pressed send. "I'll FedEx them the originals tomorrow, so they'll have them when they go to court."

"Good. I'll pin a few copies of the jeweler's receipt on the bulletin boards in town, starting with the board at the library." René grinned, an echo of the mischievous boy she'd known so long before. "That should rattle Betty June good and proper."

That evening they sat on Lisa's patio, gazing at the pile of dirt and the black-draped mourners still surrounding Bambi's open grave. Lisa said, "I'm going to move into my dad's old place out at Westport and let the county have this mess. I just don't know how to fill the hole in first."

"I'll do it. I can use my dad's little Kubota for the job, so no problem."

Tears stung her eyes. "Thank you. Thank you for your kindness and for being a friend." She wiped the corner of her eye. "I'm going to miss Bambi, and I'm going to miss Wonderland."

René laughed. "You'll always have your memories."

"And the movie." Her wicked grin faded. "I'm going to miss you."

He laughed again. "My house is on wheels. I'll visit."

Roslyn McFarland is the author of multiple Young Adult novels, including the No Sea trilogy (book 3 on the way), for which the "Fiji Mermaid" is a prequel. She specializes in fun, clean reads with a fantasy or sci-fi twist and a splash of romance. In addition, she is a freelance cover designer, and has taken on the role of editor and designer for the Color Your Own Story Book collection, written by her own daughter and illustrated by April Bullard. Already amassing a lengthy list of future series ideas, Roslyn plans to continue turning dreams into reality for many years to come.

The Fiji Mermaid

Roslyn McFarland

1962, Portland Rose Festival, Waterfront

"Step right in! Step right in!" the hawker bellows. "See the most wondrous creatures in the universe! Step right in!"

I consider his white painted face, floppy hat, fur stole, vest and bell-bottom get-up. "Ah'll pass."

"Hey! They've got a two-headed woman in there, Tim. Let's go see," my shipmate Fred urges, pushing me past the daffy at the door and straight for the ticket counter.

"But ah don't..."

"Awe come on, man. They've gotta have a cute babe or two. Let's check it out."

"There's plenty girls by the rides," I protest, but he's already handed some change to the bored-looking old lady behind the counter and received the paper entry tickets. "A freak show? Really? Ah thought those died out in the twenties."

"Then I guess we got lucky, and you Southern boys are missing out. Anyway, we have two days before we go back to the ship. Let's have some fun with our leave."

Shaking my head, Fred pushes me through the beaded curtain and into the dirt-floored hallway of the large tent.

To the left, in a small alcove, sits a man with tattoos covering every square inch of his body. I find myself revolted and fascinated all at the same time.

Moving forward, through a small doorway to the right, a man in East Indian garb is juggling swords. As we pause to watch, he selects the largest of the bunch, and proceeds to tilt his head back and swallow it.

"Holy cow, man! That thing is longer than his body! How does he do that?"

"Ah have no idea," I reply, impressed despite myself. "What ah'd like to know is what kinda crazy made him try sticking a knife down his gullet in the first place."

In the next three rooms, we view a woman with an extra face on the side of her head, both made up in garish colors, a very hairy fellow they referred to as the "Wolf Man," and a strong man lifting unrealistically large weights.

Chuckling as I cross the threshold of the final, over-decorated room, I half expect to see a three-headed purple cow. In no way could I have prepared myself for the vision before me.

Within a small alcove, decked out with glittering beads that shimmer like a waterfall, sits a large, sealed box, probably four feet wide by five feet tall and filled with water, an air tube throwing bubbles up from the bottom. Inside is a young girl.

Hair, the blonde of early morning sunlight, floats around her pale face and torso, as her arms move to modestly cover her full chest. Darkening skin at her waist morphs into dull yellow…scales, flowing into a long, flowing tail.

"Holy mackerel, Tim! It's a mermaid! A real one! Or it's the most humdinger of a con job I've ever seen, eh buddy? 'Fiji Mermaid' they call her. I wonder where…"

I barely hear him. I'm entranced. Mind blown. She is the most magnificent creature I've ever beheld. Then the girl raises her dark eyes, meeting mine, and I fall into the depths of them. I drown in her pools of sadness, hurt and longing, every sense of time and space evaporating. Somehow these eyes, the very essence of this girl, pierce me to the depths of my soul in a way I've never experienced.

Fingers snap in front of my face.

"Hey, Tim! Tim! Wake up, man. Are you coming or what? Let's go."

"Comin'? Going? Going where?" My mind is sluggish, enthralled by the raw beauty in front of me.

"Back to the rides. This honey may be juicy to gawk at, but I think we'll get more laughs with those choice bits by the Ferris wheel." He pulls a flask from his pocket, taking a swig as he heads for the exit.

"Ah, uh…yeah. Yeah. Ah'm coming."

Looking down and away, the mermaid turns from me, her chocolate tipped fins brushing the glass, her visage even more forlorn than when we arrived, if that were even possible.

"Ah'll be back," I whisper, determined. We hadn't spoken, I didn't even know her name, but the need to be with her overpowers me. "Ah promise."

Her head turns, eyes darting back toward me briefly, and I swear I can see the slightest upturn of her lips, as if she heard me.

My knees weak, feeling conflicted, backing away requires a force of will. Making myself move, I tromp after Fred to go flirt with girls I no longer have any interest in.

I will come back to my mermaid. I always keep my promises.

An hour later I ditch Fred and his giggling Navy groupies. Entering the freak show tent for the second time, I ignore all else and head straight for the back room. Unfortunately, this time there's a crowd. A family gathers around the aquarium, making appropriate noises of shock and wonder.

My eyes are only for the girl in her chamber. Somehow, she sees me enter, her expression brightening fractionally. Moving toward her as the family files out, my plans are stymied by an older couple entering the space. I find a stool in the back corner, settling in to wait for them to leave, biding my time as a series of couples and a smattering of individuals circle though. My eyes stay fixed on her, taking in every nuance, especially when she looks at me. I should feel like some strung-out zero, but I don't. Something about her is too special to dismiss or tarnish. The feelings she evokes in me are overwhelming, inexplicable, and unselfish.

Real.

A mob of laughing teenagers stumble in, probably drunk, interrupting my train of thought. Pointing, taunting and egging each other on, one boy steps forward and bangs on the glass as the girl inside cowers against the walls of her prison.

Red haze colors my vision.

"Get away from her, you damn fool!"

At nineteen, I'm not much older than they are, but I'm an athlete and have been trained by the toughest guys in the military. Still, there are five of them.

"Oh ho! Looky what we have here, boys. The fish chick has a bodyguard," the boy sneers at me, his greaser buddies turning to flank him. "What's your bag, man? Don't like us messing with your piece of *tail*?" That earns him a few guffaws.

I pause, strategizing. The lot probably wouldn't pose much of threat to me sober, let alone loaded. Of course, there's always the chance they could damage the girl's tank through sheer stupidity, and I don't want to get myself kicked out of here, either.

Spearing the ringleader with a glare, I try to talk them down first.

"You boys don't want no trouble, now. Why don't you just get on back to the carnival before you start something you'll regret."

"We'll regret? I think your hick math is wrong, Southie." He pauses to crack his knuckles, taking a step closer. "And you're the one who don't want none of this."

Dang. These boys are itchin' to get their butts beat.

"Leave now," I try again. "You can get yer kicks somewhere else."

"Nah." He makes eye contact with two of his friends. They nod. "I think we'll get our fun right here." And with that he takes a swing at me.

Clumsy and slow enough to see coming a mile away, I easily dodge the blow. A slight pull on his arm and push to his shoulder sends him crashing to the ground.

Completely losing his cool, face red and whole body shaking with anger, he spits as he yells, "Get him!"

The other four need no further encouragement, all piling in toward me, fists flying. Deflecting blow after blow, I realize their drunken imbalance may actually work against me. One or two actually land hits with their off-balance maneuvers. I back away, circling around to place myself between them and the girl. Chivalrous, but not my brightest move.

With the leader still trying to leverage himself up off the floor, the other four semi-surround me in a half circle. Two of them go for my arms while another takes a shot at my gut. Deflecting the two on the outside, I send the guy on the left into the third attacker and watch them both go down in a tangle of limbs.

"Hey! What's going on here?"

Floppy hat guy from outside is at the room entryway. His call pulls my attention away for the briefest second, long enough for drunk number four to execute a flying tackle, crashing us both backward and into the tank with a loud cracking sound. Shoving him off me, I spin in time to see the large crack in the glass grow, becoming a spiderweb of fissures. With a final groan, the wall of the tank shatters, exploding outward in a glass-peppered waterfall.

Barely managing to remain standing as my opponents are washed away, and vaguely registering the carnival barker shouting for help, my eyes are locked on the figure of the mermaid girl. Eyes terrified, she's sucked out of the jagged opening, the broken glass raking her tail as she passes over it. Instincts kicking in, I drop to my knees and stretch out my arms, barely managing to catch her before she hits the shard-littered ground.

Dazed, her dark eyes are full of pain and confusion. Her chest is wracked with convulsions as she coughs out water. Twisting and reaching up with some effort, she clutches at my shirt and collar.

"H-help. Me."

The barest breath of a sound, her plea hits me harder than any gut punch, igniting my core with protective fire. Struggling to my feet in the wet mess, I clutch her closer and step over dazed drunks and out of the room, scanning the area.

"You there! Stop!"

With angry shouts behind me, I spot a semi-hidden exit behind a large promotional poster. Hindered by the weight in my arms, I manage to rip away the rope ties and push through, finding myself in a dark back alley under one of the towns many bridges.

Not pausing to think or plan, I hold her close…and run.

I allow myself to stop only once, setting the girl down on a bench so I can strip off my pea coat and wrap her in it, heading straight for my hotel room. Luckily, the dive deals with a lot of rowdy military visitors, and no one bothers to look up as I sneak past the front desk and into the stairwell. I don't want to risk running into other guests in the elevator. While being wet may not be cause for speculation, or even carrying a half-naked woman, the large tail protruding from the bottom of my jacket probably would get a few gums flapping.

Awkwardly shifting my passenger to pluck the room key from my pocket, I unlock the door and step inside, letting it swing shut behind me. There I pause, indecisive.

"Do ah put you on the bed or in the tub?"

"On the bed is fine, though I wouldn't mind a bath later."

Startled she answered my speculation, I barely manage not to drop her, instead placing her gently onto the double bed.

Setting my coat aside and scooting herself backward, she leans into the semi-clean pillows, her beautiful locks not covering nearly enough.

Blood rushes to my face…and elsewhere. I avert my eyes from her spectacular form.

"Thank you."

"Ah, uh…what?" The ugly painting on the wall isn't much of a distraction.

I feel her hand touch my sleeve, and a shock of electricity travels straight to my heart.

"I said thank you. For saving me."

I glance sideways, "You're, ah, welcome," I respond, quickly looking away again. "What, ah, what's your name?"

"Jeesle. Jeesle de Dalan." I hear a soft rustling. "You can look now," she informs me, amusement coloring her voice. She's pulled up a blanket to cover her chest and torso. "And you? What is your name?"

"Tim. Tim Duckett, ma'am." I run my fingers through my shorn hair, uncertain of proper protocol here. "Uh, nice to meet you?"

Her laughter fills the room, a chime of lilting notes I don't think I'd ever tire of hearing. "Yes. It is most certainly nice to meet you as well."

"Ah, uh…" Encouraged at seeing some light return to her eyes, I ask, "Do you need to be wet, or somethin'? Ah can soak some towels, or there's a tub…"

"No, thank you. I can survive perfectly well out of the water for quite some time, and after being in that horrid box for so long, being dry actually feels quite lovely." She stretches, languorously. "A bath in fresh water would be nice, but maybe later."

I nod, working out some excess energy by pacing from the door to the window, and back again, hands mashed into my pockets as my brain spins.

I stole a mermaid from a dang Carnival tonight. On liberty. Ain't that a tale for the grandkids.

Jeesle watches me, both wary and trusting, a slight quirk of amusement on her lips.

I pause at the end of the bed. "Uh, beggin' your pardon, ma'am, but…what now?"

Her expression sobers. "I need to find a way home."

"Home? So…Fiji? That's near Australia, right?"

"Oh no, silly man." Her smile returns with a giggle. "The carnival people made that up for the customers."

"Then…the ocean?"

"Possibly. What city are we in? The men who moved my tank weren't very forthcoming. It was hard for me to keep track of my location."

"We're in Portland, Oregon."

"Hmmm." Tapping her lips thoughtfully with one delicate finger, a slight crease forming between her brows as she thinks. "Do you happen to have a map?"

"Uh, yeah." She looks at me expectantly. "Oh. You mean to look at it now."

"Yes, please."

I do her bidding, no question, digging through my duffle bag and handing Jeesle the tourist pamphlet I find there. Pulling out a rickety chair from the table against the wall, I sit next to the bed.

Unfolding it carefully, she smooths the paper on her lap, the blanket on her chest dipping slightly as she leans forward to study the details. Trying not to stare at her ample cleavage, I direct my gaze, instead, to the delicate finger tracing its way through streets and landmarks.

"So, um, where are ye from?"

Her lips twitch up in a tiny smile. "My home is no place you have ever been, nor anywhere you will ever travel to."

"Well that's just a bit ambiguous, ain't it? And are you sure? Ah am in the Navy, you know. We do travel some."

"I am quite certain."

"Then, where did those freak show fellers, uh, find you?"

She sighs. "Florida. I was careless. I had never been to…Florida before, and I didn't pay enough attention to my surroundings. I found a nice spot to watch the people visiting shops and on the beach, from a stream that ran into the ocean. The boat of fisherman came from behind, taking me completely by surprise. The next thing I know, there's a bag over my head and bruises all over my body. I'm only a Deusame, it was stupid of me to try my Douxgraine alone, so I was unable to get away while they held me on land."

Having no idea what those words are or what she means, I nod for her to go on anyway.

"The men passed me around for a while, then finally sold me to the carnival master, oh, I'm not sure how many months ago. He stuck me in the water box, and fed me old fish, but at least no one could touch me anymore." She doesn't look at me as she speaks, but single tear drips onto the map.

My vision burns with the scarlet images she's painted for my imagination, and I'm filled with an unearthly desire to track down and beat bloody every one of those pieces of scum who held her captive, leaving their bodies in the bone yard to rot.

"They'll never touch you again," I swear to her, fiercely protective.

Large chocolate eyes rise up to meet my blue ones, full of hope, and maybe the start of trust, remnants of unshed tears swimming in them. It's all the thanks I need.

"Now. To find somewhere you can go to find yer kind near here. Or do ah need to drive you all the way to Florida?"

"Don't you have a ship, or something, to get back to?" she asks, looking pointedly at my military garb.

"Bugger th' ship," I scoff, though my insides feel wrapped in barbed wire at the mere thought of deserting my post. I worked hard to get where I am, positioning myself to get even further up the chain, and

I've never taken my duties lightly. One look at her, though, and I know I'd throw it all away in a heartbeat if she asked me to.

She smiles, melting my heart.

"I think I have found a location somewhat closer than Florida. You'll not need to break the bonds of trust with your Navy." She points to the map. "Here. Here is where I must go."

I break my gaze away from her face with some effort to look where she's pointing. "Oswego Lake?"

"You are surprised?"

"Well, uh, yeah. Ah guess ah just thought you'd want to go to the ocean somewhere."

The air fills with her chiming laughter again. "No. Not this time. Maybe if we were closer to San Francisco." She winks at me, laughing at my baffled expression. Then her merriment is cut short by a wince.

Anxious, I move closer. "What's wrong?"

Lifting the map reveals two streaks of blood, her injuries having soaked through the blanket over her lap.

"Dang it, woman! Why didn't you tell me you were so badly hurt?"

She shrugs, looking away. "I did not realize, or think to concern you."

"Well, obviously ah'm concerned. Let me see." I slowly and gingerly lift the blanket off her tail, careful not to pull it from her torso, and examine the two gashes she received from the broken glass. "One's not too deep, but this other one looks like it could use stitches." I cock my head. "Ah gotta admit, ah'm not exactly sure how to do that with yer scales an all."

"It is fine. I will get them tended to when I get home. I'll bind the wound for now."

"Ah'll bind yer wound," I insist, standing and pulling off the top sheet from the bed. I then use the Swiss knife I always carry to slice it into strips of fabric. Jeesle lifts her tail, wincing in pain, while I use two of the strips to tightly cross bind the wound. I unsuccessfully do my best to ignore the soft smoothness of her bare flesh beneath my touch. Scales or not, her beauty ignites something inside of me. "Ah hope this'll keep till we can get you where you need to go."

"It's fine," she sighs, reaching to grab my hand and giving it a squeeze. "This feels much better, actually."

The heat between our hands electrifies every nerve, flowing

through me. "Well, uh…"

The front door swings open, banging into the wall with a resounding crash.

"Tim! My man! Where are ya?"

Reflexively, I grab the comforter and throw it back over Jeesle's tail, barely covering her before Fred comes stumbling into the main room, a giggling girl on each arm. All three are visibly loaded.

"Tim! There y'are. We were lookin' for you." Pausing to belch, Fred spots Jeesle. "Hey, hey, hey! Looks like you already got some company, eh? Nice bird! Out of sight, man."

"Uh, yeah. An' we're sort o' busy." I try my best to block his line of sight. Fred may be a skirt-chasing lush, but the guy was a whiz kid. I couldn't risk him recognizing her.

"Where'd you go? We're having a blast, I turn around and you've disappeared."

"Ah, uh…"

"Oh, that reminds me! Man, did you hear about what happened at that World of Wonders tent we went to? I guess there was a big brawl and the whole place was ripped apart. The toughs are going ape, man. I guess one of those mutants hit the road, you know what I'm saying? They're offering up all this green to whoever finds him…her…it…whatever. Like they could blend." He laughs at his own cleverness, losing his balance and taking a couple steps—just enough to see around me. "Yo, baby, haven't I seen you somewhere before…"

My stomach drops like a two-ton rock. "What do you want, Fred?" I interrupt, desperate to change the subject as I shift in front of his line of sight again. "You and the ladies."

The blitzed bimbos giggle at being called ladies, rubbing up on my friend. It's enough to distract him. Thank goodness.

"Want? Riiiight! We're getting a bite. Gotta bag some food for the brain, you know? You need to come! Plenty for all." He grabs a girl with each hand for emphasis.

"Ah don't need any of yer gut waddin' cheap eats right now." I move forward, pushing the whole group toward the exit. It's not difficult considering their intoxication. "Thanks anyway, Fred. You have a good night, now," I add, shutting the door firmly and cutting off any objections. Throwing the lock, I breathe a sigh of relief.

"Did he recognize me?"

"Ah dunno," I admit, stalking back into the bedroom. "But he was nice enough to provide us with transportation to yer lake." I hold up the ring of rental car keys I'd slipped from Fred's pocket, giving them a jingle for emphasis.

At three in the morning there's fewer possible witnesses, but I don't count on a clear exit. Considering how many sailors are around this weekend, odds are someone will be still be up and about. Creeping down the stairs, I make sure Jeesle's tail is well hidden from view by the blanket I've wrapped her in, before furtively edging through the lobby. Out the back door of the hotel, we head for the waiting rental car. I found and moved it earlier, while Jeesle was taking a bath. Donning one of my spare tee shirts to cover her top afterward, she probably should have dried off first.

As I'm settling her into the passenger seat, a cry raises up behind me.

"There! There she is! Fella's, over here!"

"Fred? That son of a lame dog." Slamming the passenger door, I practically crawl across the hood in my hurry to get to the driver's side, firing up the car and ramming it into gear. "Thanks a lot, Fred," I shout out my open window as we pass the traitor, tires squealing, wishing I could pause to beat the snot out of my shipmate.

Later, I promise myself.

"Any time, man," he calls back, waving a handful of bills at me, likely his payoff for providing info on the mermaid. Being blitzed clearly did not interfere with Fred's memory, or tighten his loose lips.

Finding my way to Lake Oswego proves pretty easy, as it's basically a straight shot out of Portland, following the river. I reach over to grip Jeesle's hand as I drive, enjoying the contact while hoping it will help her feel safer. Headlights bloom into view behind us, the raucous yells and blaring horns telling me these must be the carnies looking for their lost prize.

"They'll not get ye," I reassure her, giving her hand a squeeze and hitting the gas.

The lake is the most prominent feature of the town, and surrounded by fancy homes. Easy to find. Locating a place to park with direct access to the lake, however, is proving more challenging. The angry carnies hot on our heels aren't helping, either.

"Ah'm gonna have to drive right out onto that there dock, so you can jump from the car straight into the water."

"All right." Unwrapping the blanket, she frees her tail. I also see her strip off my shirt from the corner of my eye, and make myself focus on driving. Her voice is calm, though her expression broadcasts her fear, or excitement. I can't tell which.

Yanking hard on the wheel, I jump the curb bordering a grassy park with a small copse of trees, the tires spinning out on the dirt. I floor it, heading straight for the small dock, hoping I'm gauging the size correctly in the dark and the car will actually fit. Sounds of screeching metal, and shouts behind us, tells me our pursuers aren't pausing either.

A shot rings out.

Jeesle gasps, her fear almost palpable as her whole body locks up, her knuckles white as she grips her seat.

"You aren't hit, are you?" No response, only ragged breathing. I rip my eyes away from the brush in front of me for a brief second. "Jeesle!"

"No. No, I'm fine. Terrified, but fine."

Swerving to miss a large oak, I swear under my breath. "This ain't good. Yer gonna have no time to be messing with getting to the water. As soon as ah pull to a stop on that there fishing dock, you jump for it. Got it?"

I swerve as two more shots ring out, my own heart pounding wildly in my chest.

"Got it," she replies, her breath ragged, but she grips the door handle firmly. "Ready."

"All right then. Let's do this."

Flying around a trash can, I aim straight for the pier, flying onto the wooden planks with a bump, and only hitting the brakes when all four tires are safely on the dock. Screeching the vehicle to a halt, mere inches before the guard rail at the end, Jeesle flings open her door and launches herself out of the car.

I open my own door and stand, watching in wonder as she sails over the fencing and arcs beautifully into the water. My heart clenches, despair washing over me. "Ah didn't even say goodbye."

More shots ring out, and a bullet whizzes past my head.

"You're gonna pay for that, Squid!"

Two cars screech to a halt, blocking the dock and any possible escape. A silhouette in the headlights levels a shotgun at me, and I hear the distinctive pump action sound.

With nowhere to go, I do the only thing I can. Vaulting the rail, I take a deep breath and splash into the lake. Staying under the cover of the water, I peel off my shoes and swim deeper, butterfly kicking away from the gunman. A lifelong competition swimmer, my experience serves me well.

Over a hundred yards in, my lungs start screaming for oxygen. Angling upward, I'm about to breach the surface when my leg is caught by something, and I'm pulled back down. Mildly panicked, I look down to see what has hold of me.

Jeesle.

The mer-girl is there, keeping me from rising. Before I can think or do anything, she flicks her tail and is face to face with me, her lips meeting mine.

My head practically explodes in a mass of sensation. Warm lips, the feel of brushed silk and sweet as honey, are followed by a rush of oxygen she passes to me as her mouth opens to mine. Her fingers trace through my short hair as she grasps my head and neck, holding me close, and my own arms reflexively wrap around her.

For the first time, I allow myself to truly appreciate her curves. Her soft skin is warm, heating me through my sodden clothing, her body is pliant as she molds herself against mine. If there is such a thing as Heaven on Earth, I must be in it.

Too soon she breaks the kiss, pulling back slightly. "I'm going to help you get to a safe place."

Shocked by how well I can hear her under the water, I nod.

Smiling, she grips my shirt, and guides me in for another brief kiss before her powerful tail speeds us through the water, faster than any mere human.

Only a short while later, it feels like second but must be longer, she is pulling me up to the surface. We are in a small alcove, protected by overgrown bushes and trees, though I can see a fancy house nearby. More importantly, I can't see or hear the carnies and their guns.

"Thanks for the lift." Enveloping her in my arms, I hold her body close.

She lets me cradle her for a moment, but pulls away too soon.

"Dearest Tim. I owe you my life, but you've earned my heart." She pauses, sadly placing a hand on my cheek. "I found you, only to leave you now. I wish I could bring you with me."

I cover her small hand with mine. "Ah wish ah could ask you to stay, but…"

"It can't work. Not here, not now." Her eyes fill with tears as she brushes her lips against mine one last time. "I will never forget you," she whispers.

"Ah think it's safe to say you'll be impossible to forget, too." My own voice is thick with emotion. I can feel my soul shattering.

"Maybe someday," she offers weakly, slipping back under the water, her glowing tears winking out of existence as she disappears from my life.

"Someday." I repeat, meaning it with every fiber in my being. "Ah promise."

Tim goes on to serve his country with distinction, before leaving the military and establishing himself as an elite swim instructor and coach, never marrying and never forgetting his promise…

Steven C. Schneider is a practicing lawyer in Spokane, Washington. He listens to the stories of others for a living. His writing life started when he was fourteen with science fiction and poems for girls, two major themes that weave through his work. He has completed a trilogy, *Sweet Charlotte in the Higgs Field*, *A Small Goddess*, and *Heart String Theory* as well as non-fiction works. His current work continues exploring science fiction memoir. "After all, in a multiverse, all stories that can be told must be told."

The Monkey Bug Circus

Steven C. Schneider

The plane landed in Spokane a few hours after redrise as Sol approached forty-five degrees past its zenith. Much smaller and dimmer, Roseus shaded the horizon pink to dark purple as its larger primary descended. It was pretty, but this time of year, at this latitude anyway, it was a bit tiring. Even though he had grown up here, Dan was now used to more real darktime farther north in Nunavut; but, as the flaps went fully up, the wheels hit and braked on the tarmac, and the engines reversed and roared in protest, his excitement overtook any jetdrag to come.

In fact, as the plane taxied in toward the terminal, he was wide awake with the anticipation of meeting Meg again after so many years. Out of the plane window, he watched the late summer swarms of monkey bugs in the grass beside the runway; a sight once familiar and since forgotten; it was too cold up north for monkey bugs. But with the appearance of the odd little creatures, some attracted to the light in the plane window, he knew he was definitely on the road home.

It had started with a random search on the net when his life was in a holding pattern. His wife had left him, though she stayed close enough to raid the house for furniture and toilet paper. The divorce was dragging along but sucking him dry financially and emotionally. He was spending as much time at the law firm as he could stand for the distraction and spending the evenings on social media for entertainment.

An old friend who had moved to McMurdo, Antarctic Free State, after college had mentioned Dan's first girlfriend, Margaret Shepherd. Dan hadn't thought about Meg much in the intervening years, though he had made her part of the myth of his past, the myth of his first sexual

THE MONKEY BUG CIRCUS

experience at fourteen. When he was a teenager it seemed impressive, but, like being the star quarterback in high school, the glory rapidly faded.

In the past, what had happened to Meg had never mattered to him. She didn't come to the class reunions, was completely out of mind. But this time, searching for things that mattered before his marriage, this time inside him, something began to happen.

He was alone in the house, depressed, anxious, not sleeping and so, one day after midnight he just began searching for word of Meg. Eventually, he happened upon her, now Dr. Margaret Sheridan, Ph.D. alive and well, right there on Linked In. She had become a professional astrologer and Jungian therapist, a fitting career for a girl who wrote the horoscope column for the middle school newspaper.

And when he saw Margaret's profile photograph, saw her familiar smile, no longer innocent, now world wise with experience, he saw the young girl he had known inhabiting a woman, a miraculous incarnation outside of time with a back story he could only imagine. Suddenly, he wanted to politely thank her for being his first love, to apologize for being a jeering teenager when they broke up.

That's all he wanted. He believed he must have offended her back then. He vaguely remembered shouting her name and taunting her across the athletic field to show that he didn't care that she had hurt him.

But at that moment, forty-two years later, he just felt proud of her, for having followed her dream. He didn't stop to think *why* he had the right to feel proud of her, but the feeling of entitlement and ownership was quite clear.

Sending that first e-mail to her, he had already discarded all the years when he hadn't even given her a thought. As he clicked on 'send', and without any evidence, he had decided that underneath that veneer of sophistication, she was exactly the same girl that he had not quite finished loving.

He wasn't far off. What he did not know then, what he could not have known, was that in the scant half hour between his message at 5:18 p.m. and her response at 5:42 p.m., for her also, the same forty-two years flew past. That one boy who had stood fast and remained unchanged in her mind through all of her other regrets, stepped into the light in that improbable moment.

She responded "What a surprise, a pleasant one," kept her composure, and said appropriate things about old times and times since, comparing families and professions with studied nonchalance. While Dan had in his mind to apologize for imagined slights, Meg also had not meant to do anything other than to make amends for breaking up with him, for not telling him then that it was her parents who had made her stop seeing him.

But inside her, a woman child was becoming not so quietly amazed, about to grab a stranger by the shoulders on the street and scream, "Listen to this…I am not making this up!" as her heart fluttered into a blur.

Dan learned that Meg had never stopped thinking about him after her parents broke up their relationship, after the seemingly criminal and tragic destruction of their mutual discovery of love and sex at the age of fourteen. Being a parent himself, he understood the problem, still not conceding however, that he had been in any way typical or naive. He and Meg had *not* been like his kids; *they* had been wise and powerful initiates into something much grander; *they* had been *different*. He knew it couldn't be true, that every thirteen year old thinks they have discovered love unlike any other; that's how it should be, but *his* feelings were only his and therefore, that same ordinary subjective wonder *was* different.

She began, slowly at first, to give him gifts of their past that had disappeared from his memory. Oh, he remembered events that they had shared; a first rock concert, a trip to the Space Needle, summer nights lit by blue flyers dancing at the carnival as they kissed under the bleachers, but he didn't remember *her* in those memories. It seemed like something else that required an apology.

She gave him back a history that was, in retrospect and appropriately, a pleasant fiction, a summer of awkward joy and passion; embroidered and embellished over the years to be sure, but in light of their mutual bad luck with marriage, a pretty good myth and metaphor on which to imagine a future.

She was still married then but had reached a breaking point; her two daughters were mostly grown while she and her husband had become more formal and polite with an undercurrent of rage. But this, this version of her, none of them had seen *this* before; no one had seen her *like this* since she was fourteen.

They hadn't seen the blue fairy ballerina, wound up tight, dancing and spinning on the music box; they hadn't seen this unedited complete joy that she had somehow kept hidden from them before this day. They did not recognize this whirling dervish with no cynicism, no sarcasm, no wry joking commentary. It was all gang way and 'Oh my God', cleaning out closets and ravaging photo albums looking for...him, in a poem, a photograph, a letter. She was on her knees over a drawer, purposefully separating wheat from chaff throwing papers over her shoulder until she spotted a gem. Aha!

She lovingly unfolded his letters and her life, stared at his face over oceans of time, squinting, concentrating to catch a glimpse of him. With each artifact she imagined inhaling his essence from so long ago, his first pheromones created only for her; she does not want to exhale, will never wash that hand, watches the memories cascade from coiled neural networks that have retained their shape for this moment, unwinding and speeding to the surface, ballast jettisoned.

She sent Dan those excavated artifacts; a framed photo taken at the carnival on Krishna Bhakti, their faces peering through comic cutouts of the hanging judge and the dance hall girl, captioned, *Dan Pritchard, my first boyfriend*; a poem, a cartoon birthday card he had drawn.

Her daughters watched this excavation, worried; worried because they had heard of this boy before, Mom's first love, an icon, a metaphor, an oft repeated bedtime story, now inconveniently come to life. They looked to their Dad for a solution, reassurance, a call to 911...*something*. But, most pointedly, she had never acted this way over *him*. He decided right then that he was through with the façade and simply turned away in disgust, grabbed his car keys off the hook and just drove. Eventually, he didn't come back.

Meg barely noticed as Dan shamelessly lured her further from any safe harbor:

> He only has your body
> But do not despair.
> Now you are mine,
> Infinity jingling
> On your ankles and wrists,
> Feet lightly pretending
> To dance with gravity.

She began to think, and later said out loud in a recording attached to an e-mail:

"Daniel, I don't think I could've left this life without having told you what happened and how I felt. As more years went by, I would have

114

found you. Technology is on my side. I would have to see your face again, hear your voice, I hope, to touch your hand again. I dare to hope to touch your lips again, look deep into your eyes again, feel your body against mine, if only as an innocent hug."

With that admission and plea from her, what else could he do; really now; what else could he possibly do but fall in love? Her words exploded inside of him, magnified his current despair and created the thought of a chance of something new.

'Dr. Meg' explained it in terms of archetypes, the collective unconscious; that the holy grail of that first love is presented to the innocence of youth and then snatched away. The youth then seeks the Grail Castle through the complexity of adulthood, and if lucky, discovers the prize again in the wisdom of age. The girl inside her was sure that *she* was the subject of his Cathar crusader's quest. Either that or it was something about Saturn being in cyclical retrograde around the date of his birth. It was fine with Dan either way.

And now, at the end of that cycle, there he was on the tarmac, his house in the north sold, his worldly belongings in storage, about to tap on her bedroom window again and fan the fire aflame, imagining that he was soon to be her first and last boyfriend.

Before that moment could come however, Meg had to struggle through the end of her marriage, counsel and reassure her daughters, see one off to college, comfort the other one who clung close to her now as her world changed. Dan was also finalizing his divorce, painting and fixing up the house so it could be sold and the proceeds split, all the while working full time and teaching classes at the law school.

In spite of all that, they did not neglect each other as they continued to peel back the layers of their past. Early in their e-mail exchange, she gave him a poem written on a scrap of paper that she had saved since they were fourteen. He recognized his own handwriting but did not remember the words. There was however, no doubt; it was unmistakably, embarrassingly, exactly what he would have written.

> My love for you
> Cannot be expressed
> In word or rhyme
> Or metered verse
> Perfect in its antiquity;
> And though this in itself
> May seem antiquated,
> Still it holds.

The sentiment that she had honored by guarding that ephemeral piece of paper inspired him once again in the future and he began to feel the mad rush of poetry into his head and fingers.

He wrote:

> Only for you do I rise in the dark
> Nodding off while writing to you.
> And in the day, while writing
> To someone else, still I nod off
> Thinking of you.

It seemed as if a timeless hour had spanned the distance between the first poem and the second, an hour faster than light that had frozen them and their love, waiting for a signal, a sign, to begin the warming flow, the ticking of the clockwork algorithm that would bring them out of suspended animation, like interstellar colonists, immigrants to the future in love.

> When I taste you at last.
> Like the first time,
> Will your memory rise
> From the place it has hidden?
> Will the years dissolve
> And my tongue proclaim you mine?

> When I smell you at last
> Like the first time,
> Will soft wispy hairs
> Greet gentle inhalation

With long guarded treasure
Surfacing and crying out; mine?

When I hear you at last
Like the first time,
Will the sound of your voice
Rain down on its long
Dried shadow, forming
Only one jealous word: mine?

And when I'm inside you at last
Like the first time,
Will our wandering souls
Intertwine, dance and gyre;
Recognize and welcome home
Each other, at long last shouting, *Mine?*

How odd she thought, to be obsessed with a fourteen year old boy, the only memory she had of him, when back then she saw him, most certainly, as *her man*. She wrote: "How do you do that? How do you make heat come through the computer like that?" He simply could not help it:

Inside my heart, you dance like a bee,
The movements of your body describing
The distance, direction and intensity
Of love.

Since then, they had e-mailed and talked on the phone almost daily, commiserated, sympathized, and planned a reunion after things settled down. He was content to wait and court her long distance, to create something this time that they both hoped would last. Perhaps they didn't realize it, but in that process, it had already become real, an easy friendship poised at a familiar crossroad, a song of innocence holding experience and wisdom at bay for just a moment longer.

In the dimming red tinged sol-set, he drove from the airport in a rental car toward the old park where they had sat on the swings and discovered each other and themselves, before and after that first poem. The satellite pictures on Google Earth had shown him that the swings were still there even though the park and playing fields had been renovated over the years.

He remembered going there when, like today, a small traveling carnival hit town for Krishna Bhakti, just before the little league season started. It was the kind with a clanking miniature roller coaster, a midway, and pony rides, the kind that might pop up in a mall parking lot for the weekend or be tucked in a corner of the County Fair. As a child, he would wander alone, not a part of the crowd, but observing life, sampling exotic cuisine at concession stands; Elephant Ears and Deep Fried Twinkies, following the sweetly rank smells of hay and horse apples; talking with the blue flyers as they danced and performed with their tame monkey bugs under the bleachers.

It was a flea circus set before a special pint sized audience, children who could still be paralyzed with wonder watching monkey bugs driving a toy fire truck, climbing ladders, saving a blue flyer manifesting as a damsel in distress, and a vision in light of a tiny fire breathing dragon battling monkey bug knights, all of which grown-ups ignored and relegated to childhood nonsense.

Later, when Meg happened, they ignored the blue flyers too. The tentative young lovers sat on one of the ornate high backed benches on the carousel, in something like privacy, holding hands and feeling the heat of their bodies beginning to intertwine and equalize like a physics experiment in thermodynamics, but with infinite potential; love = mc^2.

The kids called the blue flyers 'blue fairies', in homage to stories of imaginary friends that even adults could see, could see but then forgot how essential and comforting they were when a shy and awkward kid needed kindness, wisdom, someone to confide in, someone who could talk away the sticks and stones, the bruises and loneliness of childhood. Their presence in the peripheral vision of adults sparked wistful memories just as Dan's path now stirred his memories of ancient summers.

He smiled, remembering how you couldn't catch the blue fairies no matter how hard you tried, but when you tired of trying, *they* followed *you* around incessantly and wouldn't shut up. The bullies stopped chasing them while the introverts sat down and happily, quietly, played in their world. *Smart fairies.*

Kids didn't wonder about the monkey bugs too much, but scientists were always fighting over just why the bugs had monkey faces. In truth, they were more like caricatures of hominins. The best explanation was in the fact that the blue flyers could and did manifest a face sometimes, for ease of interaction or maybe it was just their idea of sarcasm. Perhaps this talent had evolved as a camouflage mechanism early on to avoid predators, like those moths with the big eyes on their wings.

So, the scientists reasoned, some insects started to mimic the blue flyers' protection mechanism, evolving faces, confusing their own predators. Well, that was as good an explanation as any, but it was one of those things you just took for granted. There were even monkey bug marshmallows in Lucky Charms. *Magically Delicious!*

The park, playing fields, and this week the suburban carnival grounds, were next to Dan and Meg's old junior high school, now housing a Manichean fellowship mega-church. At the back of the church was a path at the edge of a canyon. He parked the rental there in the auditorium lot and began to take the path he had not walked in forty years. There used to be a creek at the bottom. Every so often a coyote or moose would show up. Once, a black bear got itself treed by pet dogs in someone's back yard. Flocks of wild turkeys would march down the center of the streets and stop traffic. All of it made the local paper.

There were cookouts, marmot hunts with bows and arrows, trails leading to who knew where, and later, construction sites with stakes to be pulled up by children in protest of encroaching civilization. But now, looking down as he walked, now there was a major road leading to neighborhoods, a community college and shopping centers where before there had only been what passed for wilderness in the mind of a child.

His morning walk to school with Meg had traced the lip of this canyon, an isolated path then. They could have walked on the sidewalk along the south edge of the park; sometimes, in the afternoon, or when she had charge of her little brother, they did walk that sidewalk home, skirting the park, another church, and their old elementary school. But when alone and intent on privacy, when her mother was still at work, or off to curling practice, they followed the canyon rim and the shortcut to the few blocks of suburban street leading to her room, the remodeled garage with its own entrance; her own private door that had opened for him that summer in 2003 when they were fourteen.

He remembered one morning in that summer when he had concocted a grand gesture, something literary and over the top, like Romeo or Cyrano de Bergerac. He rode his bicycle to her house when it was still dark, before any sane person would be up. But the blue flyers were out, somehow as excited as he was. They swarmed and made a spiraling blue comet tail behind the bike, suddenly transforming the three block journey into the hero's quest it was.

He threw pebbles up at her window until her face appeared. She was befuddled and amazed. He stood on his bicycle seat and hauled himself right through the window and into her bed. She took him under the covers and into the alien atmosphere she had made there of sweat and heat and pheromones. They made love while the blue flyers made mood lighting in the window. It was the best day of his life till then.

When he met her again as an adult, he wanted to honor the children they were and their romantic naive enthusiasm. It came to him in a dream after those first e-mails and then the memory of that morning rushed back in detail. While still in bed, in the dark again, he wrote for her:

> Just now I smelled you on the sheets.
> You were one synapse from my hunting brain.
> Short, technical inhalations identified you,
> Calculated time and distance, knew you were near.

120

The trail was lost but not desire.
In the night I pulled you from the air,
Kissed you gently, only as a lullaby,
Held you at my right side as I lay on my back,
Your head on my chest, your arms and legs around me,
My right arm holding you close, a kiss on the forehead.
And so you slept. I didn't try anything.
But I dreamt of curves and hollows offered to me.
I dreamt of you above me, crying out. I dreamt
The smallness of you, the ampleness of you;
Dreamt the feel of you into being, and awoke
Moving inside of you, and continued
In a dream, holding onto the bed, pulling.
Then I saw a vision of you above me in another bed.
In a room, through a window I appeared;
Something you had prayed for to many gods.
I still remember you in that bed, sleepy,
Happy, delighted. Somehow you knew
Everything you needed to know.
We were alive then and I smelled you all the day
And treasured that presence on my body.
I smelled that on the sheets just now
But you were gone.

Well, that sealed the deal for both of them, the reality of that moment coming back in full force as he walked, a walk he had imagined since that first e-mail in August, 2045, just one year before.

They had arranged to meet by the carousel, so he made his way along the old path, now high above the traffic and bustle. Still, it seemed like a private dream to walk those same steps again, behind the long classroom buildings, the bungalows, and the athletic fields to the edge of the park. Along the way, the familiar sounds and smells of the summer carnival and midway grew stronger and started to nudge him to move a little faster.

From the canyon edge it was downhill to the baseball diamonds and the main carnival area so that he could not immediately see the carousel, though the Ferris wheel, the Tilt a Whirl, and the Octopus poked above the rise at intervals, the screams of their riders fading in and out with the motion of the machines. As he walked toward the spot where he knew the carousel should be, the midway and rides appeared before him. He heard the calliope music, came around from behind the concession stand, and saw her standing by the ticket booth. She was looking the other way toward the street entrance and so did not immediately see him in the dim red light.

But, as he approached, she sensed something and turned. She was dressed in jeans, a light cotton blouse, linen sport coat, her light brown hair unbound, and her lips the red he remembered from her 10th Grade school picture. She took a deep breath and met his eyes.

"Mr. Justice Pritchard," she said.

"Dr. Sheridan, I presume; enchanté." He said as he kissed her hand and made a little bow.

"Why, M'lord, so formal…"

She batted her eyelashes and they laughed as she took his other hand and closed her eyes. In silence now, he deliberately put his body in front of her so that his left hip touched her right hip, placed his left cheek on hers, his right arm and hand rounding her waist, tensed at her back, and his left hand holding her right hand high, as if to begin a dance. He closed his eyes too and inhaled the smell of her neck, clearing his mind of all other perceptions.

Memories stirred as sol-set approached and Roseus at its zenith evoked the same mood of privacy and the spark of dimly remembered kisses so long ago. The blue flyers were gathering as well, maybe some of the same ones they had known as children, gathering and dancing with their pets, too polite to greet them just yet. A shared tremor went through Dan and Meg as they exhaled together.

Arm in arm now, he bought tickets and led her to the carousel, to the sanctuary of their bench. The calliope music rose in volume and the platform began to turn to the squeals of children commanding horses, tigers, and ostriches.

With their long lifespans and unfading memory, the blue flyers certainly did remember them. They shooed their monkey bugs off to play and flew in curving braided trajectories among the carved animals, ignored as usual by the excited riders and cautious parents. At the heart of their behavior however, was an undeniable attraction to human emotions and they knew how to enhance human feelings, feelings they perceived as auras merging. 'Officially,' it wasn't polite to just butt in without permission, but actually asking for permission seemed too contrived, and killed the mood to boot.

Instead, there was a kind of silent understanding, humans treating them like a warm breeze or sudden chill, things in nature that just brushed against you and enhanced or changed whatever it was you were feeling in the first place. So, with no further invitation, they approached the bench from behind and quietly wove their blue light through the auras of Dan and Meg, causing a shared rush of breathlessness that erased the years as they held hands. As the ride ended, the moon was just coming up, bloodied by Roseus as it began its dive toward the opposite horizon.

"The house closed yesterday, she cleaned me out good in the settlement." Dan said.

"What will you do now?"

"Don't know," he joked, "I could only afford a one-way ticket."

"Well, you're in a bit of a fix, homeless, penniless, I could drop you off at the mission."

"Don't much care for soup and religion."

"Guess I'll have to take you home for a while."

"That'd be mighty kind of you Ma'am."

"Meg, please."

They laughed and she put her arm through his and pulled him tight to her side. They got up from the bench and watched as the blue flyers buzzed off nonchalantly like nothing was up. They then walked toward Meg's car noting the same old monkey bug circus mesmerizing a new generation of babies under the bleachers and began to speak of sharing a life in the world.

KateMarie Collins is the author of 20 fantasy titles, ranging from short stories to novels. She has garnered international recognition while remaining a lifelong PNW resident. A lover of cats, coffee, history, and family, she resides in the Seattle area. She is currently working on her 21st title.

The Unmasking

KateMarie Collins

Veronica tried to ignore the ache in her back. It didn't matter. It *shouldn't* matter. The delivery would be here soon. Even if the inside of the house was dismal, the front step had to be pristine.

At nineteen, she'd missed Carnival last time. She'd only been fourteen. The delivery driver had smiled at her, told her not yet. Her time would come. And then handed over one box to her sister.

The dress was the most beautiful thing Veronica had ever seen. Satin and lace, a wide ribbon lacing it up in the back. All in shades of yellow. Heidi's face glowed with hope and pride when she'd held it against her body, twirling around. When she'd tried to touch a single bell that dangled off a cord on the sleeve, her sister had slapped her hand away. "No!" She all but screamed.

Veronica hadn't seen the dress after that until the day the carriage came. It was the only day she saw the mask, as well.

And it was the last day she saw Heidi.

The day after Carnival, a liveried servant arrived. Said that Heidi was to be the wife of a man whose holdings were on the other side of the valley. A man rich enough that their small home was an embarrassment. Heidi had sent the servant not to collect her things, but to tell them never to visit.

Sitting back on her heels, she fussed with her hair. One brown curl never wanted to stay in place. As always, the sight of Mount Rainier made her smile. Tilting her head, the sound of horses approaching brought a fresh surge of excitement. Veronica bolted to her feet. "Ma! Pa!" She screamed. "They're coming!" She shook her skirts, bits of dirt and grass flying off.

The door of the cottage opened. "Hand it here, girl," her mother demanded. "Quick, now. Go brush your hair out. You have to look your best, so they give you a good box."

Veronica pulled at the leather piece that held her hair back as she darted behind the curtain that separated her sleeping area from the rest of the house. Quickly, she grabbed the wide tooth comb and ran it through her long hair. "Nonononono," she muttered as she glanced down. The soapy water had left stains on her skirt.

"Veronica! Hurry! They're with Jonas now!"

"Coming, Ma!" She twisted the waistband of her skirt, spinning the stained part to the back. Grabbing the sleeveless duster that rested on a peg, she donned it as she sprinted from behind the curtain.

Her mother stood in the door, waving her to hurry. Pa was outside already, waiting for the delivery to arrive. "Your day's here at last, Veronica," she said as she fussed over her hair. "Whatever the future holds for you, you'll learn it soon enough."

"Do you think it'll be as grand as Heidi's outfit was?"

A shadow crossed her mother's face. "Grand isn't what matters. It's the mask. It's enchanted. You can look at it, but don't put it on until you head to Carnival tomorrow night. It learns who you are, who you should be."

"Daniel! Is your youngest home?" A deep voice called out above the din of the horses.

"Aye, she is. Veronica!" Her father called out.

It was time.

Taking a deep breath, Veronica stepped back out into the midday sun. Clasping her hands in front of her, she looked at the driver. "I am here."

The man climbed down from the front of the wagon, leaving the driver alone. His hand clenched a piece of parchment. Unfolding it, he read aloud in a monotone voice. "The time of Carnival has come. Veronica di Contini, you are now of age for your fate to be determined. Wear what is in this box, enjoy your youth one last time. At midnight, your future will be revealed." He went around to the back of the wagon. Veronica heard him move boxes around before he came forward with one.

She said nothing as he placed the large, white box across her outstretched arms. A cream-colored ribbon held it closed. Her arms drooped slightly from the weight, but she didn't drop it. Her future lay within, for good or bad.

Veronica stared at her reflection in the hammered copper sheet that served as a mirror. The gown she wore danced with color. Muted tones of red blended seamlessly with greens and blues. Metallic threads made everything shimmer with the slightest movement. There was no lace on the dress itself, but the necklace that came with it was a delicate gold mesh. Small, clear stones that erupted with fire when light hit them lay embedded within the pattern.

Her mother had encouraged her to put her brown hair up. Shifting her attention to her face, she scrunched her features in disgust. It wasn't her. The braiding was too tight, too neat. Raising her hands before she lost her courage, she pulled out the multitude of pins and shook her curls loose. They settled across her bare shoulders. *There*, she thought. *That's who I am.*

Only two things left. The shoes, which sat at the foot of her small bed. And the mask.

She slipped her feet into the shoes first. Dancing slippers, really. Soft leather that hugged her feet and promised comfort.

"Veronica? Are you ready? The coach is coming."

"Almost, Ma." Taking a deep breath, she reached for the velvet box that rested at the bottom. Placing it on top of her small dresser, she raised the lid.

Nestled inside was her mask. The black leather was surrounded by small crystals. Peacock feathers sprayed out from the edges. A wide, black ribbon was attached on each side.

Veronica stopped breathing. The mask was more stunning than the dress itself. Her fingers lightly stroked the feathers, tracing the iridescent colors. Was this how Heidi felt when she saw her mask? Full of hope and terror at the same time? What kind of future would this reveal for her?

"Veronica? Is everything okay?" Her Pa's voice was soft.

Glancing at him, she smiled. "Yes, Pa. I'm ready," she told him as she shut the box. The mask wasn't supposed to go on until the last moment before she left her home.

Pa crossed the room and held out his hands. "Know that, whatever tonight brings you, we are proud of you. You are loved. Carnival is a rite we must all go through, but it doesn't mean you must turn your back on your past."

"I won't, Pa. I won't do what Heidi did."

He smiled and raised his hand to smooth one curl. "I know you won't. You took your hair down because this is you. The other...well, it's your ma. Not that she means you ill. She just—"

"She's Ma."

He drew his breath and stopped. A horse whinnied, followed by a bell ringing out once. The coach had arrived.

Fear gripped her for a moment and her chest tightened. Was that a tear in Pa's eye? Whatever it was, it left without a word. Instead, he squeezed her hand in parting and left.

Her heart raced in her chest. Lifting the lid again, she removed the mask. Before she could stop herself, she put it on her face and secured the ribbon.

The leather was smooth against her skin. As she lowered her arms, it felt...strange. While nothing moved, the mask seemed to melt into her skin.

Carnival had begun.

The carriage somehow avoided the ruts in the road, making the ride smooth. Two others sat opposite her. Young men. Jonas was one, of that she was certain. They'd known each other their entire lives. She'd know him anywhere, even wearing a mask.

The other one she couldn't quite decide who it was. Not that it mattered. Carnival was about being anonymous, hidden. Letting the real person out while pretending no one knew who you were. Tonight, the manners their parents had drilled into them could be put aside.

Veronica kept silent during the ride. She sat with her back to the driver, her voluminous skirts taking up the entire bench. The village slowly faded into the night. A few lanterns and fires let travelers know someone lived there, but nothing else.

"Wow," Jonas' voice was filled with awe as he stared past her.

She turned around to see. The manor house on the hill had always been special. The majestic pillars and archways looked down on Ashford, both protective and intimidating. As they drew closer, though, she saw the lights.

Thousands of them, most barely larger than one of the crystals on her necklace, covered the gated entry. They flickered and glimmered, dancing in the moonlight. The effect took her breath away. As the carriage passed through the entrance, her eyes grew wider.

The courtyard was even brighter, but the light never went past the gates. A dozen or more carriages danced around each other, waiting as the rest of the participants got out. She turned back around and nervously smoothed the front of her skirt.

Glancing up, she caught Jonas staring at her. His blue eyes danced with mischief. She smiled in return. Knowing he wasn't scared gave her strength.

When their carriage stopped in front of the wide steps, a uniformed man came forward and unfolded a small set of metal steps from the undercarriage. Opening the door, he held a hand toward Veronica.

She looked his way as she placed her hand in his, but he wore a mask. Not nearly as elaborate as the one the party goers had been given, but enough to hide his identity. *What did you expect?* She chided herself as she stepped out of the carriage. *Of course they're masked. No one talks about Carnival night. They don't want us to know who they are after it's over.*

Lifting her skirts so she didn't trip, she began the climb up the wide stairs.

The majestic doors opened up to a ballroom. Veronica stopped, her jaw slightly open. The room was massive. Their small home could fit in it a dozen or more times over. Chandeliers full of crystals reflected the light from thousands of candles. Colors bounced off the polished wood floor. One side was lined with tables laden with food. A fountain sat atop a table, an amber liquid flowing nonstop. Chairs were scattered about.

The curtains were pulled back, and ornate doors opened up to a balcony. Curious, she took a step toward one. Was there a garden it overlooked? A hidden grove?

A crescendo of sound echoed through the room, drawing her attention upward. Circling the room was a balcony. Book-filled shelves and doors dotted the walkway. At the far end, above the food, a small group of musicians played.

Standing in front of them was a single robed figure.

Glancing around, Veronica saw the entry doors shutting as the last of the guests came into the room. They all looked up at the figure. Expectation, excitement, and fear filled the room.

"Welcome to each of you. Tonight is your Carnival. For the next few hours, you have no rules. You have no expectations to meet. Dance, eat, drink. Talk to your friends, if you can find them." The figure laughed. "At the stroke of midnight, I will return. Your fates will be revealed, and you will be bound to those. Maestro!" They waived a hand at the band's leader and melted into the dark recesses of the balcony.

As the music resumed, Veronica found herself dancing. She was passed from partner to partner for a good hour. Everyone was trying to figure out who was behind the masks.

Tired, she retreated out to the balcony at last. It overlooked a small garden. The white stone pathways and benches stood out in the moonlight. One deep breath and she let the aroma of the pine forests fill her lungs.

"Why aren't you dancing?" Jonas asked as he leaned against the rail next to her.

"Got tired," she replied. Only, that wasn't quite it. She'd felt like she was being evaluated, judged even, by every partner she'd had.

"Well," he sighed, "I suppose that's a good reason. You really should get back out there, though. It's our last night before things change. You gotta take risks while you still can."

He moved closer to her. There was something in his stance, the tone of his voice, that didn't seem right. "What do you mean, Jonas?"

Without warning, his hands grabbed her arms and pulled her closer to him. His lips pressed insistently against hers. She raised her hands and pushed him away from her. "Jonas! What do you think you're doing?"

His mouth twisted. "What? Don't pretend you didn't like that. I know you did." He took a step toward her again.

"Stay away from me," she spat at him. Picking up her skirts, she ran back into the ballroom.

Her heart raced. What was he doing, kissing her like that? She'd never even thought of him that way! It was possible, yes, that their fates would be intertwined. But that wasn't love he'd offered her just now.

Leaning one arm against the paneled wall, she placed a hand on her chest, willing her heart to calm down. Was this what happened to Heidi? Did her first kiss come here, forced on her?

The room was too loud. The laughter was shrill, forced. She couldn't think. She leaned even more against the panel. The wall gave way slightly, startling her. A small gap appeared. Desperate to escape the party and find somewhere to quiet her mind, she pushed it open a bit more. There was a small room back there, with a spiral staircase. Veronica glanced around the party to make sure no one was watching her and lifted a candle out of the holder closest to her. Sliding into the secret room, she closed the door behind her.

The meager light showed no dust or cobwebs. The passage was clean and bare, except for the steps leading upward. Bunching her skirts into one hand, she took her time climbing the winding staircase.

At the top, the landing opened up to a small study. A fire was going in the fireplace, making the room comfortable. One wall was transparent, as if made from glass. She could see the party happening below her, but the sound never breached the room.

Placing the candle in a holder on the table, she watched through the window, mesmerized. She could see their faces so clearly from here, even through the masks they wore. Shadows followed them, mimicking their movements with precise accuracy.

"Fascinating, isn't it? Seeing your friends as they truly are instead of what they show us?"

Veronica spun around. The hooded figure rose from a chair hidden in a corner. "I'm sorry," she stammered. "I didn't mean to intrude on your solitude. It was just that…"

The hood fell back as they stood up. The woman's face was wrinkled, weathered. "It's fine, Veronica. Calm yourself. If I wasn't willing to have you here, I wouldn't have unlocked the door."

Veronica blinked. "You…you opened the secret door?"

The woman smiled. "Of course I did. This is my house, after all. I know all the passages. If I didn't need to talk to you, you'd never have found it."

She moved closer to Veronica. "Tell me, child, what do you see down there?" She waved at the party down below.

Veronica turned back to the window. "I see young people, having fun."

"What else? Look closer."

"There's…something else. You'd probably think I was strange if I told you."

A small chuckle escaped the older woman. "Not likely. Don't overthink it, just describe what you see."

She drew in a deep breath. "Everyone has a shadow with them, something that mimics their every move. Wait, no." She paused and stretched out a hand. "Over there. That shadow looks like it's whispering in the ear of that person." She stepped back. "And then he attacked the girl he was dancing with."

"Yes, he did. But what did her shadow do?"

Moving back to the window, she searched for the couple again. The girl wasn't fighting off the boy's advances, and her shadow was cowering next to her. "It's curled up, on the floor. She's not fighting back."

"That's too bad. I'd hoped she'd have been stronger." The woman moved away from the window. "Come away now, Veronica. The party's likely to get worse before midnight. And you and I have things to discuss first."

Turning away, she followed the woman and sat in a chair near the fire. "How do you know my name?"

"I learn about my guests before they come to Carnival. It helps me make decisions."

"Your guests? You mean…"

"Yes, Veronica. I'm the one behind all this. Or, rather, I have been. My time is almost up. I'm needed elsewhere. But I can't leave until I've trained my successor." She levelled a direct look at Veronica.

"Me? I'm not anyone special."

"Oh, but you are. You can see who people really are. Every time for the last three Carnivals, I've summoned someone up here. You're the only one to see the shadows, see how they react.

"Those shadows are who we really are. Your friend, Jonas. He's had a crush on you for years now. But he was afraid of what your Pa would do if he tried anything. Carnival meant he could give into that desire, and he thought you'd be flattered. Instead, you didn't cower. You didn't let his shadow overpower yours. You stayed true to who you are.

And that's the key."

"Key to what?"

"To living a life worth living. You're going to be given a choice, Veronica. The rest aren't expecting that. They want to be told. You don't."

She listened to the woman's words closely. She was right. She wasn't ready to settle for a life that was dictated to her. "What's the choice?"

"You can go back downstairs, rejoin the party, and see what I choose for you. Or you can take off that mask now and become my apprentice. Learn how to guide your fellow villagers to paths that will be beneficial. Run Carnival when I move on."

"What about Ma and Pa?"

"Excellent question, and one worthy of an apprentice. You show compassion for those around you." She rose and went to one of the shelves lining the room. Pulling a book out, she opened it. "Ah, here we are." She handed the book to Veronica. "Read this part here," she tapped part of the page.

Taking it, she read the paragraph. "An apprentice, or sorceress, must live apart from those she presides over. Should they be the youngest, and the parties are in agreement, the parents are allowed to visit. But such visits must be done in secret, so that others cannot learn of the relationship." She closed the book. "I don't understand."

Settling back into her chair, the woman replied. "It's not that hard. You must remain neutral. If it came out that your parents were able to visit or contact you, other families would try to bribe them to get advantageous marriages or careers for their children. It's simply not a good idea. You can do things to provide for them. That's not forbidden. But direct contact must be kept secret."

"What would you choose for me? If I went back downstairs?"

"Well," she sighed and folded her hands in her lap. "It's not decided, but it's possible you'd end up married to Jonas. He certainly wanted you bad enough."

The memory of how little passion she felt when he kissed her flooded back through her. He was a good person, but did she really know him? Would she be able to be a good wife to him? She rose and went back to the window, searching for him below.

Finally, she spied him. He'd pinned a girl against a wall. His shadow was dark, almost pitch black now. Hers was barely visible.

She made up her mind. She needed to protect the world. Being married to Jonas, or anyone else, wasn't part of that. Reaching behind her head, she undid the ribbon and pulled the mask away from her face.

"So, what do I call you? Mistress?"

"I prefer Gaia."

The chimes of midnight began to ring, echoing through Veronica's soul.

Sheila Deeth is the author of the *Mathemafiction* contemporary novels, the *Five-Minute Bible Story* series, *Tails of Mystery*, and other stories, poems, and books for children and adults. She is an English American, Catholic Protestant, mathematician writer with a math degree from Cambridge University England and a life-long love of words. Find her near Portland Oregon in the real world, or at sheiladeeth.com or sheiladeethbooks.com in the virtual.

Cat Carnival

Sheila Deeth

Alice's cat had the knack of disappearing. Sometimes Alice's mother sounded like she was pleased at its absence, as if the cat were just another mouth to feed. Of course, Mom didn't understand.

Alice's cat was black as night, green-eyed as leaves, red-mouthed as holly berries on a Christmas wreath. It always came back, and it never needed to be fed.

But it wasn't Alice's cat. It was *cat* when it wanted to be cat. And Alice was the human who belonged to it.

Alice lived in a human place of gray-ground streets, gloomy-sounding hawkers, red-brick and stone, dark tenements, and cesspit smells, where sharp-edged wheels bore carriages that rattled and rolled. Gray skies dropped rain on the crowded city, and nothing green would grow because their paradise had been paved with hunger, misery and pain. Alice's brothers, the older ones, took jobs, lost jobs, found money, lost money, lost shirts, came home, hid away from the unexpected birth of their new baby brother, and rued the day their father died when they became the helpless wage-earners. Meanwhile Alice, the one with the cat, was the only one whose face and fingers were clean because the cat cleaned them, and because…but only Alice knew that other *because*.

One day Alice's mother declared she'd found passage to something she called *a better place*, somewhere safe to raise her family. The cat wondered where they were headed this time, having come from Ireland's green to America's gray, exchanging the lack of potatoes for the lack of everything else, and black of wasted soil for the soil of waste. Alice's cat disappeared in haste, determined to learn the answer.

West. That's where they were going. West to a city not yet born, to a town surrounded by trees, fronds as green as a cat's eye, tall as the sky, wet as the ocean but almost dry beneath. Rich-fibred loam covered the sheltered ground. Nursery redwoods harbored tangled boughs of cottonwood and alder. Hemlock's feathered branches twitched under the weight of mossy cloaks. And every scent of green and life was like the morning light, pouring down on the bright arena of *cats*.

Kittens ran like children's giggling laughter, up over logs, splashing through water, swinging from a branch, and flying to land four-footed and firm. In the twinkling of an eye, these young cats seemed to change into boys and girls astride a racing carnival ride. Music played and painted horses neighed their equine pride. "This way, this way," the carny called, and the children, kittens all, lined themselves around his feet then bounced into their seats. The carousel turned. The lights flashed winter and spring.

A kitling yowled from the top of a tree, unable to climb down. Then a twisting slide appeared so cat-child laughed and rolled as he flowed to earth. More flashing lights. More merriment and mirth.

Alice's cat joined a team of dusky shades around a pot. Like witches, they tossed their cloaks and stirred their brew. Scents of eternity lingered in the air.

"You'll bring her here when they arrive."

"Yes, of course."

A cry distracted the secretive group. A well-thrown acorn hit its target in the coconut sky. Then the witches continued, "Bring her soon."

"They've got their tickets. They're on their way."

"Bring her now."

The cat disappeared. Behind her, she knew, the carnival continued to play in the green of its western forest, a different land. But the cat reappeared in that unforested city, gray with human tenements, loud with horse and carriage, dark where only stunted misery found root.

The people packed their bags, and Alice packed her cat. They went to the station where a fire-breathing dragon awaited to carry them over metal rails, dark-drawn like scars on the land. The train, the train, that ran then halted, then waited, then ran again and stopped again…in nowhere, neither West not East, that waiting yet again…

Their transport, not a dragon after all despite Alice's dream, had been shunted aside. The wheels were still, the carriages immovable, and the people were running out of food. Of course no one starved; neighbors shared, and hawkers eagerly sold their wares, but with so little to go around, no-one offered snacks to train-travelling cats not even meant to be there…whether the cats were purely feline or curiously something more. The train moved and stopped and was shunted aside again, so merchants and presidents could hog the line.

This posed no problem for Alice's cat. Her small human was dreaming again, with black eyes wide awake. The dust-bitten carriage faded into glorious, palatial splendor, flaked paint giving way to the colors of rainbows riding on velvet curtains that lined the marble-columned walls. Black cat transformed into a beautiful servant, skin the same shining, exotic, gloriously glowing color. She offered her mistress—and shared—wide plates filled with human delicacies: cakes, sandwiches sliced wafer-thin just like the rich folk ate, and sips of juice that the child pretended was wine. Alice begged to share with her mother and brothers too, but, even when she screwed up her eyes to imagine them there, they sat like sleepers unable to wake while she feasted.

"It's not fair," she complained.

Alice's mother pulled her out of the dream. Trembling palace walls crumpled at once like breadcrumbs revealing gray decay. "What's not fair, child?" Mother snarled, then continued, her usual refrain. "Nothing's fair in life. You should know that by now."

Alice knew. The cat knew too. But not the oldest brother, who complained, spotting his sister's black companion which had so carefully hidden until now, "Not fair! You were meant to leave that thing behind, stupid girl."

Alice wasn't stupid; she was magical. She closed her eyes and the black cat disappeared.

Transforming into a mouse was easy for a wise familiar. Staying alive as a mouse was another story. Alice wasn't the only child to have smuggled a pet aboard. Indeed—the cat-mouse quivered its whiskers and twitched its tail—the railway people should be pleased, else third-class carriages would be overrun with rodents.

Chased by a speckled feline with bright teeth and claws, mouse-cat ran under a seat, shuffled from her borrowed skin, and became a bird, which flew up and out through the window. A wide-winged eagle swooped down on her, so she transformed again, fur-feathers to scales, and chased it away. Someone shouted below, "Do they have griffins out West?" Then whistle shrieked, engine stirred, and wheels began to move. The train was on its way, and the cat on the wing.

She flew her griffin-body down, hooking claws into the wooden roof of their carriage. From here she could listen to all that occurred below. She watched her child and caught the continuing complaints of fellow passengers. And she dreamed, with griffin head tilted to one side, pondering a future she couldn't yet see. Not even a *familiar* could answer if there were truly griffins in America's West. None in the forest nor at the carnival, at least none that she'd seen. But elsewhere? Maybe.

The carriage was shunted aside again, with still too few miles covered. Everything had to wait so valuable goods could be transported along the line. A faster train with rich passengers followed, wheels rattling while they rolled. Alice leaned out the window to wave, scarcely noticing that nobody waved back. Why would they? They were the rich, eating at linen-covered tables, enjoying freshly heated snacks, real wine, succulent meats with gravy, and puddings that wobbled on cloudy cream like castles in the sky.

Alice had probably spotted the feast. She was hungry again. Her eyes turned black, and the griffin-cat slipped back inside to meet her. Alone of her family, Alice had food that no one else could see, and drink they couldn't share. She didn't clutch her stomach with hunger pangs, nor lick dried lips and drip rainwater-pans' sparse offerings into her mouth.

If only *their* eyes could change. The cat scratched softly at the leg of her younger brother, still scarcely more than a baby. Perhaps *he* could try.

In Alice's dream, the cat-ebonied servant bent over the sleeping child, proffering fragrant soup under the little boy's nose. Steam arose, and Alice saw her brother stir. "Wake up," she whispered, afraid to break the spell. "Wake up, Michael. Please..."

Michael shuffled his body on the hard wooden bench. *He wriggled and squirmed on the cushions of Alice's palace.*

He rubbed sleepy eyes with a questing, grubby hand. *He lifted both hands, almost begging to drink from the magical cup.*

Then he looked up, black-eyed and beautiful, hurriedly swallowing the gift the black-skinned woman offered. He smiled at his sister. "How? What? Why?"

Alice moved to sit beside him, holding a tiny cake to his quivering lips. "Eat this, and don't ask so many questions."

Michael ate till he was full. His eyes still black, his gaze still quizzical, he asked again, "How? What? Why?"

Then Alice pointed to her friend who trembled, swiftly shifting from servant to griffin to cat. "It's your heritage," the cat replied, once she had Michael's closest attention. "You have the power, you just never knew where to find it. Your sister has it too, but your brothers have forgotten. You simply have to dream."

"Am I dreaming?" Michael asked.

"Dreaming and real," said the cat. "The food was real. You'll feel full when you wake. But this place..." Alice's castle began to tremble again. "This place is your sister's dream and you're sharing it."

"How?"

"She invited you in."

Around them the rest of Alice's family sat stubbornly still. Their eyes had lost the blackness of youth; their brains lacked the elasticity of dreams. Plus they didn't like cats.

Alice's cat disappeared again, seeking the path from train to destination. The metal railway lines turned south instead of north, to a bay called San Francisco instead of Portland, Oregon. Once beautiful, its hills were scarred now with tenements almost as gray as the eastern city they'd left behind. Perhaps this detour was a test, to see how determined the cat might be to bring her human friend to the Cat Carnival.

She smelled the salt of San Francisco's water, an evil scent that reminded her of their journey from Ireland's shore. *Please, let's not play that game again.* But the ships on this bay were smaller, their bellies less filled with human detritus and pain. People were happy and mobile here, open to change, with many delighting in plans to head north along the coast. They sailed their cargoes out of the bay, along the ragged seashore to another river's wide and gaping mouth, then fought their way upstream to the port that waited beneath forest gleam. They talked, with loud voices and harsh sounds, of stumps and mess and mud. But they knew nothing of the Cat Carnival. These people weren't magical. They were contented, but they weren't cats.

Except…one delicate feline crept toward Alice's cat…pale as a ghost, blue-eyed as the sky, thin-furred, long-tailed and gorgeously beautiful… She touched her nose to Alice's cat, twitched whiskers, ruffled her fur, then feathered herself and flew toward Alice's train.

Both cats appeared in the aisle where baggage tumbled, wheels rumbled, and passengers stumbled half-asleep. The gray-white cat stepped like a dainty princess toward Alice's brother where he slept. She slipped her body sleekly alongside his ankles, and purred to his delight.

Soon, soon, the two cats promised, then disappeared again. The lure of the carnival called them. The green of moss that dripped like rain, of sunlight twinkling with festival colors, or birds that sang the tinkling of loose change in the carny's bag, and castled trees transforming to the cats' imagined scene.

Gray cat and black, they laughed like girl and boy, rode the carousel's horses together, sang their caterwauling song, then returned invigorated to their train-bourn human family. This gray-white ghost would be Michael's familiar, and together the felines would lead their people here. Their family would pay passage with work on the ships, as those unmagical siblings were so well-equipped to do—might as well use the muscles of the mighty, light-eyed brothers who couldn't see or believe but could surely labor in such a good cause.

The cats had it all planned out.

When their carriage shunted to a halt in the station, Alice's cat jumped out into the rain. Alice chased it all the way from station to port, through splashing puddles and wretched town, down hills toward the shore where gray of sky gave way to foggy white. Michael chased the ghost he'd decided just had to be his cat. Big brothers, mother carrying baby and bags, everyone raced the same way too, dripping wet with coats over their heads, until they came to the place where ships stirred soft on the wide clean bay with its blue sky and ocean and trees beyond the town, and its promise of more.

The cats leapt aboard while the family joined a line in deep conversation, comparing plots and plans, and pots and pans, discussing charges and labor, making promises, displaying muscles, then finally striding or stumbling up the plank.

No cats were meant to sail on the ship, of course, but Alice's and Michael's familiars took wing like seagulls and sat together on the rail. They saw it was going to be a hungry trip for the humans, the sailors having no food to spare, even for working passengers; but the two young siblings ate in their magical palace, leaving more of Mom's depleted supplies for the brothers. Everyone, even children, had to work on this busy boat, but palace time wasn't real and it gave them both relief. Meanwhile they questioned where their travels would end, while seagulls flew ahead to watch, and coasts of endless trees slipped greenly by.

They anchored close to a river, waiting for the tide. Mom wasn't sure they should stay aboard, but Alice and Michael said, "Please." Their bird-cats had whispered that the fast-growing town inland was a city of trees. The name the locals gave, Stumptown, sounded rather less attractive; people said, "It's all mud." But Alice claimed the beach was also mud. Big brother Sam expected more jobs in a city. And Pete would do whatever Sam declared.

In Stumptown, when they arrived, the remnants of trees proved altogether too broken and too real. Houses were mostly wood; streets mostly mud. Uninviting to say the least, but there was room for Alice's palace...and squirrels to feed two cats (who liked real food too)...trees... magic...even mystical hemlock's billowing boughs and fronds on the outskirts of town.

The cats declared, as planned, that the family had to move on. "Up the hill, into the forest," they said as they wore their servant guises, one black, one white, in Alice's palace. "We've things to do and places to go. You'll love our Cat Carnival. Come under the trees."

The desperate pleas of magical children do have some mystical power. Mother and brothers might not have wished to move out of town, but they obeyed. They couldn't hear the carnival though, just the twittering of birds. They couldn't see the glorious festive lights, just the colors of flowers and the twinkle of stars through leaves. They couldn't sense the slipping of slides, the swinging of rides, the swirling of carousel. But they sensed joy—even they, unmagical, could sense *that* wondrous taste—and that was enough.

Meanwhile Alice and Michael, wide-eyed in amazement, rode the carousel in magical time. Around and around on mystical horses they rose up and down, ears filled with the glorious cacophony of sound, mouths filled with sweets and glamorous treats, noses twitching to vanilla and cherry above the scent of grass and pine and leaf. They ran to the organ grinder, played with his monkey, chased up a slide and helter-skeltered down. Around, around, around and around. Music and cats welcomed them to a party without end. Cat Carnival was real. Cat Carnival was more than they could have imagined.

"Good," declared the witch to Alice's cat as they stood together, watching the cauldron, watching the future bubble in its depths.

"Good," purred Michael's cat, her blue eyes dancing to see the children play.

"Good," whispered the flame beneath the cauldron with dragon-smile. Fire licked over the heated edge, as if to gaze within. "Yes, this will be good," he said.

"A good place for them."

"A safe place for strangers."

"A sacred place one day."

"Sanctuary."

"A forest too."

In real time, Alice and Michael learned to dream food that stayed tangible, so the family could eat. They purified water with their visions; cooked meals over open fires. They shifted winds and breezes away until their cabin was sound, then tilled the soil, grew crops without dreams, took city jobs that promised hope and paid a just reward, and delighted in the growing of a brand new place, Boston or Portland its name—really, who cared? It was Stumptown to them.

It was their town. Its busy streets would be home to people of every shape and kind, made welcome by cats, even if human thought took a little more time to catch up. Its river would carry flaming dragons with glorious lights to shine their festival. And its green Forest Park, protected by love and by law, would remain the home of the Cat Carnival, delight of American dreams and familiars.

The Carnival is still there, guarded by cats, green with delights all hidden to those whose eyes can no longer turn black, but present to babies and the wise. Rain-dripped, sun-sipped, time-slipped, a mystical place where reality flips into magic and music plays.

If you're young enough, if your eyes can still change and your heart isn't hardened yet to mystery, if you dream very carefully and deep, and let the sound of magic catch your sleep, and if a cat's nearby, you just might find...Forest Park's Cat Carnival.

Jennifer Courtney writes as jl courtney. She lost her capitals in a sadistic line editing accident where all her darlings were cut—even those normally attached to her. She's the aging mom of three and the managing editor at Postcard Poems & Prose. Jennifer ghost writes, beta reads, and works as a developmental editor. She has been published at Page & Spine, Black Heart Magazine, Feathertale, and others. If you're pure of heart and have a silver bridle, she can be found at: jlcourtney.com.

Stark Naked

jl courtney

Shrugging into her uniform top and hoping unlaced boots counted as dressed, Louise answered the door with her biggest, fakest smile.

Her Team Leader, Sergeant Gray, was using the overhang to avoid the drizzle. He managed not to topple into her room as she jerked the door open—probably a good thing. She hadn't been his soldier long. Dropping him on his butt in a puddle wouldn't exactly color her as high-speed.

Gray kept his feet, but lost his clipboard. Louise snatched it out of a puddle and dried it on her pants leg before handing it over.

"Another wet one today, isn't it Sergeant?" she was smiling so hard her teeth hurt.

Her Sergeant frowned. "Stark, what the hell is wrong with you? You look guilty."

"That's just my face, Sergeant," Louise said. "You've heard of resting bitch face, right? I have resting guilt face."

Whatever the male equivalent of resting bitch face was, Sergeant Gray had it. Louise called it his I'm-still-ten-years-to-retirement look—called it that to herself, not out loud. Day or night, Gray strolled around, three quarters honey badger and one quarter wet cat.

Tonight though, Louise couldn't help but notice Sergeant's expression was a shade closer to I-think-this-might-put-me-in-the-ground.

"I'm here on a health and welfare check. Got anything in your room I need to know about?"

"Define 'anything.'"

149

Sergeant Gray barely glanced up from his clipboard. "Are you drunk again, Stark?"

"This early?" She pantomimed a halo above her head. "I just got off shift five minutes ago. How am I going to be drunk already?"

"Stick around a couple days." He tapped the rank on his chest. "You'll learn things." Gray might have been kidding, but Louise thought he probably wasn't.

"Last chance for the amnesty box," he said, "Do you have anything in your room that shouldn't be there?"

"Some drugs. And…a body. But, it's fresh so that makes it less weird," Louise turned to holler over her shoulder at the room behind her, "We're busted. Grab the mime and the goats and *run*." She turned back to face Sergeant Gray. "Strictly for research purposes, how big is that amnesty box?"

"You're hilarious, soldier." Her Team Leader shouldered past, leaving the door hanging open. "I'm coming in. Do me a favor and don't call, 'At ease.' I've still got the rest of these rooms to search. Some of these fuckers might actually *have* goats or drugs—or drugged goats. I don't want them getting a heads-up that I'm here."

"So, for the record, goats and drugs are a no, but the body is okay, yeah?"

In reply, he poked into a couple of drawers and thumbed through a stack of notebooks.

Louise drummed her fingers against her leg. "Not to rush you, Sergeant, but is this going to take long? We're on twelve-hour shifts. Tomorrow will be my first day off in seven days. There's perfectly good alcohol I could be drinking."

He pulled her closet open, but didn't do more than glance in before shutting it. "You got a suitemate, Stark?"

"Yeah, you know her. It's Briggs from second squad."

He made a face. "Yet another problem child. She in?"

"You're checking soldiers' rooms who aren't yours. That's a little weird."

He didn't respond, but he did frown over at her nightstand. "What in the name of high-holy science fair experimentation is in that coffeepot?"

"Want some? I'm trying to make a brew strong enough to get me through shift. I can add some Jack to it."

"The coffeepot shouldn't be next to the bed. It definitely shouldn't be left on for however long you've had it cooking. If you catch the barracks on fire you'll be living in the parking lot—in a tent." Not a hint of joking in his voice.

"I thought *mandatory* health and welfare checks came with *mandatory* notices a few weeks out—for strategic goat-hiding and coffeepot scrubbing purposes?"

Sergeant Gray sighed and glanced over at her still open door.

"C'mon Sergeant, what gives? Surprise barracks inspections, is that even allowed?"

The lines in her Team Leader's face seemed deeper than usual. His eyes held shadows. "You're older than most people your rank, Stark." He squinted down at the clipboard and then at her. "Hell, you're older than me." He picked up one of her textbooks, opened it, and snapped it closed. Opened it. Snapped it closed. "Your story is your own. And, it's none of my business. I don't need to know why you're here or what you're running from that put you here in the first place." He tossed the book down and turned to leave. "Watch yourself. I'm out—other rooms to check."

"Wait," Louise called, putting out a hand. "I was hungry."

He waited.

"I joined because I was hungry," she explained. "That, and I wanted to finish college. Got in just before they lowered the max age. Later in the year and I wouldn't have been able to." She gestured at the book Gray had tossed. "Most of the time it's worth it, even with the long shifts. School's free as long as I keep my grades up. Sometime I think I'm too old for this shit, though."

"Fair enough," he said, "Why Army?"

"Dad was Army."

"Yeah?"

"Well, that *and* the Army was the only branch that would take an old lady."

For the first time, her Team Leader almost-smiled. "You're mostly good people, Stark. And you're not old—just older than most. Go find some friends your age."

"I have friends. There's Gimcrack. He's good people."

Sergeant Gray gave her another almost-smile. "The whole circus to choose from and she picks the clown."

"He acts more mature than I do."

"Well," Sergeant Gray replied, "I can't really argue with that." He tapped his clipboard against his leg. "When I leave, lock your door. Someone knocks, be sure you know who it is before you open up."

"Is there something going on, Sergeant?"

"That answer is above your paygrade. Above mine, too. Just keep your door locked."

Within days, Louise had almost forgotten the room inspection. Shifts were long and frantic. When she added in PT—boring stretching, a run, random push-ups, sit-ups, more boring stretching—and school, it was easy to slip into dazed routine.

Online classes were the only kind she could manage with shift work. There were discussion questions to answer. Tests to study for. Papers to write. Online didn't mean easy, it meant she got a lot less sleep.

If she hit the bottle to help make the studying a little more entertaining, what did it matter? Everyone else drank, too—it was kind of a prerequisite for the job.

She was studying—nodding off, really—when a knock startled her half out of her chair. Sergeant Gray's image popped into her head, even though this knock sounded nothing like his.

The knock came again, hesitant, almost shy.

She jerked the door open without looking through the peep hole.

Sergeant Gray filled the space, his uniform ripped and filthy. He reeked of mildew and vinegar. The scent filled her mouth. Louise staggered back, gagging.

He grinned and his jaw gaped, wide, wider, unhinged, his tongue lolling. A rope of spit hung from his chin down to his name tag. He reached out with one hand and grabbed her wrist.

Louise woke flailing.

A lake of drool graced her *Marginalized Voices* text. Sharon Old's poem would never read the same.

Louise took a shaky breath and willed her heart to stop clattering. Her study aid was still uncapped. She didn't bother with a shot glass, just swigged the vodka straight.

A knock at her door—that same bashful tap as in her dream—forced her head up and around.

There wasn't much in her barracks room she could use as a weapon. The vodka bottle was the closest to hand. She polished off the dregs and hefted it. Solid, trustworthy.

Her pulse hadn't slowed a bit.

Tap, tap, tap. The knock at the door and her heart danced a little two-step.

"Stark, you up?"

The voice wasn't Sergeant Gray's. It wasn't a zombie, either—Louise was pretty sure they mostly mumbled or groaned. At the very least, they'd roll their r's and wouldn't sound prepubescent and over-anxious.

She didn't bother putting the bottle down before opening the door.

Gimcrack stood outside with a full bottle. "Hey loser." He saw the empty she was holding and grinned. "Call me your knight in shining armor. It looks like I got here in the nick of time."

Louise waved with her empty bottle and staggered back to her desk.

He cracked open the new one and took a swig before handing it over. "What took so long to answer the door? I knocked for a good minute. I thought you'd fallen asleep."

"I did." Louise ran a hand through her hair. "And I had a crappy dream."

"Sounds like you need to drink more."

"Best advice ever." Louise took another long swallow and rested her cheek against the bottle.

They'd downed half the bottle and were arguing the finer points of *Magic: the Gathering* versus *D&D* for the four-hundredth time. Times like these, when she'd shoved the bookwork aside, when there were a couple days off to look forward to, and she had Gimcrack to argue with, she felt like the old Louise—the civilian Louise—before she'd raised her hand and forgotten what it felt like to be called by a first name.

She stretched out across her bed, occasionally reaching over to the popcorn bowl. "I don't care how good your blue deck is, Gimcrack. My new green one is going to stomp it. Crash and smash. All the strategy and spells in the world won't save you."

"*Magic* again." Gimcrack threw a piece of popcorn at her. "I already told you we're running my D&D campaign first."

"Yeah?" She grabbed a handful of popcorn and chucked it at him. "Good luck with that. Half our party just PCSed. The way people come in and out of here, we're lucky to get a handful of campaigns in before someone has to move."

He shook popcorn off his shirt. "Don't waste food."

"Why? Are we saving it for the imaginary crowd coming over to play *D&D*?"

Gimcrack picked the popcorn off the floor and tossed it back into the bowl. "Actually *they* are feeding *us*. I found us some guys in Lakewood. It's going to be epic."

"Which part of Lakewood?"

"How should I know? Why does it matter? We are going to them. They're cooking. Besides, we don't want them over here. You're a slob."

Louise drew herself up. "I am not. Gray just came through the rooms and gave me a thumbs up—except the coffee pot—which I *moved* and *scrubbed*. I bet you didn't even notice. Now, I have to go out to the common area and talk to Briggs when I need my go-go juice."

Gimcrack shuddered. "Briggs. What a problem child."

Louise snorted. "You've been spending too much time with Sergeant Gray. You sound just like him."

"I'd need to drink twice as much."

"More than twice, probably."

Gimcrack pointed at the near-empty bottle. "The way you go

through those bottles, you could give him a run for his money."

"Whatever." Louise began to pick up the kernels Gimcrack had missed. "You know you left a bigger mess than I made, right? So, how did you do, Mr. Clean?"

"With what?"

"The barracks inspection. The one were just talking about." She showed him a handful of kernels she'd picked off the floor. "I've seen your room. You don't exactly pay attention to detail."

Gimcrack looked blank. "I thought you were joking."

"Nope, he came through the rooms."

"When was this?"

"I don't know—a few days ago."

"He didn't go through mine."

They were quiet for a few minutes. Gimcrack dug through Louise's books, looking for something he hadn't read yet. Louise finished cleaning the mess they'd made with the popcorn and bagged up her trash.

There were more empties in the can than she remembered drinking.

"So, when is the epic game in Lakewood supposed to take place?"

"Tomorrow."

"No dice. There's a children's fest on post. We're going."

"Stark?" Gimcrack stared at her over his book. "Neither of us have kids."

"Maybe I want to relive my childhood."

"You want to get drunk and jump in the bounce house, don't you?"

"We," Louise announced, holding a bottle aloft, "Are going to need more vodka."

The children's fest had a carnival theme. Hordes of munchkins swarmed, flitting from the face painting to the game booths, to the snack tables, in and around the bounce houses, and all over the kiddie carney rides. Louise had to admit, as much as it must suck to be a military brat, there were times, like this, when it seemed to have its perks.

Colors and sounds whirled around her. Children's laughter seemed to have a tint and texture and Louise swam in it all. Usually vodka put a nice soft glow around things and mellowed the suck. This was different. This was a thrumming excitement.

She rushed through the crowd, chasing kids dressed like butterflies.

Gimcrack struggled to keep up.

She turned and grabbed his arm. "Hey," she said, eyes a little too round, "Hey, I just saw Sergeant Gray. He was wearing stilts and an Uncle Sam beard."

"Sergeant Gray?" Gimcrack followed Louise's slightly wobbly point. "I don't see him."

She gave him a goofy grin and dove back into the crowd. "He's this way. You have to see. He was actually smiling—with teeth."

"Stark, how much did you drink?"

She didn't answer. She ran.

The world blurred and whirled. She felt like cotton candy—wrapped around and around the carnival—stretched out into a billion thin wisps of colored sugar and air. She ran and laughed, following one group of kids and then another, letting the crowd guide her, until finally she stopped to rest in front of an inflatable bounce castle the color of a fresh bruise.

A few seconds later, Gimcrack panted up next to her. "Holy crap. You run fast for an old lady."

The shadows next to the bounce house shuddered. A darker blob peeled away and stepped toward her. It was a woman dressed in uniform. A mardi gras mask hid her face.

It wasn't a real uniform, but one of those cheap Halloween-store jobs. The kind that usually showed a pouting blonde on the package and had the words *hot, sexy,* or *naughty* preceding whatever it was they were supposed to be.

"You kids wanna play? The woman slurred.

"I know why she's wearing that mask." Louise nudged Gimcrack hard in the ribs. "If someone sees her dressed like that around all these kids, and they recognize her, then she's going to get her face stomped in later."

Gimcrack elbowed her right back, just as hard. "Shut up, Stark."

"Well look at her, am I wrong?" Louise grabbed Gimcrack's arm. "She's fucking drunk."

"So are you," he hissed, barely above a whisper.

The woman's eyes seemed amused under her feathered mask—amused and familiar. "Are you going to play or not? It's empty—no one's been by here for almost an hour." She chuckled, low and dark. "This is your chance."

"Hell yeah, we'll play." Louise didn't wait for Gimcrack to nay-say. She dove in, dragging him behind.

Louise jumped, a huge springing leap, expecting to come down on cushiony air. Instead, her feet hit cement. The bounce house was gone. The carnival was gone. The familiar brickwork of Fort Lewis was gone.

Louise stood in a dark parking lot. Behind her, Gimcrack puked into a row of bushes.

Across the street, a darkened restaurant promised *hof* and chicken during business hours. She knew the place. The burnt orange paint needed a touch-up, and it was plastered with advertisements, but it had great food.

She recognized this parking lot. It was the hotel she'd lived at when she'd first gotten into town. She'd stayed a week, burning up a little leave, before she got her room in the barracks.

They were in Lakewood, about fifteen minutes from home.

Louise let Gimcrack finish puking, before grilling him. "Why are we in Lakewood? How did we get here? Did I black out?"

He waved a hand at her, dry-heaved, and then lay down with his head pillowed on the curve.

At a loss, and much more sober than she'd like to be, Louise walked into the hotel to get them a room.

Gimcrack made himself scarce for about a week, before crawling back with a bottle of the top-shelf stuff and a sheepish apology.

"But what happened that night?" Louise asked.

"We both got blitzed out of our minds—that's what happened."

"The jump. How did we make the jump? One second we were climbing into the bounce house and the next we were in Lakewood. And what about that weird lady—the slut—something about her seemed familiar."

Gimcrack just shrugged. "Hell if I know. Maybe you dated her. You kind of have a type, and she's it."

"You're saying I only date sluts?"

"I'm saying you have a type—you can take that however you want."

"How did we get there, genius? To Lakewood? We sure as hell didn't walk down I-5."

He held up his phone. "Maybe we called a cab. We were probably trying to find those *D&D* guys."

"Yeah. Okay." Louise frowned and studied her nails. They were ragged and gross. "I need to do something about this. My nails are ate-up."

Gimcrack glanced down at his own nails. "Yeah, yours look even nastier than mine. We could go to the PX."

"Yep, we can. And, we should." Louise reached for the top-shelf bottle with a grin. "But not sober."

For Louise, the PX, or Walmart, or Costco, or any big box store, was a lot more fun to visit when wasted. The shiny was ever so much shinier that way.

She forgot all about her nails, roamed the aisles, chuckling at the play of light on sanitary napkins and plastic forks, T.V.s and coffeepots, jewelry and kid's shoes. That top-shelf stuff was no joke, she hadn't even finished the bottle.

She wandered, taking in the tidal rush of shoppers desperate to be parted from their disposable income. Gimcrack trailed behind, considerably more sober and less spellbound.

"Where are you going?" he asked her.

But she didn't answer. She knew she should, that she was probably worrying him, but the world had the same cotton candy sweetness as the carnival had. If she spoke, the feeling might melt away.

She passed a little glass case of resin figurines—a circus scene. One of the little figures had a mardi gras mask and a really short outfit. She made it three steps away before her brain caught up to her feet and she turned to double check.

It was the woman from the bounce house. The little statuette had the same sexy soldier outfit. The same strangely familiar eyes. The same feathered mask.

Louise leaned in toward the case closer, closer, *closer*—

Wind.
Dark.
Nothing.

Louise was above the ground. Not high up—but high enough that her head swam for a minute. She tried to get her bearings.

"Gimcrack?" Her voice sounded hollow. "Gimcrack, you here?"

Whatever she was sitting on was plastic-y. She slid down, hung by her finger tips for a quick second and then dropped to the ground.

It was a climbing boulder.

There was mulch under her feet and swings in front of her, but no Gimcrack.

A quick spattering of rain made her hair stick against her cheek and slicked the surfaces all around. She saw herself reflected in the droplets, each a fun house mirror. Short, tall, fat, thin, funny, and masked.

She leaned closer. The tiny masked reflection mimicked her. Closer and closer still, until her nose almost touched the droplet. The masked figure seemed to cock its head quizzically.

There was a noise from behind her, almost a sigh.

Louise spun.

The uniformed woman from the bounce house was standing so close, Louise could have reached out and embraced her—if she'd been in an embracing mood.

"You get lost, honey?" The woman reached out and smoothed Louise's hair where it stuck against her cheek. She tucked the damp strands behind Louise's ear.

"Where am I?" Louise's voice only shook a little.

"You're at a park, honey. Can't you tell? In Ft. Steilacoom." The woman's familiar eyes smiled behind the mask. "Don't you want to play?"

"How did I get here?"

The woman smiled wider. The lips stretched, so wide her face was sure to split; so wide, Louise was scared to keep looking, and more scared to look away. "You're here because you want to be. You brought yourself, honey."

And then, the woman lunged.

Louise fell hard. Her head hit something that wasn't mulch or plastic climbing boulder. She didn't feel pain, not exactly, but she felt the impact. It should have hurt, but didn't, and for a second that was the scariest thing of all.

There was a stillness. Everything receded. The woman on top of her, the mulch under her back, the playground all around, it all faded to gray.

The woman's hands were on her throat and Louise couldn't breathe and suddenly things mattered again. She struggled and scooted and got her legs around the woman, but still couldn't pry those hands off her throat.

No air.

Fingers scrabbling, Louise reached up, grabbed the mask, and yanked.

The woman let go of her throat. She pushed Louise's legs away and stood, offering a hand up.

The woman was her. A perfect doppelgänger. She flashed Louise a crooked smile. "Do you see, honey, I'm—"

Louise's first punch flattened the woman's nose against her face. After a few more punches, the resemblance was less than passing.

Louise woke up to Sergeant Gray's voice. He was yelling at someone, but she was pretty sure it wasn't her.

She tried to turn to see what was going on and something beeped.

Sergeant Gray's face swam into her field of vision. "Look who decided to grace us with her presence," he said.

"Hey Sergeant," Louise replied. Her voice sounded weird.

"Don't 'Hey Sergeant' me. The second these doctors release you, they're going to need to call for a gurney, because I'm going to put you right back in here."

"You're in a hospital," Gimcrack's voice added, helpfully.

Louise tried to flip him off, but her fingers wouldn't work right.

"You were holding this when we found you," Gimcrack waved a feathered mardi gras mask a few inches from her nose. "I saved it for you."

Louise didn't have the energy to jerk away, but she didn't really think she needed to. It was a sad, bedraggled, piece of trash—nothing else. "Toss it. It's garbage."

161

"Stark," her Team Leader asked, his face settling into its customary frown. "Has anyone ever told you that you're you own worst enemy?"

Louise felt the grin coming on, but couldn't stop. It stretched and stretched, despite the pain. Cracked and broken. Self-aware.

Suzanne Hagelin has lived as varied and interesting a life as she could manage—growing up in Mexico City, living in the Middle East, traveling and exploring the world, learning languages, working in IT, family, exchange students, teaching, volunteering, and translating. She settled in the Seattle area where she runs an indie publishing company, Varida Press, with a small group of authors, and teaches language on the side. Her books include the sci-fi *Body Suit* and contemporary fiction *The Artist*.

The Last Beer

Suzanne Hagelin

"Welcome to the ECJF Carnival!" a booming, circus style voice projected in Ray's direction. He had been screened and recognized as a legitimate registrant of the Annual Emerald City Job Fair.

Several people in line behind him hooted, trilled their tongues, or belted out mariachi calls, cheering him on as he stepped successfully through the break in the laser net.

Bells and whistles blasted, colorful lights whirled, and the pink and purple gates dropped into the ground before him. Ray trotted through just in time before it slammed shut with a simulated dungeon door crash and macabre cackling. The chaos in the waiting line outside was nothing to the jamboree within. Jazz music from multiple bands rolled around, melding and vibrating; laughter, like cymbals and drums breaking through the din; costumes that bridged all human history and creativity in a sea of gaudy regalia.

This was the place where everyone gathered to celebrate their job wins and the excitement in the air was tangible and intoxicating. To hear their own propaganda, the ECJF Carnival was a wildly successful event where dreams came true and impossible matches were made. Serfs and imperial-worthy companies faced off in good-natured encounters where all job and employee interview norms were irrelevant.

Many people claimed the costume was the key and spent months researching and creating the outfit they believed could get them the job they wanted. One guy he knew had landed a position testing mattresses in orbit, which included regular trips into space, by donning a 1920's gentleman of leisure's smoking robe, slippers, and a monocle. The glass of whiskey and curled mustache were clever, but it was his air of self-indulgence with a hint of arrogant amusement that charmed his employer as he strolled around finding chairs to relax in.

Ray's only attempt at adornment was a black beret with a small green feather added to his usual office garb: slacks and a shirt. No mask or makeup. He hoped to win job offers on merit rather than getup.

Popping in the program-guide contact lenses provided at the door, he scanned the map of the Seattle Center.

"Not the food court!" he murmured, though he would be hungry soon. There were a ton of opportunities for interplanetary food service workers, but he hated the carnival insanity of the court's jousting tourneys and food fights. And he didn't cook. The dancing arena was a lot of fun but there wasn't a single company there he cared to check out.

"Where would I find off-world opportunities?" he queried the guide in a whisper. A number of events and competitions flashed on the visual, all taking place in the amusement park.

Hmm...CE was running trials at the Spacer, a popular Seattle Center ride that Ray had spent a fair amount of time at in the past. Groups of applicants would be cycling through every twenty minutes trying out for trans-orbit piloting jobs.

The Gravity Hall of Mirrors, built on the site of the old Experience Space Project, was a completely new ride opening that very day. It would be run for the evening by an interplanetary head hunter scoping out candidates for a variety of opportunities.

He scrolled down a ways. "The Drowners' Trap," he vocalized, "Sounds like space vacuum work...Maybe?"

A human whip of party goers swept past him, linking his arm and swirling him into the crowd. He disengaged himself with a chuckle and made his way out of the party toward the rides. Buttered popcorn, cotton candy, and caramel apples filled the air with aromas that made his stomach growl.

"Flinger" was the scariest ride in the center and he went there first. It seemed like a good place to prove his ability to handle space challenges. The stream of people moved quickly down the line, were sent in, elevated up twenty meters while the harness was attached to their torsos, and then at the top they were flung out across the surroundings in something of a boomerang arc; crazy gees, a gut-wrenching yank, and a tug back to the descent tower. All the rebound momentum was absorbed by the slam-cushion, then a corkscrew slide shunted them back to ground level.

"I'm gonna yell," a guy in front of him announced. "You gotta get their attention." He was wearing all yellow with a black band across his eyes. Ray didn't care much for the banana look but then he hadn't tried at all.

Some people shrieked when they were flung, others wailed. Ray gasped when it was his turn but made no other sound. He tried to pose his body as if he had some measure of control but crumpled miserably at the yank, like a puppet on strings, limbs flailing. And he was unable to recover his poise before the slam and dump down the slide.

Springing to his feet at the bottom, he grinned and looked around on several sides. Robots stood by, ready to invite applicants for interviews. People continued to come down the slide, and several were called, but Ray was ignored.

"Move along, Contestant," a voice admonished him. He had no idea what he should have done or not done, or if it even mattered.

"Was there some...?" He left the question unfinished as robotic cilia on the walls coaxed him to the exit.

Ka-ching! A bell sounded as he went out the swinging door.

You have three job offers in the Seattle Port Authority Warehouse division! The words flashed in his carnival contact lenses. *They have now been added to your carnival portfolio. Return to the PARTY to celebrate or try for bigger wins!*

Consolation jobs for losers. That's how they could advertise that everyone goes home a winner.

It's not a big deal, he told himself. Chances are he wouldn't really like a job that expected you to excel at being flung out and snapped back. What kind of work would even need that? For a moment, speculation along those lines distracted him but a current of partiers—obviously with newly awarded jobs—was sweeping him in the direction of another ride.

"Roll and dive! Climb and fall! Show your expertise in the Spacer!" A larger than life hologram boomed in the distance, probably someone famous that most fans would recognize, but Ray couldn't quite place him with the flamboyant eye patch.

He found himself picking up speed and clipping around some of the slower walkers, as if getting ahead of them gave him an advantage. It felt good, like cruising in the fast lane past the slower hover cars.

"Only the best can tackle the course and prove themselves worthy!" a beautiful, woman-like robot, glittering in sequins and voluminous folds of velvet, proclaimed in his direction as he pushed through the door. "Are you one of the few?"

"Yes!" he belted out with more confidence than he felt.

She waved an arm draped with fabric and the passageway opened underneath her booted feet. Down he went, into the twinkly sparkle of a starry night, brutally cold, past nebula, burning stars, and light-wreathed black holes, as if floating through space. Soon he was strapping into the spacer car and gripping the wheel.

"Time is of the essence," a deep voice urged. "Find the way and rescue the crew of the Opal transport from certain death by asphyxiation." A bonus game challenge. Low, rhythmic music thrummed in the vehicle walls and vibrated through his body.

Foot poised, eyes wide, Ray squeezed the wheel tightly, waiting, holding his breath. This was good. He had clocked a number of runs on this ride. Then the second the doors pinged open, he pounced, foot slammed into the accelerator, leaning into the dashboard as he shot out.

The maze changed every single day and no two paths were alike, but there was a familiarity to it that he had learned through practice. Zooming, turning, rolling to the left, accelerating up and over a planet on the right, dropping down into blackness where he knew an opening had to be. Exhilarating, heady, fun. And near the end, in the final stretch, where he knew there was enough room, he executed a flawless forward roll and braked forcefully to zero just before the crash cushion.

The Opal has been found in time and 85% of the crew will live... streamed marquee-style in his contact lenses and he wondered if the percent mattered.

"Forward," a robot instructed as he leapt from the spacer, gesturing to a brown door on his left.

Ray burst through the door as if the aura of the spacer had left a residue, adrenaline still pumping, eyes darting around. *Yes!* He knew his racing put him up there in the rankings. *Ha, ha!*

Over thirty others were in the room, moving slowly and finding places to sit while the hall filled. This was a bit discouraging.

After ten or fifteen minutes and the arrival of a handful more people, the lights dimmed. Ray found himself noticing the costumes in the room as color faded. Not as many sequins or feathers...or faux fur... people were, as a group, less adorned here.

"Congratulations!" A voice broadcast cheerily. "You are in the upper third of the Spacer runners this evening and have been inducted into the minor league pool of potential spaceflight pilot candidates! Well done! These credentials have been added to your portfolio and will open many doors for you!"

Ray's mouth dropped open and a wave of disappointment surged through him. A number of voices around him echoed his sentiment, some cursing, some moaning, some resigned.

The doors that opened *today* led back to the carnival. A scrolling list of inferior, earthside job openings flitted in the column of his contacts. There was a sour, metallic taste in his mouth.

"I should've had a chance," a voice nearby complained. "I was good."

Others were better.

The Drowners' Trap proved to be a frustrating and nerve-wracking ordeal. If wallowing in black water, in a vast tank devoid of light, in a crushingly claustrophobic steel helmet, fumbling with a maze of connectors and tubes, assembling a functioning system, that you have to guess at, working with strangers around you that you can't hear or understand—if that's what he had to do to get a job off-world—then he wouldn't.

The exit to that one had a number of vexed faces and murmuring malcontents. No sequins at all. Ray assumed the optimistically decorated folk were too smart to waste their time here.

But the failure galled him. He hated not being able to stand out and it was beginning to feel like his fate this night, wrapping him with seaweed and dragging him down into his own Drowners' Trap.

"I hate it," he mumbled bitterly as underwater construction job ads were inserted like junk mail into his portfolio.

Stopping by several minor stalls, he made his way around the park, not quite gaining the prize in shooting, or snagging the holographic ring toss, or nailing the speed racing on scooter skates—*what jobs would those get you?*—and found himself sinking into a spot on a bench with a tofu dog and chips.

Keep at it or give up and go home? He wondered as he chewed in time to the nearest band playing the latest version of "On Broadway".

"Well, if nothing else," he reminded himself, "Persistence pays off in any field." Somehow, somewhere, there must be a door, or a window.

*Not the slammer balls, though…*people encased in rubber balls, rolling around bumping into everyone else. The place was filled with aggressive punks and chaos and was just plain stupid.

In the next ten minutes, he was sucked into a 'Bunny Hop' line that pulled him off track a few meters, accosted by two overly friendly androids he was able to escape without offense, presented with offers of wine tasting and fire-walking which he declined, and found himself back on the path to off-world job opportunities again.

By the time he got to the Mystery Mansion he was out of sorts. The carnival wasn't fun anymore.

He was soon standing in the Mystery Mansion game hall with about twenty others of all sizes, shapes, and colors, muttering to himself.

"What's the point?" he complained to no one in particular.

"You're not having a good time?" a guy nearby, looking out of place in jeans and a flannel shirt, quirked a corner of his mouth.

"Am I supposed to be?"

"I don't know. A lot of people are."

A jester nearby laughed suddenly as if to punctuate the fact.

"I don't think they're actually here for the jobs. Maybe they already have jobs they like and are competing for fun. And if they get a good offer, they might take it..." Ray couldn't keep the frustration out of his voice.

The guy in jeans looked at him with a hint of sympathy. "What have you tried for?"

"Spacer, Flinger, a few others." He dropped his chin, staring down at the floor as the lights began flashing around them.

"Looking for off-world jobs?" The guy, lean, hands shoved in his front pockets, seemed well-balanced, as if he wouldn't tip over in a storm.

"Yeah," Ray shrugged and tried to smile. He didn't really care, and it didn't matter. "My earth job just doesn't...whatever...It's fine. I have a paycheck. They like me. I exist and get by." It came out more bitterly than he'd intended, and the strobing red and green flashes made him feel he was being jostled.

"Yeah?" the guy responded, un-jostled. "What would you do if you could?"

Ray stared at him for a moment, searching for the right words. *Anything*, was what he wanted to say, but it wasn't true. He wanted to do something important, find adventure, be involved in something great. And he wanted to have fun while doing it.

The strobing lights swirled faster and the wall in front of them melted away. The mystery had begun and there were puzzles to solve, mazes to negotiate, and spies to identify.

Ray hesitated.

The guy waited, gazing into his eyes knowingly and finally nodded. "I get it," he said. "It's hard to put into words. We should get going, though. Some of these are timed."

"Yeah, I enjoy timed tests…" he replied as they shot forward, the guy inches ahead of him.

It was more fun having an acquaintance to compete with, and he made excellent time through the various challenges, even the untimed ones. Never quite putting much distance between the guy and himself in either direction, ahead or behind. The one chance he had, he wasted, when an overly zealous contestant blasted through, knocking them both aside, and the guy in jeans went flat on his back. Ray decided to help him up. It was instinct. Later the hit-and-run character was kicked out for some reason and Ray couldn't resist a moment of gloating. That was also instinct.

They ended up scoring among the top third. Decent…again. Achievements would be noted in their portfolios and *many doors* would open for them…again.

But no one invited them to an interview.

The Gravity Hall of Mirrors awaited, like a beacon of solemnity anchored at the edge of the park. The final challenge, the last opportunity, the true test of mettle. And there were sixty-four prime space positions to fill. Ray felt his heart soaring unreasonably at the sight of it.

He had a chance in that one.

Looking around casually, he realized he'd gotten separated from the guy in jeans and for a moment regretted not asking his name. Maybe if he hadn't started jogging.

"You got this, Ray," he muttered to himself, clenching and unclenching his fists, loosening his shoulders as he loped along.

Entrance to the ride was restricted and whole mobs were being turned away for intoxicants in their bloodstream. Ray experienced a moment of smug delight at the carnival revelry.

Gravity.

Anyone with off-world experience would already have *space-legs*, keeping their head straight, no matter how the sense of up and down changed. For them, the only challenge would be the mirrors. But this was a night for amateurs.

"Do you agree to absolve the Seattle Center, the Planetary Solar Flare Human Assets organization, and the individuals running this event from all liability for any and all…"

Blah. Blah. Blah. *Yes! Yes! Get on with it!* He agreed as soon as the Legal-gram gave him a chance and stepped through the scanner.

He was alone at one end of a hallway, and the place where he stood grew dark while the opposite end glowed like a setting sun, smooth, flowing waves of color wafting toward him…then it began. The first shift pulled him forward gently and grew in strength as the air sped up and what had been a breeze became a torrent. He was ready when the full drop engaged and landed on his feet at the sunny end of the hall, on what had been a side wall.

Mirrors unfolded around him and he saw multiple, moving images of himself, bathed in orange and red sunlight. He made a few advances before finding an opening and stepped into the next chamber. It began rotating, or maybe it was just the gravity field shifting, and he started to slide. Thousands of reflecting images of his own body, framed in Greek columns, fanned around him. He knew they were optical illusions but somewhere a clue would lead him.

Down was easiest, but not the best way to go. He clawed at the columns and found a real one he could grasp after a few tries. It bore his weight as the chamber continued to roll and left him swinging. He swung back and forth, looking around and decided to fling caution to the wind —*pun intended*, he narrated to himself—and vault himself as high as he could toward some of the mirrors and columns.

Gravity rewarded him with a strong tug just as his feet arched up, before he began to fall, and he found himself in a new chamber with a completely different world.

"Aahh!" he uttered, stunned by the joy and beauty of it all. So much light and structure and sound! Music and ocean waves, the murmuring of voices. He stood and gazed around in amazement as people milled around him. Were they real? Were there thousands or only a few caught in a mirrored chamber that seemed to have no end?

There was a fountain in the middle of the chamber. Ray sat down on the wide edge designed for that and just stared around, fascinated by the canopy overhead of mirrored stars and planets, intersected with clouds and dark blue sky, as if the sun were setting on Earth and the galaxy was spreading across in its place. That one room painted the picture for him. The dream. All fractured in hexagonal reflections on all sides.

"Hey!" the guy in jeans showed up, pausing next to him. "How'd you get here ahead of me?"

"What?" Ray asked, eyes focusing, recognizing him. "Am I?"

"I thought I made good timing."

"Oh," he shrugged, wondering how long he had sat there. "I don't know. I was a little disappointed with the last one, so I got here faster, I guess."

"And sat down for a rest?" the guy grinned, shaking his head a little. "So, you're not trying for the timed thing then?"

"This one isn't timed," Ray smiled back. "I just wanted to relax a minute and get some perspective. It was good."

"Yeah, but you never know what may give you an edge." He sat down as though he agreed, as if he wanted a break, too; as if he wanted to savor the place a little before moving on.

Ray stood up, rocked on his toes, and decided to get moving again.

"Good luck," the guy in jeans said.

"Wait," Ray stopped in mid-turn and looked back. "What's your name?"

"Stan," he answered, stretching out a hand for a firm shake. Solid. Steady.

"Ray," he replied, "I hope you make it out there, Stan."

"You, too."

The rest of the challenge was tough, stretching him, accelerating his heart, revving up his focus, using all his skills and talent. He told himself as he dove over the final bar, pulled his body into a fetal curl, gees shifting, and stretched out to plant his feet and land in a crouch on solid ground—he told himself the experience alone was worth it. He would remember it forever. Dream about it. And he almost believed himself.

But when he walked out into the room and saw the "Top Third" award flashing in his face, it was almost more than he could bear. The most crushing moment of his life.

Good at everything. Top third, in fact, but just not quite good enough to matter.

Exiting the final challenge of the carnival, he almost ran into a bundle of shrieking partiers, all dressed alike in pink, who went running by chattering noisily about their big break into holographic vaudeville.

Ray watched them for a moment. Vaudeville would never be something he cared about, and he couldn't be jealous of their opportunity. But he did envy the thrill of the *win*. Bitterly.

The door swung open behind him and the guy in jeans came out, eyes on the ground, hands in pockets, not celebrating. He stopped when he noticed Ray's feet and looked up, recognition flashing in his eyes with a hint of surprise.

"No?" he questioned.

Ray shook his head.

"How about a beer?" Stan suggested. "Somewhere else."

"Yeah," Ray nodded. "I know a place," and led him out the nearest exit.

Outside the walls a chilly wind blew, and dead leaves tossed across the streets and sidewalks. A rat scurried by on the street with something in its teeth and distant hover cars hummed overhead. Their footsteps sounded crisply on the pavement as they made their way to the tavern.

"You didn't make it either," Stan commiserated, once they were settled at the bar, tipping his beer, taking a swallow.

"No." One word, loaded with meaning. Turns in the path of life can be abrupt.

"There's always next year." Stan leaned back. Not turning.

"I'm never trying again," Ray said, scraping carelessly at a spot on his glass. Sometimes the soul makes vows deep in the gut and barely a ripple shows through on the surface.

"You don't mean that." He tested him with those words.

"I always thought..." Ray drew shapes with his finger on the counter. "...the day would come. That I was supposed to be out there. That I couldn't go through my whole life without ever making it into space." Time to cut off the dream. Live here, with the known, and the tavern, and the bar stool.

Stan stared at him, one of those rare looks where the listener *knows* what you mean even if you say it badly.

"You thought it was destiny, but now..." As though he'd been there.

"I know. It's stupid." Ray held his glass, almost empty.

"Is life here that bad?" Stan waved a hand toward the world outside the bar.

Ray shook his head. "It's fine." He struggled to find the right words. "I just longed for something more...I don't know why it had to be out there." He had been ready. For years. But not any longer.

"I know what that's like," Stan said. "Feeling like there isn't any life here anymore. Just the one out there. The one you have to get to somehow."

"Why haven't you given up yet?" Ray lifted empty eyes to search his face.

"Can't. Won't."

They nodded and drank.

"Found a way," Stan added carelessly.

"A way?"

"Yeah," he shrugged and stared at his half-full glass. "Going prospecting on the asteroids."

"No one will hire you for that." Ray made a flat line with his lips. "There's no insurance. No loans. Risks are too high."

"A death sentence, if you're insane," Stan swirled the amber liquid. "Risky, if you're smart."

Ray stared at him. Numb.

"I found a few investors," Stan went on. "And a ship. I've got most of my team put together." Another swallow. "There's a place for you, if you want it. I can't pay you or promise you anything but whatever we bring back, we share evenly."

"No pay..." Ray echoed, holding his glass.

"You'd have to bring your own gear, pay your own transport into orbit. Once we're out there, it's all covered. We're thinking eight months, maybe longer, then the paycheck. And at that point, the whole solar system would be open to you as a seasoned explorer. You could have any job you want."

Ray glanced at his empty glass. Set it down. Let go of it.

"If you could tie up loose ends fast enough to join us when we leave."

"When would that be?" Ray responded. Dream-like. Hand reaching, fingers closing slowly onto the idea.

"Monday. Could you manage it in three days? Quit your job, get the gear, get out of the lease, sell the hover car. Whatever you have to do to be ready. Can you do that? Do you want to?"

"Uh...by Monday?" It was surreal. The axes of his life shifting, pivoting on three planes, degree by degree.

"We'll meet up at CE Dock 34 at noon, transport to orbit, then on to space-dock where the ship is."

They were standing and paying, walking out the door.

"Are you in?" Stan's eyes beckoned, challenged, dared.

Human souls are forged in moments like these.

Ray smiled.

Eric Little spent his formative years in the mountains of central Mexico, the deserts of Arizona, and the rainforests of the Pacific Northwest. He slings wine by day as a wine steward with a culinary background, and by night writes about the world of long lost Summer, a paradise hiding out in the desolate regions of the Chaos Sea. His first published work of fiction is *Summerlight*, the first volume of an epic sci-fi series about galactic war that will include *Summerstead*, *Summertime*, and *Summerwar*.

The Night the Carnival Came to Town

Eric Little

Ko remained motionless, patiently waiting for Bella to give the all clear. He raked the road in front of him with eyes that had been trained to see everything. Then Bella whispered in his ear and they dashed across the ancient roadway without being seen. They had to get out of here, away from District Twelve.

The wastelands outside the Seattle/Vancouver metroplex were divided into thirty-eight lawless districts. The D street boys ran this district, and unfortunately, they wanted both Ko's head and Bella's hardware. Bella suddenly gave the command to hit dirt and Ko became one with the ground, just another rubbish pile among many.

A strange procession of colorful but beat-up trucks and busses cruised by, their shields protecting them from the myriad potholes and IED craters. They had to frequently back up and detour—it had been a long time since anyone had driven this road. What excited Ko—he was almost seven—was that he couldn't remember *ever* seeing that much bright color in one place!

He clicked an enquiry to Bella, and she whispered, "It's a Carnival" in his ear.

"A Carnival!" he repeated, attempting to remember just what that was. He couldn't stop looking. "Where are they going?" he whispered back.

She didn't answer. Bella did that sometimes, he was used to it. The sun was drooping toward the horizon in sullen crimson and orange—it would be dark soon. They had to find shelter before then, but they had been on the run for two days and didn't know their way around this district. Bella detected a burned out residential enclave with an outlying rubble pile that might have been some kind of security bunker. Ko had his doubts—it looked too good to be true. That usually meant bad things.

The last garishly-colored vehicle crept by and Ko reluctantly watched it disappear into the gloom of a rainy sunset. Then Bella whistled 'move out', and they began carefully making their way through the chaotic mishmash of burned out buildings and stands of hemlock-studded pine.

It *was* too good to be true.

Bella spotted the sentry unit nestled into the building's former roof before Ko could see anything, and whispered, "five heat signatures—at least one auto-sentry." Five was too many, even without the sentry. They were going to have to find some place else.

Ko's thoughts were still inflamed by the visual-overload of the Carnival convoy, and he found his feet moving in the direction the trucks had gone before he realized it.

"No, boy—where are you going?" Bella demanded, probably because it was too close to the Hive, but for once he was the one who didn't answer. The siren call of the Carnival pulled him along as if he were one of the pied piper's drones, whose implants had been jacked and forced to dance until they literally dropped dead. Ko wasn't old enough for an implant yet; at least that's what Bella said. She should know. She was a child of Electron, an intelligent fighting knife that had a little brain damage. Ko couldn't remember a time without her, although he used to wonder how she came to be his mom.

Rain Hive had acquired a dark reputation that intimidated everyone, even the gangs running the Districts. They said that no one who entered it ever returned, and it was mostly true. Auntie Tao encouraged these stories. Contrary to rumors, the Hive was a place where there were no bullies, or cruel jokes, no child abuse or outcasts. It was a place where everyone fit and had a job that suited them, a place without hunger, or loneliness. Auntie Tao had built it a long time ago, when she realized that no one else cared about the poor. Auntie Tao was a child of Electron, and over the past millennia had amassed a database of knowledge and wealth that allowed her to do anything she deemed necessary.

Inside the Hive, everyone wore implants of her design, and she saw everything through their eyes, heard every word they uttered. She spoke gently in each worker's implant, always encouraging the right decisions, keeping the bad things from ever happening. In the Hive, every child has a best friend to whisper their secrets to.

Auntie Tao also played her worker's hormones and chemical-based emotions with the hand of a master conductor. She found that this is what it takes to produce happiness in these difficult times. Her people worshiped her for it, and if they didn't—well, that was adjustable too.

Rain Hive is built like an iceberg, with only a small portion showing above ground. The part everyone can see has twenty-meter high walls, shining pearly white across the rubble around it in District Twelve. Nobody defaces its walls; thirty-centimeter-long bioengineered wasps live high within those walls and are quite territorial. Those were just the deterrents you could see. Inside the walls, the grounds are jammed with orchards and gardens. Nobody actually lives up there, but the Hive finds quite a market for all those organic veggies and fruits in the wastelands. The ground in front of Rain Hive had become an open-air market of sorts, where weapons and food could be traded safely. Auntie Tao made sure of this; her giant wasps didn't care for violence unless they were the ones performing it. Hundreds of her eye-gnats patrolled the market unnoticed, all the while watching everyone and everything.

Ko and Bella walked carefully in Dune-step, the small random noises of their passage quiet enough not to attract attention. It took several hours, and the huge silver moon had sliced the broken land into bright grey and velvet before they caught up. The trucks had circled and began setting up opposite the massive ivory-walled structure of the Rain Hive that almost blotted out the drooping ancient moon. Both strangely distorted people and ordinary moes swarmed everywhere, erecting brightly colored tents and security barriers around the whole bee hive of activity. Ko and Bella barely made it through before the walls were up; a street rat can be very stealthy when needed. Bella found a place where the tent walls of a smaller attraction overlapped, creating a warm pocket of darkness. He was smiling when he fell asleep, something he rarely did. She stayed awake, watching over him, as was her custom.

An irresistible aroma of popcorn and butter woke him. His stomach rumbled a bit and his mouth began to water. He had slept all day, and the Carnival was blooming, coming to life all around him. Ko ventured out into the space between the tents carefully, but he needn't have worried. All around him swirled a colorful chaos, and there were hundreds of people wandering by, wastelanders just like him. Sprinkled among the carnival goers were brightly clad girls on stilts in swirling dresses of prismatic hue, showing shapely legs and strange bird-like masks. Two sturdy elephant-men from off-world strode by eating pretzels that looked small in their stubby hands, but were bigger than Ko's head. He hid a smile when the closest alien discarded a half-eaten one on top of a trash can, and soon was happily munching down on the still warm, salt-studded bread. It was one of best things he'd ever tasted. Even Bella seemed happy, if a little quiet; he began looking for a power supply so they could siphon off some juice and Bella could eat too.

He stuck to the sides of the tents and kept low, but everyone completely ignored him. Eventually he began to drift with the crowd, swept along from attraction to attraction. Here, a skinny-legged man balanced on dark hooves, exhaling long streams of flame to the gasps of the crowd. There, people were invited to wager if the frenetic otter-guy could guess their weight. He was always right, so Ko crept under the stage to find a carefully concealed mass-detector.

Two young cut-purses came too close and he bared ten centimeters of Bella's blade. They took the hint and moved on in search of easier prey. Ko looked up to meet the eyes of a vendor selling bird-on-a-stick. It smelled amazing and his mouth began to water again. The towering vendor tossed Ko an approving smile and a roast bird-on-a-stick as he made his way downstream, singing his offerings in a strange, lilting cadence. Ko felt oddly lightheaded, but didn't mind, he was having a wonderful time. The roast foul was delicious while it lasted. Ko smacked his lips and straightened up a bit, and continued to wander down the midway.

A rich, meaty aroma wafted his way, piercing the smelly throng and irresistibly pulling him to the other side of the midway where a small crowd gathered. He was able to dodge around the larger spectators' legs and see what was going on. A large wood and glass box with an open side held the entire roasted head of some creature—he thought it was called a pig. The vendor would take an order, then carefully slice off a piece of cheek or snout, catching them neatly in a small round flatbread. Then he would spoon in chopped onions, chilies, and green herbs, roll the taco with one deft hand, and present it to the customers.

Someone crowded Ko and he quickly punched the offender in the groin twice. You just didn't let someone get that close; bad things could happen. The offender grunted and staggered back, rebuked. Ko caught a glimpse of a grinning face reflected in the glass of the roasting-box and it took him a moment to recognize himself, looking happy. It was dangerous to look like that—bad-guys tended to take an interest. He watched the taco vendor's skill for a while longer, then wandered back to the show-tents. He was smiling again. This was the most fun he'd ever had.

The Carnival had set up on the other side of the market from Rain Hive. This provided safe access, without getting any nearer to that spooky place than necessary. Nobody realized that the eye-gnats went everywhere and saw everything. Auntie Tao was watching.

Ko felt the D street boys a blink before he saw them. They slouched down the midway in perfect sync, bonded by illegally amped implants and fight music that played their body chemistry with a heavy hand. Ko's heart sank as he counted them; he lost track at fifteen bad guys. Somehow, they must have found him and Bella. His mom had drilled tactics into him his whole life, he knew they wouldn't have shown up in force unless they were closing in on them.

Unless! Maybe they were only here to shake down the carnival and have some fun? Ko shuddered at the thought of what some of them considered fun. His stomach growled, despite having eaten only a little bit ago. He winced, afraid that the D street boys had heard him, but of course they hadn't. Bella however, had.

"Quiet son, the enemy is close, and our munitions are low," she mumbled. Mom did that sometimes, she seemed to be reliving a past she could not fully remember. Ko brushed his hand across her hilt in the sheath which he wore across his right shoulder so she could easily whisper in his ear. It seemed to calm her. He willed his stomach to be quiet; it didn't listen.

The carnival barkers watched the gangsters out of the corner of their eyes but continued to pitch their shows and games to the ragged audience that had braved the night. Entertainment is crude and scarce in the wastelands. Something like this doesn't come along often, and nobody wanted to miss it. The heavily armed auto-sentries above each attraction's tent looked as if they were about to have a breakdown as they spun back and forth, covering the most heavily armed of the gang. Ko wondered when the D street bully-boys would inevitably start trouble. He could see the Carnival had its own bully-boys, and they looked like mountains someone had strapped up with the biggest guns they could find. He was pretty sure they would quickly take down any troublemakers in thunderous ways that would be, in their own manner, as exciting as some of the shows everyone had to pay to get into. Still, he was worried—the D street boys were dangerous on a completely different level.

The eerie coordination of heavily armed gangsters pouring through the crowd literally shook the soil beneath everyone's feet. Each one's step was mirrored by the others, producing the illusion that it was one massive organism with forty legs and forty eyes flowing down the midway. All those crazed eyes looking for Ko was enough to produce a chill, way down in his guts. He didn't know how they were going to get out of this one.

They didn't.

Auntie Tao hadn't lived for thousands of years by taking her eyes off the dangerous ones. She watched closely as the D street boys flowed down the midway like some toxic mud-slide. She saw when they found their prey, a skinny little boy who looked like he was made of baling wire and sticks. He was quite dirty, and wore hundreds of rags as camouflage, a sort of urban ghillie suit that resembled just another pile of garbage when he squatted. There was something generating Signal tucked into his right shoulder, too. Auntie Tao scanned it and found another child of Electron, if damaged and starved for power. That explained a few things. She sent a few of her wasps high over the Carnival, where they would be unnoticed in the night sky. She rarely interfered with the Outside world in a way could be seen by the unwashed. But if someone came to her she would take them in, shelter them and adopt the lost soul into her flock. Watching with a thousand tiny eyes, she waited to see what the poor boy would do.

Bella screamed "Run!" when the bad-guys found them. Ko dodged and skidded around the beast with forty legs, losing part of his right ear when he came too close to one of the gangsters. He felt cold air on his right shoulder, and suddenly realized he couldn't hear Bella. Then he did, and it sent ice down his spine as she shrieked from the wicked grasp of a bad-guy.

"Run, go to the Hive! She'll help!" The cold laughter of the D street boys buffeted his shocked body. He couldn't leave his mom in this horrible situation!

"Yes, go to the Hive," mocked one of the D street boys. "They'll eat you and grind your bones for their pretty gardens! Run, little rat!" All of them were laughing now.

Bella shrieked "Go!" one more time, and then went quiet, her power levels exhausted. Ko stumbled out the Carnival gate, the D street boys making no move to stop him. The gangsters weren't even watching him—they all were intently looking up at the moon! Ko sobbed once, for the first time since he was three. Then he obeyed his mom and ran across the silent marketplace until he found himself in front of the door to the shining white enclave. A circular opening dilated noiselessly, and he numbly stepped inside. He never saw the giant wasps guarding him overhead, but the D street boys certainly had.

She took a soft, white cloth, cleaner than he had ever seen, and began to dry the silent tears streaming down his face. The steel-eyed woman crouched to bring her flawless face to his level. "I'm Auntie Tao, honey, and I'm going to be your new mother," she said softly.

"Like hell you are," replied little Ko, just as softly.

A Los Angeles native, S.L. Brown loves watching his hometown teams play. He is a retired combat veteran with 22 years combined service in the US Air Force, Navy, and Army. A world traveler, he served in Europe, Asia, and the Middle East. Teaching dance fitness rounds out his professional resume. Oh, did we mention he is an author, blogger, and motivational speaker? When he is not inspiring others with his common sense approach to life, he lives in western Washington with his wife and son. In 2017, he published his first book, *Just a Thought*, his musings on everything.

Captivating Luna

S.L. Brown

The wind whips through my small town across from the Naval Shipyard in Bremerton. The whistling of the gusts usually keeps me at ease at this time of night but not tonight. Tonight is different and I am sure my life will never be the same no matter how cliché that sounds. As the rain spatters the glass and the wind sings its unobstructed melody, in my green light, I am left to recount how I got here.

This little town of Port Orchard is quaint and fairly quiet compared to the big cities. There isn't much to do on a Friday night, which, I did not mention it was. Yes, Friday night in a small-town USA where hitting the bowling alley to bowl or a local bar to drink is the night's highlight. To be honest, I spend most Friday nights at home relaxing, crushing candies on the Internet. By the end of this day my ho-hum Friday will be nothing near ho-hum.

As I drive the dark streets heading home my phone lights up with an incoming call. "Oh man!" I see the face of my pretty, sassy friend Marie. The phone rings again as I debate if I should answer or not. Marie always gets me into something. Not always bad but always something. She's a wild soul who ensures everyone has a good time. Another ring and I make my choice to click the Answer button. The conversation starts off as usual.

"Hola, my spicy Chicana," I say.

"Hola, my caramel Papi. *¿Como estás?*" she giggles back.

"Bien, bien! Alright, you know that's it for Spanish for me. What's up, love?"

Marie tells me about this wild masquerade party she was invited to and wants to know if I want to go. Marie always gets her way but I still protest.

"I'm almost home, and you know you always get us in trouble with your crazy ass."

"Papi, did you hear me say masquerade?"

Of course I did. I start thinking about all the ladies who might be there in sexy outfits and mask.

Marie knows me well. "Yes, there'll be lots of sexy women!"

Damn her. She does it every time to me.

I protest again, "You don't know me like that, but alright. I'm in." My ho-hum Friday could very well be much more thanks to Marie. I end with, "Love you my spicy Chica."

To which she replies, "You better or I'll cut you. Love you more, Papi!"

I hit the End button, continuing homeward with a new mission on my mind. Women, mask, drinks, and dancing? Yes, please!

I get home and get showered, shaved and looking good. As I leave, Marie texts me saying she'll meet me at the party. I'm annoyed by this turn initially, but in true Marie fashion, she softens the blow.

"You may need to give someone a ride home and I don't want to cramp your style stud." She sends me the address and says she'll meet me there in about an hour.

I jump in the car, flick on the wipers, crank up the radio and head out following the phone's directions. The night's potential was getting better and better.

The map says it'll take me 15 minutes to get to the house. My mask rides shotgun in the passenger seat. I look good in my black pants, blue button up shirt and black shoes. I feel good and the evening mood is feeling more optimistic. Let's see what happens tonight.

As the lights of the city start to fade, I find the strategically placed streetlights of the paved roads to be calming. Each bright glow fades to darkness, then I hit the next light. The rhythm is mesmerizing.

The voice on my GPS interrupts my deep reflection of the roadway's lighting system as she commands, "Turn left in one-quarter mile onto Mystery Road!"

Hmm, Mystery Road is a funny name for a road, I think.

"Turn right in 600 feet."

"Yes, Ma'am!" I replied as the road approached. Turning further into the country I went.

The dark, bumpy, and, a-little-bit-scary-if-I-am-being-honest-

186

with-myself road was quiet. I decrease my speed while wondering if a bear, lion or winged hell-demon will jump out at anytime and murder me. As the thought passes, I realize I spend a lot of time thinking of how bad something could be. Not tonight! Tonight, I'll be positive, full of curiosity and see where the night takes me.

I veer left one more time. The trees part to reveal a big farmhouse surrounded by giant wooden gates. I push a button on the keypad at the gate. The ring echoes through the woods. Otherwise, it's deathly quiet.

A girl's voice excitedly chimes in over the speaker, "Welcome, Loyce. We've been expecting you. Come on in!" The gates glide open, granting me access to this secluded place.

We've been expecting you. As I drive down the dirt driveway to the rear of the house, I wonder about that statement. How could they have been expecting me? I've never been here before and, as far as I know, Marie isn'tt here yet.

I finally see life as I reach the back of the old Victorian country house. I pull up next to a barn where other cars are parked.

A stunning young woman stands in the road waving at me. I assume it's the girl from the intercom. I park and she greets me with a big hug. To say she was a bit cheery, forward and, well like I said, stunning, would be an understatement.

I try to play it cool but stumble right past cool to horrible pick-up-line guy saying, "Wow, you are as pretty as the moon!"

Even now, I'm embarrassed for myself having uttered those words. but tha's not important.

She laughs, confirming that my line was horrible, but I'm cute and it's okay.

Awkward failure aside, I say to her, "You know my name but I don't know yours."

"Luna."

I laugh at the irony of my horrible pick up line and her namesake. We head toward the rear of the property.

Luna's long curly black hair seems to float behind her as we walk. Her petite yet curvy frame glides along the path as if she is floating. She's stunning! The most amazing thing about Luna is her dark brown, deep-as-the-night-forest eyes that captivate me so much I don't notice her carnival mask. I could get lost in those eyes. I'm sure of it.

"Put your mask on, stud."

Which I do.

Her mask is black and red lace and hides what I assume are stunning features. The thought crosses my mind that she could also be a disfigured alien behind it. Wouldn't that be a shock to my system? Being the optimist, I choose to believe she's gorgeous because frankly, disfigured alien seems a little too likely way out here where no one can hear me scream.

"You look like Batman," Luna says with a grin.

"I'm going for a Mr. Grey from 50-shades kind of mysterious sexy look. Without all the money though. Is there a broke version of Mr. Grey? Maybe Mr. Brown?"

Her laugh tickles me, as it's both full of simple joy and mischievousness. I wonder how great this night will be especially if Luna is included in the outcome. Time will tell, that's for sure.

As Luna and I walk deeper into the property, I feel like we're Hansel and Gretel ominously heading to the witch's house. *Should I lay out breadcrumbs?* Again, my imagination is getting the best of me, yet I still follow this vision of beauty.

Every 20 steps, lanterns with flames light the way. We make small talk through the trees. Finally, we come to another opening where my reaction makes Luna smirk at me.

A giant outdoor tent stands at the center of a big open field. It would rival any big top tent at any world-class circus event. As we enter, the tent is in full swing with music, games and even rides like merry-go-round and bumper cars.

Latin music blares throughout the tent and people are dancing everywhere. The only lights in the place are from games, lanterns and strobes. It's festive and my sexy dance moves are begging to get out. It seems I'm not the only one as Luna leads me toward that back area where the darkened dance floor is located.

The people are all shapes and sizes. Walking through the tent, it feels like being in Brazil in the crowded party streets of the Samba nation. Men and women are in all various styles of clothing "optional" states. To my surprise, the only mandatory article of clothing is the facial covering from simple eye mask to partial mask and partial face paint to full-face mask. Bodies are dripping sweat, smiling, laughing, dancing, and touching. Some grind in unmentionable ways, not bothering to hide it.

It's definitely a party in the woods.

Luna hands me a drink as we enter the darkened dance section. The floor is packed. People spin, step, rock, touch, and groove to the blaring music. I'm amazed at not only the dancing but the amount of people on the floor. It's nightclub-worthy.

"I don't suppose you Salsa dance, Loyce?" Luna asks.

I roll my shoulders and neck, smile, wink at her, and laugh. "Oh, I don't know if I can do this very well" I sheepishly say to her.

As she begins to speak again I grab her hand and drag her to the dance floor. We make our way through the crowd and find our space. I'm smiling and looking around as the next song comes on. Is that Marie walking out by the DJ booth with some guy? As I check out the other girl, the song changes from Salsa to a Bachata song.

Luna says, "This is my favorite style."

I instantly forget about the girl in the distance and reply, "Let me see if I can get this down."

Luna doesn't know that Bachata is also my favorite style of Salsa dancing.

I pull Luna close to me. My right hand grabs her left hand, my left hand slips to her waist. Her left hand rests on my chest. As the Bachata rhythm bangs through the system, Luna and I get a groove going. We three-step and spin, turn, glide, and make dancing-style Latin love on the dance floor. We simply melt into each other like great dancers do. I feel like I have danced with her all my life.

As with any song, I wait for the breakdown to bring her closer to me. Our bodies melt into each other. Sweat moistens our clothes. The heat of us is intoxicating. I am lost in the moment.

She leans close to my ear and says, "You have an amazing energy and aura."

I smile then say, "That's how sexy works you know!"

Before she comments again, I spin us around.

She digs her nails into my back ever so slightly as I read her lips, "You're so tasty!"

Who doesn't like to be tasty? With this woman in my arms time means nothing and I have no cares in the world.

After dancing a few more songs, we leave the dance area and head for the food. We pass booths with seasoned chicken and beef sizzling in hot pans and vats of grease. The smells of the meat are drool-worthy and remind me of walking through the carnivals as a kid.

Along with the meats cooking, there are also booths with drinks, giant bags of junk food, and assortments of gut busting creations if one would dare try something like Ghost Pepper Ice Cream.

I point to it and shake my head emphatically no.

Luna laughs at me. "I don't like it either. How about some cotton candy? It's out of this world."

Can I really resist "out of this world" cotton candy? No, I cannot. "Lets go" I say.

Onward we go. Then I remember Marie and wonder if the girl I saw was actually her, having a good time.

As we walk to the booth I pull out my phone to check on Marie. Damn! I didn't have a signal at all.

Luna shook her head. "No phone signals out here! In fact, even your camera won't work."

I don't believe her, so I switch my phone to camera mode. The screen brightens and I turn it to Luna. Her sultry eyes pierce my screen as I professionally snap a photo of her. My phone does nothing. I hit the button again. Nothing. One more time and still nothing.

Through my screen, I see Luna's amazing smile. "I told you so, now come on!"

Why doesn't the camera work? That doesn't make any sense. Does it?

Luna snatches my hand and tugs. "Come on!"

Forget the camera. I'll find Marie later if she's here. I switch my phone off and we head for the cotton candy. I'm pretty sure I'd follow this woman to the depths of hell if she asked. Thankfully, I only have to watch her hips sway toward the cotton candy booth. The struggle is real, I think to myself.

The people coming and going are festive. The drinks are cold and the mood is fire hot. I have been hugged and kissed, had my butt smacked, and been danced with by a dozen people just walking the few hundred feet from the dancing area to the cotton candy stand. Luna laughs at me. I take it in stride.

Yes, it's a good day. If Marie's here I know she's enjoying this crowd. They're right up her fun-loving alley. As I think about it, with all these people wearing masks she could stand right next to me and I might not notice. That's definitely a game she would play. She could also still be home or hung up somewhere. With her, anything is possible.

Deep down, I think she's already here, having a great time. I'm sure our paths will cross before the night's over. Heck, she'd have to come just to give me crap about Luna. Yes, I'll see her before the night's over, I'm sure.

As I let go of that thought, a different one crosses my mind. There are a lot of people at this place but, if memory serves, there weren't a lot of cars where I parked.

"Luna, where did everyone park their cars?"

"This is a traveling carnival. Most of the people aren't from around here. Once a year, we converge on a different town, deep in the woods where no prying eyes will bother us." She leans against me and smiles. "Only a select few attend every year. The oldest members choose which new people to invite, and everyone is sworn to secrecy. By dusk tomorrow, all this will disappear without a trace."

This all seems very cloak and dagger. Mystery Road, indeed.

I can't imagine why they let Marie invite me. "How did I get picked?"

Luna grabs my hand, pulls me close, and kisses me so deeply that my knees almost buckle. I'm high like one of those damsels in a 1960's romance film where the hero finally kisses her. As our kiss breaks, she whispers in my ear, "I think it's because you're so tasty!"

I give her this much—she has a sick sense of humor. Add another check mark on the perfect girl list that in my head.

She bites my ear, winks, smiles, and pulls me onward to the cotton candy. I can still taste her on my lips. Select group? Out of town? I think to myself, Loyce, shut up with all the questions and enjoy the ride with this woman. I follow with a stupid smile plastered across my face and a desire to finish that kiss.

At the cotton candy booth, Luna walks up to gray-haired lady with her back to us and gives her big hug. "Nani, I brought a tasty treat for you!" She turns to me and I swear she wants to devour me. I'm ready for that.

The old lady whips around and greets me with a big jovial smile. After sizing me up, she says, "Indeed, he'll do. He will do."

To my shock, she grabs my butt and gives it a squeeze.

At this point, I'm not sure whether to be flattered or scared. I do know this would be a really odd threesome. Maybe I'm mean for thinking it, but she seems a little old for me.

Lucky for me, the old lady laughs, hearty and joyful. "We're just joking with you, boy."

I'm pretty sure they both could feel my sigh of relief.

"This is La'Star the Maker," Luna says. "My grandmother."

I've never met anyone with a title before. "What an interesting name you have."

La'Star prods me in the gut with a knobby finger. "We're all named for heavenly objects. It's a family tradition. We venerate the night sky, like some people do the earth. You might even say we're part of it."

Night owls are my kind of people—I can't stand morning people. "Now I understand why your name is Luna."

"Actually, it's Luna the Provider."

What an intriguing family I've met. The joker in me couldn't help but say, "I guess you provide the maker with the goods, huh?"

La'Star pats me on the thigh and grins. "That's where you come in, tasty!" As she winks, we all laugh.

Behind La'Star is an old-time carnival booth. It reminds me of the ones the snake oil salesmen used in the old movies. The only exception is the side facing me. It looks like a window, but I can't see in it. Above the window is a sign that reads, *Tastiest and Unique Cotton Candy...Out of this WOOOOORLD Flavor!*

On the front edge is a cutout that I assume the cotton candy comes from. Right next to that, where La'Star stands, are a few knobs, levers, and controls. Evenly spaced red and blue lights evenly frame the cutout.

"Nani," Luna says, "I told Loyce he needs to have some of your out of this world cotton candy."

La'Star clicks on the machine. It hums and rumbles. Behind the dark glass, faint green tinted lights glow. Giant mixing bowls rise and spin.

Why would a cotton candy machine have a one-way mirror only usable from the inside? The idea reminds me of a corny horror movie. Maybe there's a monster inside, and it comes out when called to deliver the candy.

My imagination is trying to ruin a great night with a gorgeous woman. I tell it to shut up.

A paper cone slides out of the opening. The machine spins cotton candy onto it. Luna hands it to me when it's done.

I tear off a piece and stuff it into my mouth. The sweetness I expect dissolves on my tongue. A moment later, I'm bowled over by a burst of unexpected flavor. How did they make it taste like so many things other than sugar at once? Maple syrup, bacon, and some kind of Spanish spices I know but can't name dance on my tongue.

I'm confounded by what I'm eating here but I love it.

Both La'Star and Luna beam at me as I ravage this amazing concoction.

"This is the best thing I've ever eaten. It's like manna from Heaven!"

La'Star glows from my praise. "Why thank you, dear. I've been making it for decades. Of course, what really does the trick are fresh, local ingredients."

I have no idea what kind of ingredients go into cotton candy besides sugar, but I don't care. "You're a goddess among mortals, ma'am."

La'Star chuckles.

Luna takes my hand. "Come dance with me again, Loyce."

Like I'd turn her down.

Now I have to admit I forgot about Marie. Luna has my full attention. She lifts my hand and runs her tongue up one sticky finger. I whimper. Trying to play it cool, I watch her clean my fingers of cotton candy and wonder when we can find some privacy. Call me old-fashioned, but I don't want to do anything too risqué where all these people can see.

When we reach the dance floor, a slow song begins. Luna pulls me close. My hands wrap around her waist. Our bodies move to the rhythm of the music. The lights around me soften and swirl like I'm in a romance movie.

The world narrows to Luna and me. No one else matters. I can barely hear anything but the soft exhale of her breath. Heat flushes my cheeks while a chill shivers down my spine. Every touch of Luna's fingers raises gooseflesh. I've never wanted anyone the way I want Luna.

Luna presses her lips to my ear. "Come with me," she whispers. "I want tp show you something."

Wherever she wants to lead, I'll follow.

Luna leads me across the dance floor. Though the spell of dancing is broken, the lights still seem fuzzy. Masks blend into each other as we pass people. I shake my head. It doesn't help.

Bodies haze in and out of static like the picture on an old TV set. Did I have a drink? I don't remember anything but the cotton candy. Maybe I did. Maybe I had one when I first arrived?

Confusing everything, some people don't blur like others. They stare, watching me with every feature razor-sharp.

But I'm watching Luna's backside. She sways her hips, enticing me onward. I stumble after her, sure I'd lose her if she didn't hold my hand.

We pass a man who grins and nods at me. He knows where we're headed and why. I think I return the nod, though I'm not sure. I know I can't stop grinning like a fool.

Luna leads me into the night. The moment I step outside the barn, she yanks me close and kisses me. Her mouth covers mine like she's going to eat me. My head spins. I feel dizzy. My hands seem thick and stupid. Am I pawing her like a teenage boy?

She breaks off the kiss and I feel like I can't breathe anymore, like she's the air and I'm drowning. Her smile changes. The world spins. Her lips move. Words come out. I can't understand them. My body feels like someone draped a lead weight over it.

Leaning close, I think Luna wants to kiss me again. Her lips brush my ear. "So tasty," she murmurs.

My eyelids droop. I fall to my knees. Nothing will do what I want. Unable to keep my eyes open, I let them drift shut. Nothing sounds right. I'm floating. No, wait. I'm being carried.

I want to sleep. Something about that seems like a bad idea, though I can't figure out what.

Maybe I pass out.

When I open my eyes, everything is blurry and I hear a low hum under my feet. Through a dark haze, I see Luna and La'Star watching me. Something in my mouth feels damp and thick. It's not my tongue. I smell copper. My arms hurt. Why are my hands over my head? Why do my wrists hurt? Why can't I feel the ground beneath my feet?

Is that whimpering coming from me?

I try to move my body. I can't. I try to yell. I can't. I try to do anything other than dangle like a side of beef. I can't.

La'Star and Luna keep watching. Together, they crack identical dark grins. They can see me, I know it. La'Star reaches to the side and pushes something. Green lights flare into bright life over my head.

What I see in the harsh glare makes no sense.

My naked body hangs inside a large metal bowl, the sides high enough to reach my waist. Something dark binds my ankles and knees. It reminds me of seaweed but I can't break it. Tilting my head as far back as I can, I see the same dark stuff binding my wrists and holding me on a thick metal hook. Plastic tubes holding something dark snake into my wrists.

Close to me, a machine whirs into noisy life. I can't hear anything else.

Outside, masked people form a line behind Luna. Some look to my left, definitely focused on something I can't see because my arm is in the way. Others seem oblivious.

I wiggle and squirm, trying to see what those people see.

I wish I hadn't.

As my body turns to the left, my gaze meets Marie's. She's crying, scared and in pain. Another wide bowl holds her, more tubes stick into her wrists, more seaweed is stuffed into her mouth. Her head isn't at the same level as mine, though. Her chin is at the bowl rim.

I try to tell her without words that we'll be okay, that I'll think of something. It'll be brilliant, I tell her in my head. We'll laugh about this later over her amazing paella.

The machine get louder, and it's coming from inside her bowl. Marie's hook lowers. The noise changes. Marie's gag muffles her scream.

I've heard a sound like that before. It reminds me of a chainsaw cutting through wood. More copper fills the air. Something dark and wet spatters on the glass. A squeegee on a robotic arm shoots down and cleans it.

The squeegee distracts me from Marie's descent. Outside, La'Star holds a paper cone pointed at the machine. She lifts it to show me cotton candy.

Luna holds up a piece of paper for me. Blocky letters spell out words. *New recipe! Tastier than ever, Out of this World cotton candy!*

Tasty.

The pieces click into place.

I'm inside the cotton candy machine. So is Marie. Spanish spice.

Not so long ago, I stood outside the machine like these oblivious idiots on the other side of the glass and ate cotton candy. Marie watched me.

I try to scream. My seaweed gag keeps me quiet. I try to rock back and forth. My bindings keep me from gaining momentum. I try to do anything other than dangle like a side of beef. My body can't manage it.

Which leaves me hanging from a hook on a windy and rainy night under the harsh glow of a green light. I said I'd explain how I got here.

Someone points to Luna's new sign and says something. I can't hear anything over the sound of the machine. Luna nods and pats La'Star's shoulder. La'Star meets my gaze with a dark, wicked grin. She pushes something.

I can't look anymore. Meeting Marie's gaze, I try to tell her without words again that I'll find a way out of this. We'll make it, I promise. She shakes her head. Tears stream down her cheeks.

Beneath my feet, a panel slides aside. I don't want to look, but I can't help it. Circles of blades rise. They separate, rotate and spin until all I see are whirring circles from hell.

Definitely won't be the same after this.

L iam RW Doyle moved to Portland, Oregon far too late in life but is making up for it by finding as much adventure as the Pacific Northwest has to offer. He has a Master in English and a long career in I.T., but aspires to be a street-corner busker playing the songs that inspire for fleeting and lost moments. He has published several stories and one science fiction adventure novel and is working on its sequel—when he is not wasting time learning guitar. His antics can be seen at Tragic-Sans.com.

Round and Round She Goes

Liam RW Doyle

The faceless carny handed the two weary boys the prize they'd won by facing their fears. He loomed over the two children, casting a shadow that ate the light. Sickly green and yellow lights from the merry-go-round were unable to cut through the shadow as they laid swaths over the tableau. The two young boys stepped backward, away from the sinewy man in tattered overalls and plaid shirt, until they found the courage to turn their backs to him and, with their treasure, ran from the abandoned carnival. Back to their bucolic town where in the morning no one would remember the carnival being there. Even the boys would question the memory of their experience.

The figure watched them run off, beyond where the strings of bare bulbs defined the boundary of the carnival with wan light. His form shifted, shuddered, and relaxed into a different shape. A black suit and bow tie, silk top hat, and lacquered cane with a silver skull handle. A face with a hawk nose and waxed mustache emerged from the blank space. He was now the Ticket Taker.

He announced the arrival of the carnival in many forms: as a clown, a magician, a Chinook shaman, a crone lurking in shadows—all dependent on what the person who beckoned him, who had need, desire, would respond to. Despite distance in time, through the human decades that it was a carnival—sprung from the place the land's first people called *tamanass máhkook*, reappearing or always there and constantly forgotten —humans usually referred to him in this role as the Harbinger. But it was this current form, the Ticket Taker, that they would first see when they actually came to the carnival.

But now, it was he who had some kind of need or desire. Well, he always did, in some formless way, that made him what he is—servant of the carnival. A need and desire to bring people, cajole them and bargain or taunt or terrorize or please them, as needed, by the carnival. But now, there was something else, something new. Something that had been growing stronger, and even that thought was unsettling.

Time didn't exist in the carnival in the same way he knew it existed in the outside world, the world of people. Even so, he felt the weight of it on him: time, and this growing need he couldn't name. He had been feeling it more and more, heavier and insistent. Would he say it'd been days, months, years, that he'd been feeling it? He couldn't tell, the Ticket Taker—the Harbinger, the Carny, the Fortune-Teller, the Stranger—had no frame of reference. He, she, it…they, just always was. Before, time was meaningless, there was no difference between past and future and nothing as defined as "days." Even the ideas of "before" and "now" were difficult to comprehend.

Yet, he was becoming aware of it all the same.

"Are you…are you the Ticket Taker?" the yellow-haired young woman with doe eyes now standing before him said, pulling him from his thoughts. She hadn't been there a moment ago. Yet, it must have been she who was the reason he had changed from faceless carny through shadow to this form now. She, her need, her arrival to the carnival, manifested him as this.

"I…I am The Ticket Taker, young miss." The words flowed from him, gaining strength as he spoke from eons of repetition, words that were his but not from him. Did they come from the people he spoke to? Why would he wonder such a thing that he never had wondered before? "You are in search of something, a wish fulfilled? A loss restored, I sense. Is that the truth of it, young miss?"

The girl looked at the sawdust and wood chips under her feet, shy, nervous. "He's dead, he died, and…and he shouldn't have. I…I was told, I read…the Book. You can help me."

He suddenly knew what he needed to know, as if he'd always known it, but actually didn't until she spoke. He knew the Book was one of the many artifacts in the outside world that connected the carnival to people. And he knew the boy's name was Brian, knew he died in an accident—in a car…fire and violence. Knew her sadness and her anger, and her guilt. It was usually either greed or guilt that brought people to the carnival. Or, maybe, brought the carnival to people? He had never thought of it like that before. The people, just always were. As they spoke to him, he would always know their hearts, their minds. The reasons they were there. Knowledge he would use to make the trades, the deals, to take from them what the carnival needed.

He reached his arm out from under his cape, caressed her face, hot with life. She shivered but didn't recoil. "Have you a ticket, my dear? The carnival," he gestured grandly around him, and in response, the carnival illuminated with garish intensity, "can provide you the prize you seek!" The carousel turned riderless horses and elephants and hippogriffs while warped music in a minor key played them around their endless path. The midway glowed with yellow light that looked more lonely than enticing, sourceless sounds of pellet guns and balls thrown against milk cans filled the air. The hellmouth leading to the Haunted Maze emitted smoke and malevolent laughter. The squeal and whine of a teacup ride cut through the night and the distant echoing prater of a sideshow barker edged under the grinding sound.

"I have the coin—" the girl began practiced words as she held out her hand, palm up, with a gold coin that did not represent any human money now or in the past, and he saw the blood-soaked bandages around her wrist. That became old scars. That became the unblemished pink skin of the girl before him now. The wrists of countless desperate girls before her, not this one, but she was all of them at once, as all people to him blended and faded into each other. But...no...no, not this one. Like the concept, the sensation of time, this girl, this singular girl, stood out in his consciousness, as an individual.

He grabbed her wrist, causing the coin to fall to the ground and he sensed her gasp was more in reaction to this breach in protocol than from the contact. Or, perhaps, of equal cause. A shock, a surge of energy shot through his own hand and through his body. He had never felt a sensation like it before. As quickly as it coursed through his bones, it was gone.

He caressed his thumb across her unmarred wrist. He knew things. But he didn't know if the ghost of other hands and wrists were of other girls that have come before, or would come after her, or was her in another time. He looked at her face and saw her elderly, an old human woman with gray hair and deep lines. Or was this someone else? An old woman with a lost life and dreams and old love, almost forgotten, she wanted to return to. So many who came before, or would come, who wanted to ride the carnival rides to return to youth. So many that the carnival drained the souls from and sapped those restored years. One of the many payments the carnival took.

No, this young woman would never be old, he saw.

The old woman he had seen in her was the crone he became when it was needed. The crone that contained within her withered form all those fears and loss and tragedy that he took from visitors like her. Each of his forms was borne and sustained by what he took from them.

The Ticket Taker backed away from this girl. There was something wrong, with her, with himself. He backed away and she looked at him, puzzled. She stammered, "I…I don't know what I'm supposed to do now. The Book—" With each step back, the strings of yellow lights dimmed and allowed the darkness to grow thicker. The girl was only steps away but already appeared far in the distance. He turned and flew from her, away from the carnival's entrance. To the Mirrors—that is where he knew he needed to go.

He bolted around the ouroboros of the merry-go-round. The carousel of accusing eyes, painted by no human hand, watched him go. The ghost of discordant music and laughter and screams clung to him like mist and let go regretfully as he put the ride behind him. Why had he never heard it like that before? He knew it had always been that way, but he was hearing it, sensing it, now for the first time. Perhaps as a guest would.

Past the entrance to the sideshow, the promises of "never before seen grotesques and mysteries" beckoned to him. He had never before felt their pull. He had forever been the one to urge visitors to see what they never wanted to see but knew they must.

To the clapboard shack with peeling paint and warped boards. Without breaking stride, he stepped through the open doorway and saw a twisted, misshapen wretch of a figure nearly run directly into him. He stopped, hands out, and felt glass. It was a mirror. It was he. He looked around and saw fragments and slices of various people, each stepping into corners and thin lines where glass joined, like birds scattering from a threat. Leaving him alone. The mirror before him, now empty. No crone, no Ticket Taker, either. Nothing.

He ran his hand over the glass: smooth, cold. He didn't wonder if it was a mirror or just sheet glass as it didn't matter, it never mattered. It would be what it needed to be for the guest. The Hall of Mirrors was where visitors found uncomfortable truths, saw things they either already knew but didn't want to face, or had always been hidden but needed to be revealed. To push them to make decisions.

He stepped to the right, farther into the maze, to a new set of glass, new angles and edges and planes, and still no reflection. He followed the path, knew it shifted and moved without him seeing, as it always did for the human visitors. Encouraging them deeper, more lost and confused, seeing glimpses and shards of themselves. He did not see anything but confusing layer after layer of shine and reflections of more glass and mirrors. Why didn't he see anything? Why didn't he see the waxed moustache and top hat, or mud-streaked robes, matted gray hair, or alluring dress with coins stitched in, or long thin business suit, or overalls, or visage of any of the forms he took? Why nothing?

The lack of his reflection among the reflections was disorienting. Being disoriented was unnerving, and being unnerved was disturbing and on the cycle of unfamiliar feelings went as he stumbled quicker through the glass passage. He understood these feelings at a distance, from the guests he brought in, sent in, or had drawn into, the Hall of Mirrors. What they ended up seeing was always brought from deep within them, sometimes twisted and distorted, sometimes with unwanted clarity. Always leaving the guest running or spilling out of the maze, stammering and shaken. He always saw, he laughed or he scowled at them as needed, as was drawn from him by the guest's need or the carnival's want. Now, with increasingly banged nose, elbows, knuckles, he saw himself acting as a guest, but without seeing anything reflected back at him.

Except…fire? The flickering illumination of fire, around a corner. Ahead? Behind? He spun on the reflection, and the flicker was gone. No, there it was, from another angle, around a corner of mirrors, the actual flames hidden but its illumination through an infinity of reflections of reflections, of unseen flames all around and into the distance. Was he moving farther away from the fire, or would the next turn of the corner bring him into it? Chasing him? Drawing him?

He staggered and spun through empty multitudes of corners and turns until his outstretched hand hit cold air and he plunged beyond the glass and into the night that smelled of rotting wood and burning machine grease. He turned to look at the Hall of Mirrors and did not see fire. He saw only the dim pall of reflections of lights taunting him from beyond the wooden doorway.

The girl. He needed the girl, he knew. She was connected

somehow. This started with her.

And he saw her, sitting back toward him, on the ground by the road that wasn't there an instant ago. But now she was there and the carnival wasn't. Blood covered her arms, dripped off her hands. She was silhouetted by a twisted car on fire, surrounded by pines and cedar. Glass among the leaves on the ground twinkled the firelight back at him. Glass in her hands. Her boyfriend, broken, sprawled in front of her.

Alerted, she turned to him. Her face wet with tears and blood. Her eyes wide and glassy. She saw him and looked shocked, but not surprised. He knew he was not now the Ticket Taker, but was something else. She saw him as something he didn't recall being before. A shadow, smoke, soot in the shape of a figure. His elongated hands wrapped fully around a tree as he peered at her.

She opened her mouth, closed it again. Opened, and creaked, "Yes, alright."

And then they stood again at the entrance to the carnival, his long but definitely flesh and bone hand wrapped around her wrist as before, coin still on the ground. Fresh, ragged scars on her wrists that weren't there the first time. This time, he kept hold of her and pulled her with him into the carnival.

"The coin—" she gasped, moving to retrieve it from the ground but he pulled her away before she could grab it. Around the carousel and the judgmental gaze of the creatures forever impaled by brass poles. He pulled her past the Sideshow, to the Hall of Mirrors. Where it had always been.

Where it no longer was.

Instead, it was the hellmouth of the Haunted Maze. A wide psychopathic smile of twisted glee taunted them. It was made of wood and paint and had a haphazard, childishly distorted look to it. Absurdly wide mouth with crooked teeth like stalactites and stalagmites, chipped and faded white paint. A gap of missing bottom teeth where the guest would walk through. Fire flickered behind an undulating black curtain, peeking through wavering gaps as it moved in a breeze he couldn't feel. Smoke curled lazily from underneath the curtain. That unnerved feeling hit him in a wave, and again, magnified by the fact he is never, was never before, unnerved. He's not meant to be. He's always been the one in control, knowing all and never surprised. Manifest by the carnival, which could never be surprised or unnerved.

The girl gaped at the hellmouth, then cocked her head. "It's..." but she didn't finish. She looked around, almost more frustrated than intimidated. He knew she sensed something was wrong, was off. She was human, a guest, alien to this place—everything should be wrong to her. And yet, she could tell something was not right by the rules in which the carnival, he, operated. She could not say how or why, or why she could even feel it. He should have known, however, should have been able to read her, her surface thoughts and deepest desires. But she was now an enigma to him, as obscure as the reason why the carnival was becoming a stranger to him as well.

He looked around, back to where the hellmouth had always been, expecting to see the Hall of Mirrors there instead. No, the path of tents and shacks no longer went that direction. The layout was entirely different. The merry-go-round was no longer behind them. The Sideshow was no longer over there. They were at the end of the Midway, now, but he had not led her through it to get to where they stood.

The girl looked up at him and he met her gaze. She no longer feared him. No longer was in awe of him. The girl pulled her hand away and he did not resist. "I know you," she said, half in question.

"You…we must go in." He felt like he was speaking for the very first time, having to form words from thought on his own where before (again that idea, "before") the words just came and he had simply been a conduit. "Come with me, into the—"

"I don't want it," she said.

He turned back to her. She was gone. He felt afraid, unsure for the first time of what to do. Or why. He knew something he needed was in the hellmouth. No, that wasn't right—he knew something needed him to go into the hellmouth. The two motivations did not seem distinctly different.

He walked up to the garish maw and ducked below the fangs as wide and long as a man's forearm. The air past the mouth, the curtain in front of his face, even the smoke, all smelled mouldy and wet. The light of unseen fire flickered from around the curtain, like what he saw from around the mirrors. He felt heat waft at him as the thick black curtain waved and moved. He pushed his hand through the break in the curtain and moved aside the heavy cloth and stepped through.

And was sitting in a car, in the passenger seat, as it sped through the night. He was the girl. He, now she, the girl, was sitting beside the boyfriend. He was still alive and saying something to her. The Ticket Taker, now the human girl, felt agitated, angry and scared, but they weren't his own feelings. He had walked into them as he became her…her body had already been in that state.

There was fire all around them, the flickering of it around every tree, around every object, the corner of her vision, all around them—but she could never see any flame. Everything was on fire and it couldn't be seen.

He, the boyfriend, was saying something about not being able to do "this." She, her, the girl, was pleading that Brian couldn't leave, couldn't do this to her. The words came out as if they were a conduit, exactly like it used to be, without his control. And because of it, in the midst of the girl's panic and anger he was now living, he felt relief.

He was shouting at her. She shouted back at him. They didn't see the deer in time. They hit the tree off-center and the car rolled.

She pulled him the rest of the way through the window, shards of glass slicing her arms, blood making her hands wet and tacky. Blood running into her eye.

The boyfriend no longer bled.

She sat next to him as the car burned.

A feeling, then a sound followed. She turned and saw him: the elongated creature of soot—a skeletal figure like smoke captured and shaped into rough bones, stuck together, stretched, forming a man-like creature with empty eyes and fingers as long as arms. He was hugging a tree, fingers wrapped entirely around it, barely discernible from the darkness the creature came out of.

This was the first time in days, since finding the Book, she'd actually seen the figure…at least, aside from in the corners of her vision at school and home and around town. Glimpses always accompanied by ghostly and warbling calliope music. She knew he was connected to the Book, he was a guardian of it, perhaps waited for whomever found it, to use it. And she had used it, to manipulate, to pull Brian to her, and push him away, bring him back and keep him…but, was that the Book? Or her? She didn't know. But the watcher was there, waiting for something. No, the full promise the Book offered, she had not yet accepted, not yet. Brian lay broken in front of her. Her life broken behind her. Possibly, probably, no life before her.

She opened her mouth, closed it again. Opened, and creaked, "Yes, alright."

She watched the creature of soot and bone unwrap from around the tree and darkness, and move toward her…and now was no longer the creature, but now a woman, old, ancient. In dirty mud-splattered robes and matted hair. The woman limped up to her, the sound of her shuffling through the leaves the only sound she could hear. The fire—its light creating stark and jittering shadows—she no longer heard.

The old woman reached down and took one of her wrists, slippery with blood. Her fingers were long and cold, and wrapped around her wrist like the soot creature's fingers had wrapped around the tree. The woman placed a coin, heavy, warm, in her hand. "For the Ticket Taker," the woman said, expelling smoke from her mouth with each syllable. And she was gone.

The girl closed her hand around the coin and the world started to narrow and fade at the edges, and she fell back onto the ground.

And kept falling.

And staggered back out through the curtain of the hellmouth into the sickly light of the carnival. She looked at her hands, clean of blood. Her wrists and forearms were still ragged from the wounds that happened…days ago? Weeks? She couldn't remember what happened after the accident, between then and now.

Except the coin.

She had dropped it at the entrance…when she, and the Ticket Taker, had grabbed her own wrist…

She walked back past the tents and shacks she knew well but was seeing for the first time, to the entrance. The coin lay in the dirt, somehow reflecting the light brighter than any of the actual bulbs on strings and posts around her. She picked it up. It was warm, like it had just been sitting next to a fire.

The coin felt comfortable in her hand, but she resented it. Didn't she say just a minute ago, hours maybe, that she didn't want it? She couldn't remember…or even if it was the coin she was talking about. She tried to remember but couldn't make her thoughts do what she wanted. Her thoughts, memories, were like smoke wafting and curling around hands trying to catch it.

"When did this come here," someone said, and she looked around. There were people, many people, walking around the carnival, looking around, laughing, talking. They were half there, ephemeral. Like ghosts.

There was a couple in front of her, and then she saw she wasn't herself anymore. She was dressed in a black suit and held a cane, and she couldn't remember who she was just a second ago. She was now the Ticket Taker, and he twirled his moustache and gestured with his cane, bellowing, "Welcome to the fulfillment of dreams and promises! The carnival has arrived to show you excitements, thrills, and perhaps," he said with a wink to the girl of the couple, "sights not meant for the innocent." The couple chuckled as the Ticket Taker ushered them through the entrance.

The words came unbidden, effortlessly, through him. Had he done this before? That's an odd thing to think, "before." What did that mean? He is and was and always has been the Ticket Taker, the Harbinger, the Crone, others.

He turned and gestured grandly, exclaiming to the ghosts that wandered around him, "Welcome, one and all!"

And one ghost formed more solid than the rest, cautious and unsure. The Ticket Taker knew everything he needed to know about this young man who lost someone dear to him in an accident, coming to the carnival to regain her. The Ticket Taker grinned and moved to welcome him.

April LaDelfa has been teaching literature and writing to high school students since 2001. Until recently, she kept her own writing to herself. In 2017, after helping a friend publish his book, she joined NIWA hoping to give her writing life and an authentic audience. She finds inspiration in her experiences and encounters living in various parts of the United States. Today, April enjoys life in beautiful western Washington. While poetry is her passion, she is currently working on ideas for children's books that inspire a love of nature and for ordinary people doing extraordinary things.

Essence of Her

April LaDelfa

She stood motionless by the cold waters of the Sound,
Suffocated by arrogance,
Strangled by expectation,
Alone in curiosity.

There, she met him,
In the shadows she thought she knew.
Yet he would show her a likeness
She had long kept hidden.
He brushed aside her hollow barriers,
Dismantling her facades, one by one.
Smiling. Knowing.

Freed by his words.
Exposed by his thoughts.
Unraveled by his touch.
He gave her the key to unlock the entrance
To the carnival of her mind.

Pulling back the canvas,
He revealed the artistry of her creation—

Sweet, candied vapors curling in the amber lights.
Brassy notes of the calliope ushering beasts and men.
Momentary strangers indulging in games of possibility.
Kaleidoscopic images spinning distorted dreams.
Jeweled silhouettes dancing to exotic rhythms.
Carnies singing, "Come one. Come all."

All of this she claimed as her own.
Among the freaks, where she found her soul.
She wanted him to share in the revelry.
Yet, when she turned,
He was gone—

And, as the sun broke over the waters of the Sound,
She took a deep breath and walked on.

NIWA's Mission

The path of the indie author is challenging and fraught with peril. The Northwest Independent Writer's Association sprang from a group of like-minded, optimistic fantasy and science fiction indies in Portland, Oregon who wanted to help each other succeed.

Almost a decade after its inception, NIWA claims over one hundred members across Washington and Oregon. Members write everything imaginable, including nonfiction, literary fiction, romance, horror, mystery, and, of course, fantasy and science fiction. Despite its diversity of membership, NIWA maintains that same indie spirit of working together to hone our craft and promote each other.

If you or someone you know is an aspiring author in the PNW, look us up at www.niwawriters.com. The group welcomes all those write, published or not. NIWA's members regularly appear across the region at conferences, conventions, and signings.

Thank you for reading this collection. If you enjoyed it, please take a moment to review it wherever you purchase books online.

Made in the USA
Columbia, SC
25 September 2021

45583469R00133